THE BALLADS OF NIAM

Also by Amit Verma

The Lives and the Times
The Lives and The Times II
A Quiver in the Purlieu

THE BALLADS OF NIAM

A NOVEL

AMIT VERMA

LAKE DALLAS, TEXAS

To my family

Prologue

In one version of the story, the daughter was always present, right besides, whose smiles could always be seen with the eyes, whose laughter could always be heard with the ears, whose hands could always be held in the hands. In another, the daughter disappeared with no compunctions about the effect on others. In a different version, the daughter never existed. In this version, she was but a figment of imagination, but an all-consuming one, one which caused an overwhelming, sometimes brain numbing, but not always, sense of her existence, but never her presence. This is the most consequential version.

And yet, this story is not about the daughter, nor about her father, Niam, and neither about her mother, Prisha. In one version of the story, Prisha is Niam's wife. In another, a version where Niam is not Niam, Prisha is not her. In a next version, Niam and Prisha were simply a means toward an end.

Prisha's versions and the daughter's versions are not inter-related, and neither do they draw upon a one-to-one link. All these versions are individually bereft of any purpose. They simply exist. They affect nothing and are not affected by anything. They are like heaps of different colored woolen yarns, jumbled up together, even entangled at points, but always identifiable, and even separable, sometimes with relative ease, and sometimes with patience. Anyway, disentangling their connections is not the purpose. Even understanding them is not the purpose. Showing Niam as a hapless irreprehensible victim of circumstance in all the different versions is also not the purpose. Truth, always an elusive goal, should be the purpose, but it is not.

What then is the purpose here?

For that, a good starting point is to understand what Purpose is. Purpose, the purported reason for anything and everything, for every action and for every reaction. The reason may be physical, tangible. Or it may be intangible, metaphysical perhaps too, created to satisfy the always burning desire to explain anything and everything.

But what of the story? Now, that's a completely different thing. The story has a purpose. In fact, the story is one Purpose.

BOOK I
Anomie

Life has a way of getting back at you, especially professional life. You avoid it, ignore it, but only for so long. It comes racing to you with a vengeance. This was the case with Niam the Procrastinator, which is what he liked to call himself, and felt about himself, too. But he wasn't a procrastinator, not by a long stretch. He was diligent, and almost always found himself completing his tasks before they were due. In an extreme manifestation of this proclivity, he had even tried to convince his wife Prisha to have her deliver their daughter before she was due. Niam simply assigned himself the highfalutin moniker because he always felt behind in his work. There was never a moment of satisfaction for him, never a moment of rest. He was always compelled to move from one task to another.

Prisha, on the other hand, was a little laid back. Not by much, but just enough to be able to enjoy some of the little moments of life. She was ambitious, perhaps more than Niam. She also had more patience and played a longer game with her personal and professional life. This mismatch did not create any major issues, though, and their married life, like many are wont to go, wasn't onerous.

It was a short drive from Nice to their hotel in Monaco. The weather was perfect. Clear blue sky with not a whiff of clouds from horizon to horizon. The choice was thus made. The road would be circuitous, with high chances of motion sickness, but they would still take the coastal route. It had to be done.

This was the first time Prisha was in Monaco. She was excited to experience and see everything they could, important or insignificant. They stood for nearly an hour under the unbearable heat of the summer sun to watch the much-touted changing of the guards at the palace in all its glorious pageantry. The heat was only exacerbated by the crowd that formed as the time for the event approached. They saw the march of thin, tall soldiers in immaculate white shirts, pants, and caps perform an intricate ritual. Once the ceremony had concluded and the crowd around had thinned out, they stood silently, hand-in-hand. There was nothing of any great hurry to do, nowhere to be at any time soon. They both turned their heads unconcernedly and together, first toward the numerous cannons and piles of cannon balls, and then toward the battlement overlooking the crystal-clear blue sea. They slowly drifted toward it for a better view. But sights like those are everywhere along the French Rivera, and there is something to be said about sensory saturation and the amount of admiring of similar sights one can do. They didn't stand there for long. Very soon, in silence and still holding hands, they walked down the castle wall in search of a place to eat. They were soon in a quaint little restaurant that served a wide-ranging cuisine. The long steep stairs up by the palace area, the stroll, the temperature, and the walk down to find a restaurant, had together worked up a great deal of thirst and hunger in them both. They each first ordered freshly squeezed fruit juices and a shared plate of potato gnocchi. This sated their hunger some and allowed them to relax in their seats as they waited for the main course, a medium Margherita pizza and a small garden salad, and, on a whim, a small serving of seasoned fries, all to be shared.

"What next?" Prisha asked. A thin ray of sunlight filtered through a tree from across the window they were seated near and danced over her eyes. This gave them a bright brown twinkle that seemed to light up her perfectly curved eyebrows.

"What next?" Niam asked back as he reclined further back into his seat and stretched his legs out to ease the ache from exertion from all the walking they had done. He admired the view of Prisha sitting across from him. Enchanting.

"I don't know! You're the planner. I just follow," she replied with a smile.

Niam took a shallow breath to acknowledge her compliment.

"I say we go back to Monte Carlo."

"Why? Weren't we there yesterday evening, and then once again this morning? What's more to see there?" she asked as she lightly brushed her fingers across her décolletage.

His face lit up. "Not to see. How about we gamble this time?"

"Seriously?" She frowned and stopped moving her fingers. "First lose money on the entrance fees and then lose money inside the casino. I don't like this idea."

"Oh, come on!" Niam raised both hands. "It'll be fun. Memories. Who knows. We may never come back here."

She looked at him and raised a single eyebrow, something that always brought a smile to his face. He had tried many times to copy her, but had been unsuccessful so far. Seeing that she was still in good humor he continued. "Come on! We'll take some nice pictures inside," he pleaded. "Something more for you to post and show off to your friends."

It did not take much effort by Niam to convince her. Even though she personally hated the idea of gambling, Prisha was curious about the casino. And Niam was right. They would be leaving the next morning, perhaps never to come back.

They devoured their lunch quickly with little interruption. The discussion over a single large cup of tea, again shared by them, was about their plans for the next day, and the day after. Once done, their walk to their car at the nearby underground car park took them along a pier with a crowd of docked yachts of varying sizes and looks. On the way they stopped briefly at the nondescript entrance to the International Atomic Energy Agency laboratory. They took some pictures and admired some of the splendid yachts.

"I don't understand the pleasure in owning one," Niam said. "It doesn't make sense to me. A short boating trip for which you rent one, yes. But owning one for millions and millions, getting a staff to maintain and run it and what not. Doesn't make sense."

"I think it's just something you do because others around you with the same social status do. More like a fashion statement, I suppose," Prisha said. "You can afford it, and others around you are buying it, so why not. What else will you do with all that money, anyway, if not splurge on such frivolity."

"I guess so," Niam said. "It's a very different world for them. It is."

"It is. Let's get to the hotel so we can change for the casino. We should try to sleep early tonight. Tomorrow will be a long day."

Their hotel wasn't too far off, like most things in Monaco. However, it took them a little longer than they expected to reach it because of traffic. This hotel was a lucky find for them. The room was reasonably priced and provided a great view of the sea. Once they were in the room, they worked as an efficient team. Niam called up room service and ordered coffee, while Prisha picked out the clothes for both of them. The coffee soon arrived, and they gulped it down. They hit the shower together and, for most parts, kept their hands to themselves. Drying and dressing was similarly silent and quick. Niam wore a semi-formal livid-colored jacket and a darker formal pair of pants. Prisha chose a short sleeve maxi dress with bright red flowers on a white background. They silently admired each other for a few seconds.

"Ready?" Niam asked.

"Ready," Prisha replied, and they stepped out together.

The traffic was still unusually heavy, and their drive was a crawl. But they did not mind it this time around. They were no longer hungry or tired. They were again filled with the same feeling of quietude and serenity they experienced at the top of the palace earlier in the day.

"Is that a tarot card reader?" Prisha exclaimed and pointed to a side shop by the street they were on.

"Is it? I can't see. Traffic's very bad," Niam said while keeping his eyes fixed on an expensive new model BMW car ahead of him. He had been forced to tailgate this car for the past few minutes and was not happy about it. The driver seemed very untrustworthy and impatient and was continually speeding up and breaking. "I suppose this guy is really eager to lose his money at the casino tonight?"

"How do you know he's going to the casino?" Prisha turned toward him.

"I don't. I am just guessing."

"Listen," Prisha said. "I want to go to that tarot card reader!"

"Seriously?" Niam gave her a quick startled look and went back to focusing on the road in front of him.

"Seriously!" Prisha crossed her arms. "I agreed to go with you to gamble, did I not, even though I don't enjoy it one bit? I agreed because it's your idea of fun. This is my idea of fun. You get to throw money at gambling, and I get to throw money at that clairvoyant. What's the difference?"

Niam did not respond right away. He toyed with the argument in his head for some seconds. He couldn't find anything wrong with the logic.

"Okay," he finally said. "Okay. We'll do it. In fact, how about we first go to this place you saw? The casino parking is right there, and your tarot card place seems to be walking distance. Going there first will help us kill some time. It's still pretty bright outside. I would rather go to the casino closer to the evening. Evenings just set up a better mood for such things, I think. And, you never know, we might get lucky! Come evening, we might even see a celebrity or two at the casino. That'll be awesome."

"Really? You'll do that for me?" Prisha beamed.

"Anything you ask for, of course!" Niam smiled back.

They found an underground parking area near the casino.

From there, the moving escalator brought them to Jardins de la Petite Afrique. They had been there the previous evening, but still decided to take a leisurely stroll through it, this time away from the casino and toward a fancy shopping place. Niam suggested going in there, but Prisha suggested otherwise. She wanted to reach the tarot card reader.

"Do you even know where it is?" Niam asked, feeling somewhat hot and drained. They had walked a considerable distance in the afternoon heat on the sidewalk of a sparsely populated and relatively narrow road with buildings, tall and short, abutting on both sides. "My deodorant will stop working very soon."

"Don't worry. I'll buy you a great deodorant. For now, you can use my perfume if you want. They won't throw you out of the casino for smelling like a pretty woman. Why would they want to let go of your money? They're not dumb." Prisha grabbed his arm more firmly, eager to continue with their search for the tarot reader.

"Don't hold me. It's so hot."

"Alright, alright!" Prisha exclaimed and let go of him. "This is the street. It's here somewhere. I know I saw it."

"Saw what, exactly?" Niam asked. "Can you describe it to me?"

"Saw the tarot place, dummy," she replied. "It was just a small outlet, just like this ice cream place here."

She picked up speed. A few seconds later something caught her attention. She stopped and grabbed his arm again.

"There!" She pointed with the free hand. "I told you it was here. Let's go!"

She flitted to the intersection ahead of her, pulling Niam along, and crossed to the other side of the road. They reached what could best be described as a cubbyhole nestled between a grocery store and a coffee shop. It had a dark-tinted glass door with an elegantly carved, polished, wooden handle. The handle was sticking out as a sharp, jarring contrast to the otherwise mostly bland environ

Niam now found himself in. The other jarring thing were the words, "Tarot Card Reader, Palmist, Mind-Healer" all in bold white, and in English, French, and German, written across the glass door. Niam opened the door and they both entered. The closing door behind them did an outstanding job of keeping the street noise out. It also kept the light out.

Prisha and Niam took a short time to get used to the absence of noise, and to a dimly lit narrow but short passageway. Above, there was a single hanging lamp hanging from the side wall. It had its light directed away from the entrance and toward the other end of the passageway, lighting up a closed door.

"Hello!" Prisha said out loud to announce their presence to whomever might be behind the closed door.

"*Nina? Nina, c'est toi?*" came the response in a loud but euphonious female voice.

"*Sí.*" Prisha glanced at Niam and raised her eyebrows. "Visitors." Prisha said again.

"I don't know what she said," she whispered to Niam. "I don't know any French. She spoke French, right?"

"I think it was French," Niam whispered back and smiled. "Something about some Nina. And maybe you said something in Spanish or German."

"It's not my fault I don't know any of those languages," Prisha whispered, somewhat louder this time. "What's happening here? Is she going to show up or what, or should we leave?"

As if to answer her questions, there was the sound of rustling from the other side of the door, a couple of thuds, and chairs being moved. Then the door opened and the light from the single wall lamp fell on the woman who just happened to have a profound connection with their lives.

Niam was never the one to turn away from anything that sounded even remotely exciting. When he was asked by his company if he wanted a posting in France for a project that would take anywhere from two to three years, he took it. Their last trip across southern Europe to celebrate their wedding anniversary had left them both with indelible memories from the trip, and a yearning to revisit. The company also agreed to allow Prisha to work part of the year remotely from France. This worked somewhat well for the first few months, but became difficult when they were away from each other. Fortunately, Niam was able to move some levers for them to be together. He found a longer-term project for her in the same office too. It was during this time that his work with a technology news website brought him some minor attention. An online news and views publisher approached him to contribute opinion articles on technology, and on any other themes he was interested in. This fitted very well with his interests. He had always viewed himself as at least a dilettante if not an outright multipotentialite. He knew he had potential to make a mark in the technology industry, and he felt that he had potential to contribute as a journalist too.

When they were finally together, Niam and Prisha used that opportunity for over a year to travel across many parts of France and Europe, on as many weekends and holidays as they could. Sometimes they travelled by train or plane, but on most occasions they drove. Driving gave them the flexibility to make and change plans on the go—stopping by small towns and villages, detouring through picturesque spots, or extending or shortening their stays at any place. But they never felt the desire to visit the south of France. Whenever the discussion on a next trip would come up, it would always be somewhere else. It's not that they actively chose to ignore or overrule the French Rivera. The very thought of that place simply never crossed or stayed on their minds. When any of their acquaintances would suggest visiting the French Rivera, they would nod, but would never act on the advice. Some place more exciting and enticing would always pop up.

Niam also got into the habit of carrying a small notebook with him everywhere he went. Whether it was strolling through Quartier Latin, around the neighborhood of the relatively inexpensive but also small apartment they were very fortunate to find, sitting at a coffee shop, buying groceries at a small, crammed store, or taking the bus to and from his nearby office, or on their trips around Paris and beyond, the notebook was always with him. In it he made copious short and long observations of anything that caught his fancy—an interesting building, or an interesting conversation or interaction he came across. Whenever he could, be it during a lull time at his office, or late evenings at his apartment, he would open the notebook and peruse its contents thoroughly, oftentimes repeatedly over that sitting, or spread out over days. Sometimes some of those notes would make a connection for an article. He would then spend a few days composing the article and sending it off to the online news publisher. Most of those articles focused on helping people like him—foreigners working in and around Paris for short and long extents—to make sense of the place and to adjust to the life. Some of his work devolved into a critiquing of restaurants, too, but he mostly tried to focus on the larger cultural aspects. These included dos and don'ts as a nod to idiosyncrasies of the Parisian and French culture, and racial issues that he found to crop up around him and in the media.

"Don't believe for a second that the common person here does not harbor some racial predisposition or another," his friend, Hamoon, once said to him.

Hamoon was an American citizen of Afghani parentage. His father was a young doctor, and his mother was a starting middle school math teacher in Kabul around the time when the Soviet Union invaded. Hamoon was a late child. His parents had tried to conceive for some years before he was born and were unsuccessful after him. They viewed him as a blessing.

As the situation in Afghanistan was unfolding around

Kabul, Hamoon's father sensed it devolving into complete chaos from what was happening in the capital, and his interactions with his patients who traveled from around to see him for treatment. He decided to use his savings to buy his family's way out of the country. The family crossed the border into Pakistan and made their way to Peshawar. In Peshawar, they were helped in settling down by close relatives. But they did not spend too long there.

A few short years later, they were in Karachi. They did not stay long there either. A relative of theirs helped Hamoon's mother find a job as a teacher at a school in Doha. The salary seemed lucrative enough to support the three of them very easily, and then some. So, in just a couple of more years, about the age when Hamoon was beginning to make some sense of the world around him and make friends, they found themselves on the move again.

Qatar at that time was an exciting place to be. It was on a path of attempting to use its oil wealth wisely in building the economy up, and there were lots of opportunities. Hamoon's father soon found a job through friends as a manager at a small pharmacy. Shortly after, he entered into a partnership with the store owner to open up another store, with an agreement to manage them both. Thus, Doha was where they settled for a length of time after many chaotic years on the move.

Hamoon's parents were very frugal, perhaps even obsessively so. They led a very simple life, stayed in small cheap homes, and rarely went out. They mostly bought cheap, utilitarian things —utensils, clothes, furniture, and anything of necessity—but usually nothing else. They saved as much as they could. The country, while run by immigrants, was only welcoming to them to the extent that it needed them for fulfilling specific tasks and no more. Growing roots and settling down in the country was not something that Qatar wanted the immigrant working population to do. Hamoon's parents were well aware that they could be asked to pack up and leave the country. Going back to Afghanistan was not an option for them. They wanted to have enough in savings to buy their way to anywhere else if they needed to.

Fortunately for them, their worst fears never materialized. Hamoon's mother stayed as a teacher. Hamoon's father built upon his experience and opened up two restaurants in partnership with relatives. By this time, Hamoon was also nearing the end of his schooling years. He was the only child, with one parent a former doctor and another a teacher in a school. This meant that his education was a prime focus in the family, and Hamoon graduated from school with good grades. After that, he was sent off to a small university in North Carolina with a relatively low tuition and a relatively good reputation. He emerged four years later with a degree in computer science, just when the industry was taking off in a big way.

Many years later, Hamoon and Niam found each other working on the same project in Paris. They were drawn to each other from the beginning in spite of the age gap between them, or perhaps partly because of it. They shared a common love of eating out and trying different cuisines, and spending time at different coffee shops. They enjoyed sharing anecdotes and experiences from their various travels. A lot of times, they simply enjoyed complaining and whining about stuff—coworkers, higher ups, anything else that came to mind. This was their guilty pleasure, a chance to blow off some steam in confidence. This came about after they had gone out for lunch a few times.

"Why do you say that? I mean, I know some people do, but a big number?" Niam asked.

"Don't get me wrong. I don't mean people are racist in the racist sense, you know, the extreme sense. You might meet some of the extreme ones, or maybe you already have," Hamoon replied. "But those are not what I'm talking about. I'm talking about many of the regular folks you'll see. They'll ask you where you're from, and will doggedly try to dig up your roots going all the way back to Adam and Eve. This one day I was in a train going to Thonon-les-Bains..."

"Oh, yes? How was it?" Niam interrupted. "We've been wanting to go there!"

"It's great. I've been there a couple of times. I love it. It's a great place to sit back and relax for a couple of days. And things are reasonably priced. Not too far away from Geneva too, if you want to drop by for some big city excitement."

"Yeah, I've heard about it. Maybe Prisha and I will go there next."

"When you do, make sure to talk to me first. I've learned a few things about that place which will help you save some money and make things easier," Hamoon said.

"Thanks," Niam said. "Sorry. I didn't mean to interrupt you. What were you saying about the train ride to that place?"

"Yes. About that! As I was saying, I found I was going to be totally by myself on this one weekend, with nothing specific to do. So, I called a friend of mine who works in Zurich. He suggested we meet up at Thonon-les-Bains and spend a couple of days just hanging out. Basically, doing nothing. While I was on the train, this person sitting next to me decided to chat. About a minute or two into our conversation, he asked me, very politely, where I was from, and I replied, very politely too, that I was from the USA. That should have been it, right? But no. He asked, 'No, but where are you originally from?' I mentioned that my parents are originally from Afghanistan. Then he asks, 'So, were you born there or in the USA?' At that point I was beginning to feel uncomfortable. I replied Afghanistan, and then excused myself to go to the bathroom. I took my time to come back and spent the rest of the trip trying not to lift my head from a magazine I had."

"Oh yes," Niam interjected. "Something like this has happened to me too! At least a few times. Here and in Germany. I can totally relate to your story."

12

Hamoon carried on, "I think they ask because they think it will help them somehow understand you better. If they can find out where you're originally from, they can pull out data from some stereotyped boxes or silos they have to help them to figure you out. But come on, that's really just being racist, and maybe even worse."

"What's worse than that?" Niam smiled.

"I don't know what's worse than that. Maybe being super-racist. Maybe being some racist superhero. Maybe some superhero who shoots beams of racism. I don't know. Come to think of it, why don't we have racist superheroes? Given so many of them, I would suppose there's got to be at least one who is racist, right? What do you think? Maybe even a closet racist, with raging racism bursting at the seams, trying to come out."

"That's an interesting theory. Maybe we should ask those comic book folks." Niam smiled while sipping on coffee. They were sitting outside a café not far from their office.

Prisha and Niam had gone out for dinner with Hamoon and his girlfriend a few times, and had invited each other over to their apartments. But they never really clicked as a group. Their interests and backgrounds were just too far apart. In all those occasions, Prisha and Niam and Hamoon would start talking about work and office politics, and his girlfriend would feel left out. She worked for an NGO based in California focusing on animal rights and was studying to be a veterinarian. She and Hamoon would visit each other whenever their schedules permitted, which turned out to be relatively frequent. In time the two couples simply stopped inviting each other to meet.

Hamoon became the only close friend Niam had during that time. Prisha, on the other hand, made many friends among the larger diaspora within a radius of a few blocks. They would meet every few days for meals, or for short sightseeing trips around the city. Niam did not feel left out on those occasions. He would take the opportunity to take public transport to places known and places unknown and walk around with the notebook in his hand, making observations and taking notes, sometimes copious, but often only writing a sparse few lines.

One such trip on a Saturday late morning found him in an elegant neighborhood surrounded by Haussmann buildings. Prisha, at that time, was meeting her friends for brunch at a pizzeria near their apartment, and then planned to go with them for window shopping at Champs-Elysees. Someone in their group was leaving France, perhaps for good, and wanted to take one last stroll on the street as a remembrance. This meant that Prisha would be gone for hours with an uncertain, but surely late, return. This also meant that Niam had a good bit of time to himself to roam around.

The partially cloudy warm and humid day was not proving to be particularly helpful in his walk. It hadn't been long, perhaps less than about forty-five minutes, and Niam was already thirsty and a little hungry. This made it difficult for him to admire the surroundings. And so, somewhat uncharacteristically, he decided to drop in at what looked like a patisserie from a distance. On the way he passed a small restaurant that had just opened its doors. A thin tallish blond haired young man and a nearly equally tall dark haired young woman, both dressed in well-ironed white buttoned up shirts and black pants were busy setting up outdoor seating. An older balding man with similar attire was busy inside, close to the entrance, moving a table.

A few steps away from the restaurant was a small grocery store with many types of fruits and vegetables arranged outside in boxes. An older couple, whom Niam thought to be in their seventies, were rummaging together through a box of peaches and bananas to pick out the best. Niam slowed down to look at them. He fleetingly thought of buying a couple of bananas and a soda but decided to move on.

The patisserie was next to a small boutique. The boutique had big projecting display windows on either side of a comparatively narrow glass door. The door and the windows were held in place with the help of a glossy and bold coffee-brown wooden frame that ran around the windows from one end to the other. The frame caught one's attention before the brightly colored summer dresses on four mannequins, each staring blankly at the passersby.

There wasn't much of a crowd on the street. The few people walking around Niam did not seem to be paying much attention to the boutique, or most other things for that matter. The only person who was looking at the mannequins with some interest was a woman. She was sitting on a chair outside the patisserie, and was alternately sipping on a small cup of coffee and playing with a small biscotti. When the biscotti was not in her hand being played with, it was on an equally small plate lying on a tempered glass top of a small round metal table.

As he approached the entrance to the shop, Niam and the woman gave each other a lingering glance, just short of a stare. Niam felt something familiar about her but couldn't quite place where he had seen her before. Even inside the shop, as he ordered his coffee and a fancy looking pastry using the little French he knew, he kept turning his head around to look at her, trying to remember. Once he placed his order, he decided to take one of the only four small tables inside the shop. This table was farthest from the window, but was close enough to see her. It was then, as he waited for the coffee and pastry to arrive, that he got a longer chance to look at the woman. She appeared to be in her late twenties to early thirties, with a few dark spots on one side of her face. Her upturned eyes, and the way they were placed on either side of her prominent nose, gave the impression that she was looking far away, even when she was holding up her coffee cup. The contrast between the matching white corset top and pants she was wearing, and her delicate looking shoulder-length copper red hair, gave her an elegant appearance. This was accentuated by the way she handled her cup between her thumb and index finger and brought it to her lips without the slightest movement of her head. The entire movement of her hand was so mesmerizing that it reminded him of his recent visit to a neighborhood optometrist for an eye exam. The optometrist was from mainland China, from around Beijing. Niam was convinced that at some point in her life, she had practiced calligraphy because of the way her hands seemed to float as she moved them around, asking him to follow them with only his eyes.

The woman under Niam's observation finished her coffee much before him but continued to sit and stare at the boutique. A short time later, when Niam was also about to leave, she fidgeted a little, and then reached into the black shoulder bag she had hung on the chair. From there she pulled out her phone and showed it the same delicate handling she had shown the coffee cup before. With her right index finger she appeared to scroll through the screen up and down, trying to search for something—a phone number perhaps. She tapped the screen with her finger again, smiling triumphantly. She then shifted the phone from her left hand to her right, and brought it to her ear.

At nearly the exact moment, Niam was startled by the ringing of his phone, and almost dropped the empty plate on which his pastry had arrived. He looked down at his phone and saw a call from a restricted number. He looked up at the woman. She had turned her head slightly toward him and, much to his surprise, had a slight expression of annoyance. Without him noticing, she had also pulled out a pair of sunglasses from her purse and was toying with them in her other hand. He looked down at the phone again, and on a hunch, decided not to ignore the call. He picked up the phone from the table, scrolled up on the screen to accept the call, and brought it to his ear.

"Hello," he said into the phone, a little louder than a whisper. He looked out the window toward the woman. She was saying something into her phone.

16

"Are you done with your coffee? We don't have all day, you know," a woman's voice replied.

"Excuse me?" Niam replied, still staring at the woman on the other side of the window. She spoke again.

"I asked if you're done with your coffee. Or are you going to keep me waiting some more. I don't mind waiting, but I would request you to finish up faster if you can."

Niam pressed his phone harder to his ear to make sure he was hearing her correctly.

"I am sorry, but do I know you? Do you have the right number?"

The woman sitting outside spoke again. This time Niam had a strong feeling that she was the one talking to him on the phone.

"Yes, I have the right number. Just come out when you're done. The lady has been sitting for a while and she is dying for a nice leisurely stroll. It is lovely weather, and it seems it will only get better."

"But?" Niam spoke. He took a moment break to gather his thoughts. He spoke again, "But, how do you know me? I am sorry if I don't remember."

"It's totally alright," the reply came back. This time the woman outside the window turned fully around to face him. It was thus confirmed. She was the one who was calling him. "I can believe you don't remember. I am Nina. Maybe now you remember? Maybe? And aren't you the famous one with triple triplet lines on your hand?"

"Not famous. Certainly not," Niam responded with a deep breath.

"But the triple triplet line! Come on out when you're done. I am dying for a walk."

Dumbfounded and curious to know more, Niam got up from his chair and checked his wallet. He quickly brushed his fingers through his hair. During all this, and in the few more seconds it took him to reach for the door, he tried hard not to be confused with what had just happened and what was happening. He knew the name from somewhere. He knew her. But how? Nina as a memory seemed to be deceptively within his grasp, but formless and drifting.

His amnesia did not change even when he stepped out. Niam found himself looking at a tall woman, seemingly matching his above average height. She had sharp facial features, which were accentuated by a very slight forward bend at the waist as she presented her hand to him for a handshake. Niam did not hesitate and took her hand. He held it longer than necessary as he looked at her face, trying to recollect where he had seen her.

Nina broke the silence. "If you don't mind and are not too tired, I suggest we walk a few blocks. There's a very pretty garden not far from here. I like it very much. It has a lot of seating area too."

"I don't mind," Niam spoke. He had still not taken his eyes away from her face. Nina, if she felt it, showed no outward signs of disconcertion. She let him stare at her a little longer. Then, with a look of conviviality marked by a slight movement of her eyes and a small smile, she lifted her purse over her shoulder and turned around to walk. She picked up her pace to almost a trot. This took Niam by surprise. He followed, behind her for some time, and then decided to catch up to her.

"Just a couple of blocks more," Nina said when Niam was beside her. "Isn't it a gorgeous day? I love it. The park will be beautiful. I even picked up my dress just for this occasion. What do you think? Isn't it a pretty dress?"

Niam glanced at her from top to bottom. The white corset top had two small shiny, but otherwise featureless, golden rings attached to the shoulder straps. Similar rings also hung at the front of her white pants. The mostly white sneakers with pink heels and toe cap looked very new. Niam was no expert in fashion, leave aside women's fashion. He had on a plain light brown t-shirt with khaki pants and pair of somewhat semiformal, worn, black leather shoes. He admired Prisha whenever she dressed up. He would even pretend to listen rapturously when she talked about fashion. But he would never understand it. To him, a purse is a purse, and a good-fit, good-looking dress is a good-fit, good-looking dress, and nothing more. Nina, from what little he could figure out, had expensive clothes on. Even if they were not expensive, he was certain that she had put in some thought into choosing her attire, perhaps even a lot of thought.

"Yes, it is," he replied, and meant it.

"White is my favorite color. I am sure you've figured that out! Pink too. I like pink. Maybe equally."

A few long seconds of silence followed as Niam tried to keep up with Nina.

"I am sorry, but this is all very confusing," he said when he could not control himself any further, and stopped walking. On cue, Nina stopped too and turned to face him. "I know that I know you somehow. But I cannot place it. And how is it that you have my number and, you know, it seems like you were waiting for me? How do we know each other?"

"It's okay," she replied. "I understand. Let me explain. Here, show me you hand."

Niam brought his left hand up.

"No, the other one." She held his right hand and lifted it toward her. Then she turned it palm up, and brought it closer to her face so she could look at it better. "There. Do you see? Look, look!" Her face lit up with a broad smile.

"Look at what?" Niam asked, perplexed, with a voice edging toward irritation.

"Look at your palm. The triple triplet lines." She pointed at his hand. Then without looking up, she adjusted the purse strap on her shoulder and moved closer to Niam and by his side. She stooped just a little to get a better look. "This is so very enthralling, so unique, so exciting! No matter how many times you look at it, it's not enough. Look, let me explain. Here's your lifeline.

See." And she traced out a line on his palm. "Now, look at mine. Mine is normal."

She lifted her palm and held it by the side of his palm.

"Look at how my lifeline curves around the thumb and reaches my wrist. That's normal. But now compare it to yours. Your lifeline starts normal. But then around this age for you, it branches out into three parts. All three end up on your wrist."

"But." Niam tried to interject with words he could not fully form in the very brief time Nina was silent.

"Now look at your headline. This is the headline." She pointed to it. "Compare this to mine. Mine is normal. But yours, it starts normal too, but branches out again into three parts. This is the heart line. This also divides into three parts. The three most major lines on a person's hand. All three of them on your hand have three distinct paths. But, look, you have a single, single fate line. Very prominent. Here it is." She traced her finger along a line on his hand.

"This sounds very interesting, and I am sure it likely is, but again, how do you know all this? How do I know you?" Niam gently pulled his hand from Nina, and she gave in.

"I understand it bothers you not to be able to remember," she said. "But the important thing is you know that we've met." She looked into his eyes and saw him looking at her with a frown.

"Listen, trust me," she said with a slightly pleading voice. "Let's walk to the park. We will meet Ella there. She will have something to tell us."

"Now, who's Ella?" Niam began to harbor the thought that this was some prank, and perhaps he was being recorded for a prank post on someone's social media account. Or perhaps, he thought, this was even worse. It could be a scam or an attempt to take him into some shady corner and rob him.

"I don't exactly know who Ella is," Nina said. She clasped her hands together lightly. "I ask you to trust me. You may be thinking that this is some scheme to prank or rob you. It's not.

It is not. But my explanation will sound even more bizarre than the situation you think you might be experiencing."

"It is bizarre," Niam retorted. "And I cannot go with you unless I know what I am doing. I don't want to be rude or anything. I'll take leave."

"Don't you want to know what happened there?" Nina asked just as Niam had turned around to go. He turned back to face her.

"Yes," he said.

"I thought so too," she responded. "Will it bother you much if I told you that I too don't remember much. I know we've met, but I cannot place you. I woke up today with this strong pull, something just gripping my head very tight, asking me to be at this coffee shop, and wait for you. I tried hard to resist this feeling. It didn't seem rational at all. But this thing that was urging me made me convince myself. It was going to be a pretty day. I said to myself, 'Even if this is insane and you don't show up, I can still spend some time outside and enjoy the weather in this outfit I bought a few days ago but hadn't had the chance to wear.' And so, there I was, sitting there outside. Imagine how surprised I was to see you. Then I had this urge again, completely taking over my thoughts, to call you and walk with you to the park to meet Ella. I didn't even know I had your number until I saw it on my phone."

"What's Ella going to tell us," Niam asked, his forehead creased as he tried to take in whatever Nina was saying.

"I'll take a guess. I think she will tell us something about what version this is. Or maybe what version this will become."

"Version of what?" Niam asked.

Nina took a deep breath. "Well," Nina spoke slowly and exhaled, "you have the triple triplets and one single strong, prominent fate line."

"I don't even understand what it means," Niam said. "What does it mean?"

She took a deep breath again. "I'll take a guess. I think what it means is that there are three versions. This is one of them. There are two more."

"Okay," Niam said, letting slip a small bit of skepticism.

"There are three versions. There was one single version. Then that single version became three. It's not a big deal for you. But for me, and for others, it could be."

"Why is it not a big deal for me? I don't understand," Niam responded. "And why would it be a big deal for you?"

"These are your versions. You know about them. But spare some thoughts for me. I am lost. I know nothing about them. I am the one who must struggle to figure out my role in this version of yours. Not you."

They walked the rest of way to the park in silence. There was not much to say in any case. Niam was still straining to grab at any thread of memory that floated in his mind to help him remember. In this case he wasn't even sure what it was that he had to remember. Where did he meet Nina first? How far back was it? Days, months, years? No, that wasn't it. It was about reading his palm. Was it Nina who did it? He couldn't remember, and this made him very annoyed. He had to do this, he had to go with Nina. It was the one way, he felt, his memory of meeting her might come back to him. However, if he turned around at this very point, a very reasonable thing to do, he would not know how to handle the frustration of not knowing.

The park did not seem very big, perhaps a few couple of blocks wide on each side. This seemingly secret oasis had a small pond in the center, which was likely man-made, if not completely, then at least by quite a bit. There was a dense wooded area on one side. The rest of the park was mostly well-trimmed grass with a few interspersed trees, a few flower beds where flowers had not yet blossomed, and a circuitous paved path that wound around the pond. The green water had a few idling ducks, who seemingly had nowhere important to go and nothing of any importance to do. In that they were no different than some of the people wandering around the park—a couple of old women deep in their conversation, an old couple walking silently, a young couple with a pram who were frequently taking a peek to see if their baby was okay, and an even younger couple sitting under a tree engaged in passionate canoodling. A few stone benches were also interspersed throughout the park, most of them close to the flower beds. Only one seemed to be occupied.

"That's Ella." Nina pointed to her. "I just know it is."

Niam saw a woman with short curly hair, dark brown, with a pale yellow blouse and a full-length red floral skirt sitting on the bench. She had dark glasses on that covered most of her face and added to the mystery. In one hand, she gripped a white and red guide cane.

"Ella? Hello," Nina said as they approached her.

Ella turned toward her. "Hello! Nina?"

"Yes, that's me. And Niam is also here with me."

"Good, good," she said. She lifted herself up with her free hand. She stumbled for a moment when she took a small step, but quickly got her control back. "I am not fully blind, you know, but I am getting there for sure," Ella said softly to them. "It's a genetic disorder. Runs in the family. My father is completely blind. I will be too in a few years. I started losing my eyesight around thirty-five. It's been about five years. Ten years more, I would say, and I'll be totally blind. But come now. Let's not get all depressed on my behalf. Let's take a walk. Let's enjoy what we can while we still can. We'll take at least three rounds around the pond. This should make for a good exercise. My experience is that three is the perfect number of rounds. Two makes you feel incomplete, as if something is missing. Four makes you exhausted. At least it does to me. Three is the best."

Nina and Niam did not respond. They waited for Ella to

take the lead. Ella, just like Nina, was tall, as tall as Niam. She seemed to be using her guide cane only intermittently as she walked at a slow pace. She was surefooted and walked with a steady gait. Niam thought she had a perfectly attractive face. And perhaps perfectly immediately forgettable too. There was nothing that stood out on her face to hook your attention and memory of her apart from her enormous dark glasses.

"So, how has your day been so far?" Ella turned toward them both, trying to break the silence.

"Strange. Weird. Strange, I would say," Niam said.

Ella let out a small laugh. "Not bad then, I suppose," she said. "Everyone should experience at least one strange thing a day. It makes for a better life. I used to experience many strange things every day. But now it's few and far between. I suppose you know why. It gets boring. I am so tired of my boring dreary life. Meeting you two has been the most exciting thing to have happened to me in over a week."

"What was the exciting thing that happened last week?" Nina asked.

"Now that was very strange, indeed," Ella spoke with a hint of animation. "It turns out that I know Polish! I had no idea until last week. I had a fight with someone, and that's another story for another time. She's a real pain. So, here I am, all super worked up after the argument. I get home, eat a light dinner, drink lots of wine, and go to bed. I wake up in the morning much better, but still a bit upset. I decide to get dressed and spend the morning walking around aimlessly just to take my mind off the argument from the night before. As I am rambling through the streets, I pass by two men deep in conversation. They were discussing something about filing taxes or some such boring stuff. I didn't realize it at that very instant, but I could actually understand what they were saying! It was all very weird because at that instant too, I couldn't really figure out what language they were speaking in. My first instinct was, of course, French. But that wasn't it. I then thought it could be Spanish, or German, or Romanian, all languages I know. It then suddenly struck me that it was Polish. How odd! I never knew that I knew Polish. I mean, how could I? Wouldn't you know all the languages you know? One instant I did not know that I know Polish, and the next instant, I find out that not only do I know the language, but I might be almost as good at it as any native Polish speaker, if not equal."

She then turned to Niam and asked, "How many languages do you know Niam?"

"Umm," Niam tried doing a quick calculation.

"You know three languages," Ella didn't wait for an answer. "Right, Nina?"

"Yes, three that he can read, write, and speak," Nina responded.

Niam just gazed open-mouthed at both wondering how they knew so much about him.

"I think he can somewhat understand a couple more, right?"

"Yes, I think so," Nina said.

"I am sorry," Niam interjected. "How do you know all this? Did you check my social media profile or something?"

"Oh, don't be silly," Ella smiled. "What will I do on social media? It's not easy for me to look at a screen. I would rather save the effort to watch TV or a movie."

"Forget about knowing you're a polyglot, I didn't even know I knew you 'til this morning!" Nina also smiled.

Niam gave her a wary look.

"Really. I didn't know. I just... knew," Nina said.

"Same here," Ella said.

There was silence for a couple of seconds, then Ella spoke again, "It's not a big deal. We know, and it doesn't matter. It's like me not realizing that I am fluent in Polish until last week when I overheard two men engaged in a boring chat."

"I quite like that." Nina jumped in. "I wish I could wake up one day and find out that I am fluent in many languages. The language part of my brain is broken, I think. I just can't seem to learn any language other than the two I know. I can understand a few, and I even understand some of the music in those languages, but I cannot just get around to speaking in them. I tried. But I suppose I get so self-conscious and fear embarrassing myself that I can never go beyond a couple of sentences."

"I was never like that," Ella said. "I would take it upon myself as a challenge to learn a language, and I wouldn't mind making a fool of myself if I made a mistake. This has come in handy as I lose my eyesight. You have no idea how many times I've been in situations where I shouldn't have been because I can't see very well. Knowing many languages has helped me handle them."

Niam still wasn't sure what to say. Expressing sympathies for Ella's condition did not seem like the right thing to do. He did not know her and did not know how she would react. His attempts to jog his memory to figure out who Nina and Ella were, were also proving futile.

Nina seemed to sense a growing frustration in Niam's mind. "Don't worry. You'll be okay. If anything, I should be more worked up than you. I told you I have a greater need to know than you. Ella does too. But at least she knows more than I do."

"Oh, yes, indeed. Indeed, I do," Ella said. "Over my life, and my condition... by the way, did I tell you that I am also a cancer survivor? Yes, I am. I've been in full remission for about four years. One more year, and I'll be cancer free for five years. I don't understand fully what that means, but it's a milestone. Seemingly your chance of living a long life goes up if signs and symptoms don't show up within those five years. Anyway, what was I saying?"

"You've had a tough life for someone who's still relatively young," Niam said. "Losing your eyesight, and a life-threatening illness. I admire your resilience and strength to still keep going."

"I do too!" Ella said excitedly. "I am glad we agree on this.

I like my life for whatever it is worth. You, on the other hand, don't know yet whether you like yours or not. I've gone through my share of hardships, and I've lived through my father's. I've seen others too in my family and within my circle of friends and acquaintances. I have my share of big expectations from life, and I have my sense of reality and possibilities. There is no perfect life. Life is about disaffection, unrequited desires, missed opportunities, and a few pleasures we seek and even fewer that come upon us. The one thing we should hope for is a perfect death. I wouldn't like to die any other way."

"Me too." Nina jumped in. "I don't mind dying. It's the pain and suffering that I cannot stand. It would be perfect if one goes to bed at night and simply doesn't wake up the next morning. This would be a great way to go. This is what I want for myself."

"Almost everyone thinks of death only as an ambiguous, fuzzy concept," Ella said. "Perhaps something that'll not happen to them. Or even if it will, they think they can come out on the other side still alive somehow and not dead and in control. And maybe this is not all bad. Feeling you'll live forever in one way or another is maybe why people think of the near future and the distant future, and try to plan and prepare even when they logically know they'll not be physically there anymore. Future generations benefit from this. But I don't think like that. Not me. I've been very close to dying. It's deeply part of my conscious and subconscious self. I live with death. I live with the full knowledge that I can get the news about my impending demise at any time, today, tomorrow, next week or next month. This thought is never too far from me. In some ways I am done thinking about it. If there's nothing beyond, if it's nothingness, so be it. I don't care. I try to make full use of what I have."

At this Niam turned to face them both, stopped, and grinned. Nina stopped too to face him. Ella, realizing that she had taken a few steps with no one by her side, also stopped and turned around. Niam let out a small chuckle.

"I can't believe this. An hour ago... was it an hour ago?" He looked at this watch. "Yup. Hour ago. I was drinking coffee. Now I am here in this beautiful garden walking with two lovely ladies I've never met in my life. At least I don't ever remember meeting you two. But you seem to know about me, about how many languages I know, and even intimate details about the lines on my palm. And we're also engaged in a deep philosophical somber discussion on death. Talk about strange things and days, this absolutely has to be the most bizarre day of my life."

"Most bizarre day of your life so far, and from your current perspective." Ella smiled.

"What?"

"It's not especially outlandish to me, that's what I am trying to say," Ella said. "I've experienced many things. But let's keep those for another time."

"You mean there's going to be another time?" Niam asked.

"Why not! I am enjoying our company and the occasion," Nina said.

"I'll decide on that," Niam spoke. "But first, what are we doing here? Help me unravel this."

"I know what I am doing here," Nina replied. "I am trying to figure out my role in this version of yours."

"See. Right there. That doesn't make sense to me at all. What version?" Niam asked.

"That's for you to tell us. It's your version," Ella said. "As for me, I am here trying to determine how much Stoicism I need in my life."

"But...? Really? That is quite a turnaround!"

"I cannot control how my health progresses. I can only hope. What is within my conscious control, I suppose, is how I react to it and to the world at large. I cannot also...."

"But that's all well and good," Niam interjected. "And I am deeply sorry for your condition. I can only say that I do not, and simply cannot, fathom the depths of suffering you must be

28

going through, and go through every day, day after day. Nina mentioned that you have something to tell us, maybe help me understand all this."

"I suppose I have to help you. But I have no idea how. Come, let's continue with our walk. Maybe once we're done, we can head to a pizza place nearby and get something small to eat."

They started their stroll again. This time Niam stayed a step behind them, his mind whirring.

"Tell me, you have a wife, right?" Ella asked.

"Yes."

"A daughter too?"

"No."

They both stopped and turned to look at him. Niam, on cue, stopped too.

"You don't have a daughter?" Nina asked.

"I am pretty sure I don't. I think I would know something like this, wouldn't I?"

"Maybe he doesn't have a daughter with her but with some-one else," Ella addressed Nina.

"Now, wait a minute." Niam held a hand up. "Seriously?"

"No, no," Nina responded to Ella, seemingly ignoring Niam. "It has to be with her, and no one else. She and he are together. Listen," and this time she acknowledged Niam's presence by addressing him, "you need to have a daughter with your wife as soon as you can."

"And how do you propose I have one?"

"How does one have a daughter?" Ella giggled. "You go home, and you make love to your wife. And you do it regularly until she's pregnant. Do you want us to tell you how to make love too, or is that something you already know?"

"Oh, I am sure he knows how to make love." Nina chuckled too. "You do, right?"

"Seriously?" Niam again said, his cheeks now red from embarrassment.

"Come on! We can have some fun, can't we?" Ella said.

Niam shook his head. "We haven't decided on children, if you must know. Maybe sometime in the future. I am not sure I want to have kids. My wife thinks she does, but I don't think she's very interested in children at this time. But, but, forget all this. Why did you think I have a daughter, and why should I have one?"

"I don't know. I suppose it just occurred to me that you have a daughter," Ella said.

"Same here. I just assumed you have a daughter," Nina also replied. "But it's okay if you don't have one yet."

"The stoic in me wants to tell you, or rather me, that it shouldn't affect me whether you have a daughter or not," Ella jumped in, and then looked a little angry. "I should focus on mollifying my inflamed emotions and reactions. This should be the way to go for me to make my life more fulfilling. As is, I suffer enough already. But lately I have issues with this take on life. Every once in a while, I want to cry out aloud. I want to look at the sky, and shout at it. I want to pick up whatever I can get my two hands on, in my home or outside or anywhere, and throw it against the wall. I want to blame someone for all this. I don't want to bottle up and control my emotions all the time. This makes me less of a human, I believe. I do not want to be less of a human. I want to feel. I want to affect and to be affected. I want to know that I matter to someone, anyone."

She stopped her walk. "What was I saying? I can't remember where I was before I got sidetracked by my own issues. Oh, yes. I wanted to say that I don't want to intrude in your life. But, maybe I already am intruding. Or maybe you are intruding in my life. What am I saying? It doesn't matter, does it?"

Niam looked at Ella and Nina as he thought of what next to say. He was distracted by a young mother with her baby in a pram walking past them. He looked at the sleeping baby, and then up toward the mother. Their eyes were locked very briefly.

Niam felt that she too was trying to tell him something. Perhaps she was willing him to procreate too. When he turned back, Ella had started walking again, with Nina following.

"Tell me," Nina said, when Niam was walking shoulder-to-shoulder with her, "What are your dreams? Your ambitions? Do you have any?"

Niam took a moment to think. "I don't know if I have any particular, distinct, interesting ambition. I suppose it's the same as many like me. I want to rise up in the corporate world, do work that interests me, make money, retire comfortably, maybe early, and maybe very early."

The three of them walked in silence for a very brief time. Niam thought a little more. "I guess, it's not completely correct. I do have dreams and ambitions beyond what I said. In fact, I wouldn't even call those things I just said dreams. Perhaps things I would do to aid in my dreams."

"Then what are they?" Ella asked.

"I have two burning desires. I want to be a celebrity. I want to experience the feeling of being adulated. I want people to listen to my opinions, to seek them. I want my thoughts and opinions to matter."

Niam paused after taking a deep breath. He couldn't understand why he was opening up his heart to these two strangers he had just met. He hadn't mentioned this to anyone before, including Prisha.

"Interesting," Nina filled in the silence. "What is the other burning desire?"

"I want to help the world," Niam continued. "I want to pick up a social or environmental cause that'll benefit the world. I want to leave the world a better place than what it is now. I don't know what cause I want to pick up. Maybe I'll never find a cause that I can somehow wholeheartedly jump into. But I'll keep looking. And maybe being a celebrity will help. It'll give me the platform to be heard. It'll make it easier to affect any positive changes I will seek. Perhaps these two desires are not separate after all."

"How interesting," Ella said. "I can see that you are in touch with yourself. It may be tenuous, but there is a bond. My advice is not to spend too much time dreaming about what you just mentioned. Dreams are like people. They all die, the bad ones and the good ones."

"I know," Niam said. "I am working on my ambitions. What I mean is that I am trying to figure out how to achieve them. I am trying to develop a roadmap, a plan which has the steps listed, and the milestones I need to meet. Nothing has come to mind so far. But I am sure something will. In the meanwhile, I have other things to keep me occupied—my daily professional routine, earning my living, saving for retirement, a longer-term aim to rise up the chain of command."

"Yes, there are those things too." Nina smiled.

"I think I am done with the walk for today," Ella said. "I am tired, and I should be getting home."

"How far is your home from here?" Nina asked. "Maybe we can accompany you there?"

"Thank you for the offer!" Ella said. "But I think I'll be alright. I know the way around here better than anyone else." She turned on a small path leading toward and through the canopy of trees. "I love this place. It's always so quiet. We three should do this again. Maybe just the three of us, no one else. Three is as big a group of people as I can handle. Anymore, and I don't get an opportunity to converse and understand and connect."

They were out of the park on the opposite side from which Niam and Nina had entered, and on a sidewalk of a noisy and busy road.

"I will go this way," Ella said and pointed her guide cane toward her right. "There's a bus stop there, not far from here." She pointed the cane to her left. "It was a most wonderful time I had meeting you two. We will meet again."

With that she started walking. Niam looked at her, thinking of what to say. In the end he decided to say nothing. He turned to look at Nina.

"I live some distance from here. I would like to walk," Nina said. "Let me walk with you to the bus stop."

"Thanks," Niam replied.

"I too had a wonderful time," Nina said as they walked. "I wish it could have been longer. But then we don't need to fit the entirety of all our meetings into one single long meeting. As Ella said, we will have more such wonderful times together."

"I am not too sure we'll meet again," Niam said.

"We undeniably will meet again." Nina's face lit up with an innocuous affecting smile. "Don't you see? You have helped me better understand my role. A few more conversations, and I'll be absolutely certain."

"I am not really liking all this. I still haven't understood anything. What role is it you're talking about?" Niam asked.

"You're being too harsh on yourself." Nina continued beaming. "You don't need to be. This is your version after all. If I've understood it right from you and Ella, my role is to help you navigate through, what would it be, what would it be, yes, non-existence. Non-existence. There's your bus. It should take you to the nearest metro line. Or close to it, I hope. You'll figure it out."

Niam saw her turn around and walk away before he hopped on the bus.

Niam and Prisha first met on a long-distance train. They found themselves together in the same compartment, and instantly felt a connection. Prisha was a final-year college student in Bangalore. She was returning home to Delhi for the winter break. Niam was to change trains in Delhi for a further onward journey north, to spend a couple of weeks with his family. Niam was older than Prisha by about four years. He had moved to Bangalore for a new job after working in Pune for nearly two years. He had wanted to move to Delhi to be closer to his home. However, he had not been able to find an appropriate position there so far.

Their small talk eventually led to longer conversations, and an exchange of contact information. By the end of their train ride, it was a forgone conclusion that they would meet up when they were back in Bangalore. They soon developed feelings for each other, and became even closer when Niam helped her find a starting position in his company.

Further developments in their relationship were not smooth. Their families were not very excited about their union, or any union that wasn't endogamy. Prisha's family belonged to a lower caste—urban. Outwardly, her family did not show any caste bias. However, Prisha's father, in particular, carried the weight of generations of resentment. Niam's family, on the other hand, was rustic, and carried their upper caste credentials on their sleeves. To them, Niam was supposed to take on the mantle of the family leader, and as such had to do everything per family traditions. The mutual dislike between the families was instantaneous, even before the first contact.

Prisha's family were more open to their relationship than Niam's family. Niam knew that if they got married, he would face difficulties visiting home with her. Caste distinctions in his village were very open, and intermingling was limited. Prisha would not feel welcome, and his family would have a tough time with neighbors, friends, and relatives in the village. This thought upset him, but he did not let it bother him much. He was already the most educated and successful person in his village. He was certain that eventually his help and advice would be sought after. As for himself, he had left the village for education and work, and did not think he would ever settle back there.

They got married in Delhi. The wedding ceremony was a small affair. Niam's parents and siblings, and a few friends were there. Prisha's family and neighborhood had a larger showing. Right after the ceremony they left for their honeymoon for Goa. It was in this distant state, that they consummated their marriage, and both lost their virginity.

Prisha had always intended to save herself for marriage. She and Niam had often engaged in intimacies and heavy petting, sometimes without clothes. Emotions would also occasionally reach some heights. However, on all such occasions, she, more than Niam, would show the greater restraint. Niam was on the whole patient and mostly in control of himself and respected her boundaries. In many ways, this practice brought them even closer. Trust and respect aside, they learned a lot about their own and the other's body, and the many different ways of giving and receiving pleasure.

Niam had always been shy around women. However, Prisha was not the first woman he had been intimate with. With him, women would usually be the ones to take the first step. However, their interest would soon fizzle when they came up with an introverted and conflicted personality. That personality was mostly a cover. In reality he did not know how to converse freely with women. Coming from a small village and landing in a male-only college hostel, he had not interacted much with women for most of his short life thus far. He simply did not know how to approach women he liked. On the other hand, women who approached him were more aggressive than he could understand, let alone handle, and he found them intimidating.

This all changed about a year before he met Prisha. It was a late Saturday evening, and he was getting ready to settle down on the sofa to watch TV after a light dinner at his apartment. His two roommates had left for a night of drinking and partying with friends. They had tried hard to convince him to join, but on that day, he was not in the mood for it.

All by himself at the apartment, Niam decided to cook an elaborate meal for himself. He prepared basmati rice, shahi paneer with a bit of extra cream to remind him of his village and his grandmother's cooking, a scrambled egg, and a small side salad of cucumbers and onions. It was more than he would be able to eat in a single, or even two sittings, but he felt like trying. Once seated with the dinner spread in front of him, he turned the TV on to a gritty crime-drama program. In the middle of the dinner, he got up from the couch to get a cold bottle of beer from the refrigerator. Before he could open the bottle, his phone rang. He rushed back to see who was calling him. He saw a number he did not recognize and decided to ignore the call. The phone rang a couple of times and went silent. He soon returned to the couch and went back to the task of watching the program on TV while gorging on dinner and beer.

A short while later, as Niam reclined back on the couch with the remote control in his hand and while he was thinking of looking for something more interesting to watch, his phone rang again. He held it up and saw the same number. On a whim, this time, he decided to pick it up.

"Hello? he enquired, eager to know who had troubled to call him twice.

"Hello? Can I talk to Niam, please?" came a woman's voice. It sounded soft, and a little hesitant, vulnerable—attractive even.

"Yes, this is Niam," he replied, with some impatience. He had learned that doing so at the earliest point in the conversation was necessary to deter any telemarketer.

"Hello Niam. I got your number from a friend. I am in Bangalore for a couple of months and staying with close relatives. I just wanted to know if you can be my friend. We cannot meet, but we can talk on the phone. My family is very conservative. I am always being watched, and it's tough for me to meet people. I know this sounds strange. But my friend who gave me your number said you are a very nice person, and someone I can talk to during my stay here. Do you want to be my friend?"

Niam went silent to try to digest what he had just heard.

When the silence became long enough, the woman spoke again, "Hello, are you there?"

"Yes, yes, I am here. Sorry."

"It's okay. I understand. This was not a call you were expecting."

"Certainly not," Niam said.

"Why don't you think it over for a day? How about I call you tomorrow at the same time? I would love to have you as my friend and as someone I can talk to. But I'll also understand if you tell me you're not interested," she said.

"Yes, you're right. It sounds like a good plan. Let me think about this. Who gave you my number?"

"I cannot tell you. If I do, you might try to find out about me. I don't want that. Maybe we can eventually meet up. But it has to be on my terms, and in a way that will not cause my relatives to become suspicious."

"I understand," Niam said. He did not understand, but he did not want to think about all this at this very instant. He wanted to savor the strangeness of the moment, not the thoughts. "You can call me tomorrow at this time. What's your name, if I may know?"

The woman spoke with a clear elation in her voice. Niam could almost sense her smiling. "My name? It's Ella. I'll call you tomorrow, same time. Goodbye." She ended the call.

Niam found it challenging to sit steady after the call. He paced the living room for a while. He then sat down on the couch for some time to finish a couple of beers. It didn't work to calm his emotions, and he went for a walk around the apartment complex. When he came back, one of his roommates, Arun, had returned. Arun, like Niam, was more of an introvert. However, being single with a well-paying high-pressure job, and living with young men of similar age, had started to change him. He had developed a taste for rich food and heavy beer on the weekends, and going to bars with friends to be in with the crowd. During the week, though, he was very focused on his work.

Niam met Arun through the help of common friends when they were both looking for a shared apartment. Right from the first time they met, Niam reached the conclusion that Arun was not of an intellectual bent. He was gregarious and easy going, and definitely very intelligent—all wonderful qualities in someone to share living quarters with. But he had a limited worldview. That worldview, in the simplest words, Niam told a colleague he worked closely with, was a couple of variants of a single broad theme—an assumed cultural victimhood where his religion and the country were always under threat.

"I feel sorry for him sometimes," Niam had said to his colleague. "This constant feeling of being under siege. It cannot be good in the long run. He'll snap. He's otherwise such a nice, docile guy."

"They all are in person when they are by themselves," his colleague said. "It's in groups or on online forums where they bare their true inner selves. My experience with them has been darker. I would say I find such people suffering from narcissism with a perceived sense of superiority over people with a different ideology, religion, or education. It's also sociopathy perhaps with a lack of empathy for others. But if you two get along well and respect each other's boundaries, I see no reason to worry."

Niam did not see a reason to worry. There were times when Arun's hardheaded opinions would irritate him to no small extent. But Niam was a very accommodating person. He also knew that Arun and he would not be roommates forever. It was a matter of patience. Arun did his share to help keep the place clean, he paid his rent and other common expenses on time, and he did not interfere in others' lives. It also helped that they all led busy lives.

Arun, once comfortable with someone, did not shy away from conversations when talked to. Occasionally, when in the mood, he would become near garrulous. Mostly, those conversations were about people within the larger sphere that made up his world. He would not poke others to open up about their lives. His universe was large enough to keep him occupied. It also kept others involved and entertained because he was a good storyteller. He had the knack of personalizing and enlivening the lives of people he revealed, and made them far more interesting than they could ever aspire to be. It was during those conversations that Niam obtained interesting insights into his family.

The flirting with radical ideologies by Arun was mostly because of his extended family—a close-knit community of siblings and cousins and uncles and aunts and his parents, but particularly his mother. The extended family was almost functionally a secluded self-contained tribe living in a crowded world. They hung out mostly with each other regularly, took care of each other, shared each other's joys and pains, loved each other, fought and made up even more regularly, and were intensely jealous of each other. The extreme closeness left little emotional room or opportunity to bond with anyone outside the family. It also closed them from experiences and thoughts and ideas, and critically, education and ambition.

Arun's mother was more ideological than most in his family. She had married into it from a somewhat more open, smaller family. In the beginning she had found her married life overwhelming and tremendously onerous. She spent days and nights taking care of everyone, with little time and energy left to spend with her husband, Arun's father. The judging was near constant by her in-laws—what she wore, how she wore it, what she cooked, how she cooked, what she said, how she said, everything was up for discussion by everyone, oftentimes right in front of her. A rare outing to a movie theater would also draw jealous aspersions from everyone. Over a few years, this near constant state of being hostage-like developed in her a sense of helplessness and meekness and anger. Since the docility that had been beaten into her psyche prevented her from expressing this anger toward the family, it accumulated in her and took on a shapeless, nebulous form. Then it was only a matter of time that the rage found an anchor in extremist thinking. Here *others* were the cause of her suffering, though she could never clearly elucidate what she was suffering from to herself and to Arun. This did not also matter to Arun. As her child, only her anger mattered to him. From an early age, whenever she could, his mother told him that she was angry at a community, at a politician, at a religion. Arun imbibed that anger till it became his superego. He covered that angry core with layers and layers of derived docility. But it was there, with a glow strong enough to drive him. He became a vessel of her collective angers. Without that angry core, without that ideology, he would not have an identity.

Niam guessed most of this from what Arun had narrated. It was the only explanation that seemed to fit his basal personality. During the early phase of their acquaintanceship, Arun was an enigma to him. An itch that couldn't be scratched. Deciphering Arun's personality had become important for him. Niam had grown up believing that education opened one's mind, made one more agreeable to new ideas, more respectful of others' viewpoints, and less given to irrational anger. The people in the remote village that he grew up in were mostly not educated beyond basic reading and math skills, and he had found them to be anything but open-minded. By extension, he ascribed this to a lack of education. But Arun was educated. He had a master's degree. This did not fit into Niam's original worldview.

Niam soon discovered that Arun was not unique. There were many like him who held radical views.

"Look," his coworker once said, "in my experience the only difference between an educated and uneducated person is in the degree toward propensity for violence. A person with education will be less likely to engage in violence, that's all. If you look around you, a person with education may scream like a lunatic and even call for violence, but it's usually only people less educated who would go out on the streets to riot and burn and whatnot."

"You're right," Niam said.

"Of course, you agree with me!" his coworker responded. "You didn't really choose your roommates. You just somehow got stuck with them because you were in a hurry. But you chose to hang out with me. We gravitate to people we can have agreeable conversations with without feeling we are being judged."

Niam was someone who rarely judged, if at all, on most things. He wasn't passionate about politics, sports, movies, literature, fashion, or anything that ignites the emotions of large swathes of people. His discussions with others on these topics were never initiated by him. If they happened, his participation was usually perfunctory and lacked any depth. He was well-aware of this, and was not shy of declaring his deficiencies. His upbringing had trained him to lead a mostly disciplined life with little room for extremes. His taste in outings was also not like those of people around him. He loved parks, where others sought the glitz of the city. He loved short hiking or trekking trips at some distance from the city, while others dove deep into its belly. Arun and Neel, his other roommate, accompanied him on some of these trips. When they did, he had to find something easy to do. They both did not have the kind of endurance Niam had. The first time Niam got them excited about an all-day hike for a Saturday was to a small temple on a hilltop his colleague had told him about. When he first mentioned it, Arun nearly jumped up with a yes because it meant a visit to a temple. Neel said yes with great excitement because hiking sounded adventurous. It was something he had always wanted to do but had not had the opportunity to.

Niam ended up picking the most difficult climb up the hill,

one that his colleague had specifically talked against. To his colleague, this hiking route was for those who led active lifestyles and were in great shape. Niam was, and, he initially assumed, so were his roommates.

The climb wasn't perilous going up, but it was steep and full of big boulders. Some of these big rocks could only be crossed by lifting oneself up using one's hands. Niam considered this a great exercise. Arun and Neel, on the other hand, were completely exhausted within twenty minutes. The two took frequent breaks to rest and rejuvenate. Doing his best to motivate his friends, Niam had to make his way back down a few times to encourage them. To them both, going back down looked so much easier than the ever-increasing steepness of the climb up ahead of them. Nonetheless they persevered, egged on by Niam. A couple of times they were quite literally pushed and pulled up the boulders by him. Collectively it took about two hours to climb the hill that Niam, by himself, could do in under an hour. Eventually they did finally reach the top. Once there, it was only a small distance around and down to the temple.

The temple was small and not particularly impressive or fancy. The interior wasn't well lit since there was no electric line connecting to it from below. On one side, away from the cliff the temple was situated on, was a small brick house within and to the side of a small compound. The enclosure was fenced off by a neat row of small bushes, and was mostly empty except for a single cow and a calf. The cow was busy munching on hay, while the calf stood beside its mother. The dim light in the temple hall was powered by a single small solar panel on the roof of the house. A few interspersed trees provided adequate shade to the entire place and helped keep it cool. The height above the ground also helped.

"I like it!" exclaimed Arun when they saw the temple. He managed a genuine smile on his haggard face. "It's peaceful and quiet and pastoral. How did you even know about this place?"

"I heard about it from a colleague," Niam replied. "He's been here a couple of times. He told me something interesting about this temple, which he heard from others. So, this is just hearsay. He said if you climb up the difficult path, the one we took to reach this temple, you will get an easy visa and a big project to a big foreign country, and with a chance to make a lot of money. Isn't that great! When we go back down, we will all have a project and a visa waiting for us!"

"Ha! That would be wonderful! But I am not sure I have the energy to go down. I need to eat and sleep, and, after I wake up, think about it for a long time," Arun said.

"Some days are just good days. Not great, not earth shatteringly awesome, just good, just perfect. I think this is one of them," Neel declared after being silent for nearly an hour.

The temple was remote enough, and reaching it arduous enough, to keep the building mostly empty. Besides the three friends, there was a young couple, and a couple with toddlers. They did not appear nearly as tired as the three because they had driven up to the temple in their cars on a narrow road. This road was in decent shape, but not the safest to drive on. At some points it was barely able to accommodate two small cars side-by-side.

From out of nowhere, the temple priest appeared. He was a short thin man, not much older than thirty. He had a full head of hair, and then some, which was pulled back and tied in a bun. A thin mustache in an otherwise clean-shaven face accentuated his upper facial features, particularly his eyes. His smile was very welcoming as he invited them all into the temple hall and proceeded to perform a small prayer ceremony. The donations from the small but regular number of temple visitors were what was keeping the place running—the only source of his income. He had to be accommodating of everyone's prayer requests— whether it was for marriage, a job, passing a competitive exam, health, the birth of a child, sometimes of a particular gender, or even a visa and a big project in a foreign land.

"Where can we get something to eat?" Arun asked the priest after he was done with the prayer and the generous doling out of blessings in proportion to the donations.

"Eat? Are you hungry? Come. Come with me," he beckoned the three. They followed him as he took them outside the temple, to a round raised stone platform with a couple of stone benches.

"Sit, please." He pointed to the platform. "*Idli, sambar? Idli, sambar?*" he asked as he looked at them.

"Sure!" Neel exclaimed.

"I'll get it for you. My wife makes those herself here and sells them for very cheap." With that he took off to the house.

"He never told us how much it would cost, did he?" Niam asked.

"How expensive can it be? Besides, I don't really care. I need a filling hot meal to give me the energy to be able to make it down," Arun said.

They stayed silent for the next ten or so minutes as they tried to recuperate from the exertion of the climb. When they had become tired of waiting, the priest emerged from the house with a big tray. The tray had three big bowls, each filled with *sambar* and four *idlis*. Much to their surprise, there were also three big glasses filled with spiced buttermilk.

"The yogurt for this is made from the milk from our cow," the priest said as he kept the tray on a bench. "For sure you'll like it."

They liked it. They also loved the *idlis*. The three were so hungry, they would have liked anything served to them. They also paid a very reasonable price for the hearty meal.

After some rest the three started their trek back down to the base of the hill. The climb down was tough too. It was less tiring, but more dangerous. Each foot had to be planted carefully before the other could be lifted. The steps had to be small. It was easy to lose one's footing and fall and even break a bone or two. If that were to happen, it would be difficult to imagine being carried to the base or back up to the temple. Fortunately, they did manage to get back to the base in one piece. From there it was a near leisurely couple of kilometers walk to the parking lot and to their waiting bikes. Among the three they had two bikes. Niam rode with Neel on his bike, while Arun rode by himself on his.

On the way back to their apartment, they stopped at an Italian restaurant Neel had been wanting to try for a while. It wasn't a super fancy restaurant, but just fancy enough to bring some hesitation in Niam when they entered. The prices listed on the menu were also much higher than his comfort zone would have allowed him to spend. More than that, there was nothing on the menu he really understood besides pasta and pizza. He decided to order the cheapest thing he could see, a Margherita pizza. He sensed Arun's discomfit too. Arun looked through the menu a few times and kept it on the table. He then looked at Neel and said, "This the first time I've been to an Italian restaurant. I don't know anything except pizza. Any suggestions?"

"I like the mushroom ravioli best here," Neel said. "I'll order it for myself, and you can share with me. Maybe try the pasta. They have a decent selection."

Arun ordered a fettucine Alfredo. In the end, all three shared their dishes with each other. Not a scrap was left on any plate, and not a drop of beer was left in any bottle.

That night, as they were getting ready to retire to their individual rooms and crash into their beds, Neel repeated what he had said earlier.

"Some days are just good days. Not great, not earth shatteringly awesome, just good, just perfect. I think this was one of them. Let's just not do something this strenuous again for a while!"

Niam had realized that Neel had a habit of repeating some phrases over a period of a few hours or days. It was as if once he came up with a phrase, he stored it in a memory bank. Later, he would retrieve it from there for use once or twice before erasing it. This time he added a short sentence at the end of the phrase: "Let's just not do something this strenuous again for a while!"

"I agree," Arun jumped in. "I think I'll hit the gym regularly from tomorrow. Give me a few months to build the kind of stamina you have. Then I can do this hike again with you."

"Me too," Neel blurted before entering his room.

They never went hiking back to the temple again. Neel and Arun both left the country for big projects a little more than a year later. Neel went to Israel, and Arun to Britain.

"You should have joined us! It was absolute fun," Arun exclaimed as soon as he saw Niam enter the apartment. "We went from one bar to the next to the next. Those guys were planning to drink even more. But I told Neel I needed to get home because of work tomorrow. He gave me his bike. He'll probably be back tomorrow morning."

"Great! I'll join you guys next time for sure. I just wasn't into going out tonight. I had a long chat with my family today. It got me into one of those moods where I needed to be by myself and take it easy," Niam replied as he got a beer out of the fridge.

"I understand," Arun said. "I have those mood swings too occasionally when I talk to my family, especially when they talk about get-togethers and all the fun they're having. I miss it."

"Yeah," Niam said. He started to move his lips to say something more but became quiet for a few seconds. Arun looked at him silently in anticipation.

"Something interesting happened this evening when you were out," Niam finally spoke.

"Oh, yes? What was that?" Arun asked as he made his way to the couch.

"I had made myself a great dinner. I used some of the *paneer* you had in the freezer, and made a few other things. I decided to go all in. And just when I was totally into it, I get the strangest of phone calls."

"Yeah? Who called you?"

Niam sighed. "Some random girl called me up and said she'd gotten my number from a mutual acquaintance, and she wants to be my friend." Niam tried to sound serious.

"What the hell?" Arun frowned a bit.

"Really. She said she's new in town and is here for just a short time. She said she cannot meet me because she's staying with her relatives and she doesn't want to create issues or something. She says we can talk over the phone for now."

"Seriously?" Arun frowned again.

"Yup," Niam responded.

"Wait, wait, let me get this straight. Some girl calls you up and wants to be your friend. This doesn't even make sense. You have her number, right?"

"Yes, it showed up on my phone."

"Then call her back. I am sure this time it's going to be picked up by some dude. This sounds like a scam or something. Or maybe someone playing a joke on you." Arun's frown deepened.

"I think so too," Niam said.

"What do you mean by 'think so'? Do it. Ring her right now."

"Nah." Niam lightly waved his hand. "This lady said she'll call me tomorrow at the same time. I don't have to do anything. If she calls, I'll talk to her, prank or no prank, scam or no scam. If she doesn't, then that's the end of it."

"Just be careful," Arun said as his frown returned. "It's easy to get scammed. You see it on the news all the time. People get fleeced for money, or even blackmailed."

"Who would blackmail me?" Niam smiled. "There's nothing to blackmail me for."

"Whatever. Maybe. Just be careful," Arun said.

The woman called back the next day at the same time. Niam had spent the evening straining to control his anxiety, or perhaps excitement, by pacing up and down the room waiting for the call.

"Hello?" Niam spoke into the phone. He was thankful that he was alone again at the apartment. Arun had not returned from his office. The project he was working on was approaching the delivery deadline. This was keeping him and others in his office very busy over evenings and weekends. Neel was out grocery shopping for the week.

Niam had spent the day trying not to think about the call. He had convinced himself it was a prank by one of his friends. But a part of him was also very curious and hoped for the call, if for nothing else than to just unravel the mystery. That part of him would have been disappointed if the call had not come in.

"Hello, Niam? How are you?" she said in a slow, soft, uncertain voice.

"Hi," Niam said while trying to keep a steady voice. "I am fine. How are you?"

"I am fine too," she replied. "Thank you for taking my call."

"You're welcome," Niam said.

An awkward silence followed. Niam thought he was expected to carry the conversation forward. However, he wasn't particularly good at striking up conversations with strangers. Fortunately, he did not need to think much about it because the woman spoke.

"Did you decide if you want to be friends with me?"

He took a pause to collect and put together the words for a response. "I haven't decided," he said. "I need to know more about you before I can even answer this question. I don't know who you are and what you do, and everything, and why me, and everything, and something more?"

She let out a small laugh. "My name's Ella. I told you that before. What more can I tell you?"

"I don't know," Niam said after a pause. "Anything you want. Maybe, why me?"

"Someone I know gave me your number. It's not easy making friends. That someone said you are trustworthy and sweet, and I should reach out to you. I know I have to earn your trust because I am the one who called."

"That's for sure," Niam said. "You're not pranking me or something, are you? Or something worse?"

"No, no," Ella replied with a deeper voice. "I wouldn't do something like this. Why would anyone want to?"

Niam tried to gauge her sincerity from the tone of her voice. Arun shouted to him very loud from deep inside his head, "Just be careful!"

"Okay," Niam replied silently to Arun's voice in his head.

"What do you know about me?" Niam steered the conversation to try to take some charge.

"Just that you work in the technology industry. Nothing more," Ella said.

"Do you have a social media account we can connect on?" Niam guessed the answer to this in the brief pause before she replied.

"I don't have a social media account. I never had one. My family does not allow it. If I were to create one, and they were to find out, they wouldn't be very happy. In case you want to know, and if you trust my judgement, I am not outstandingly beautiful, But I know I am not bad looking."

Niam did not know how to respond to her last statement, and didn't. "So, what are you doing here?" he asked, instead.

"I am studying to be a nurse. I am here for a few months working at a hospital as part of my training," Ella responded.

"And staying with your relatives who closely monitor you?"

"Yes, that's right. It gets tough, but what else can I do? My cousin drops me at the hospital every day on his way to work and picks me up in the evenings."

"It's very strange," Niam said. "You're not even allowed to go anywhere by yourself."

Niam felt the effort and exertion through her breath before she spoke, "Mostly not. I am Muslim, and my family is very conservative... Are you there?" she asked a few seconds later when she didn't hear anything from Niam.

"I'm here, I'm here," Niam replied.

"Are you okay?"

"Oh, yes, I am okay. Listen. How about we talk tomorrow? Same time? Do you want me to call you?"

"No, please don't call me, or even text me. I'll call you," Ella said.

Later that night, the three, Niam, Arun, and Neel, went to a late-night ice cream shop not too far from their apartment. Arun had returned from work exhausted and wanted to unwind before going to bed.

""We are finally getting close to completion," Arun spoke once he had freshened up. "My work is is mostly done, and now it's up to the other team to finish up. My boss said I don't have to come in early tomorrow morning. Maybe we can go out for an hour or so? If you're up for it, I'll buy you an ice cream each."

Niam and Neel had agreed. The night was hot and humid, and the ice cream was a cool treat.

When they were reclining against their parked bikes outside the ice cream shop, licking and biting the ice creams they had ordered in cones, Niam said to Arun, "Guess what? The woman called me back!"

"She did? Did you talk to her?"

"What woman?" Neel interrupted.

"There's this unknown woman who's been calling him up. Says she's in love with him and what not and wants to do it with him," Arun replied and smiled.

"Are you joking me?" Neel asked.

"No, it's not like that," Niam responded. He narrated to him the events from the past two days.

"No way!" Neel exclaimed. "Some woman calls you up and wants to be your friend? Give her my number. I can be her friend. I am great at being phone friends. And even better at phone sex, I tell you."

Niam laughed at his friend's response.

"Muslim, you said?" Arun seemingly ignored Neel.

"Who cares Muslim or what," Neel jumped back in. "Do you care? I don't care. Phone sex is phone sex. Did I tell you about this girl I used to have phone sex with for the longest time, like for eight-nine months. Man, this girl was something else!"

Arun again seemingly ignored Neel. "I am not too sure about this. What if it came out that you're talking to a girl from a conservative Muslim family? It can get complicated very fast with her family. And what if your family found out? Would they be happy?"

"Yeah, that can be a problem for sure," Neel said. "But..."

"Why get into all this trouble to begin with?" Arun jumped in before Neel could complete his thought. "I say end it. Block her number. Or simply tell her you don't want to talk to her. That is if you don't want to be rude."

"And give her my number instead!" Neel smiled and took a bite of his pistachio flavored ice cream.

"You stay out of it, or you'll get into trouble too. This seems like some conspiracy to rope in good guys and cause problems for them. They rope in girls this way too. Some man will call a woman and tell her how beautiful and sexy she is and how he's in love with her and ask her to meet him. Then he'll get her to marry him, and then convert her from her religion," Arun said, and, following Neel, took a long lick of his butterscotch ice cream.

"You think I shouldn't be talking to her?" Niam asked them both. He put what remained of his ice cream cone, with its few remaining traces of the chocolate ice cream he had ordered, into his mouth.

"Absolutely not. Hey! Be careful. You're dripping ice cream all over your shoes," Arun said.

"Oh, boy!" Neel exclaimed with dismay as he looked at his shoes. "These are my good shoes. Fuck!" He bent down to wipe the ice cream drops from his red-and-white sneakers. "It's left a mark! I'll have to figure out a way to get it off."

Arun and Niam watched him struggle to wipe away the mark. "Yeah, just stay away from this if you can," Neel said while still bent down. "I don't know about all that conversion bullshit. I don't think there'd be any trouble, but why risk it? On the other hand, if in the next couple or so months you're leaving this job and place and the country for a while, why not? I had fun talking to this chick on the phone."

"You think this conversion thing is not real?" Arun said, with an edge in his voice. "Don't talk about things you don't know anything about."

"Maybe it's real," Neel responded calmly, not taking the bait. "I have no data on it. All I am saying is it's not worth the risk."

Arun looked at him and went back to his ice cream.

"What happened with this girl you talked to on the phone?" Niam asked Neel. Neel had straightened back up after he finished cleaning his shoes the best he felt he could.

"With her? This was a few years ago. We met up on social media. I messaged her or liked her post or something. We communicated a few times. She was not from around where I was, so we started talking on the phone. Then things became super heavy soon. We ended up having super long phone sex sessions pretty much most of the time. I would lie down naked and ask her to strip off her clothes one at a time. We would start talking at like ten at night and go on sometimes till three or four in the morning. We explored everything that you can imagine. It was something else!"

"Oh, yeah? Like what?" Niam smiled. Arun just stared at Neel unblinkingly.

"Just about everything you can imagine. Group sex, bondage, lesbian sex with a close friend of hers. You name it. And during those times I might come like one or two times, but she would come multiple times. And sometimes her orgasms would last very long. I could tell that. Her orgasm would start, and she would start breathing heavily and she wouldn't be able to speak a word for like ten-fifteen minutes. I had never experienced anything like this before, or anything after. In the beginning, when I didn't know this about her, I would call out her name a few times thinking something was wrong. But then I realized she was in a bliss zone, and zoned out. Soon I learned to take this as an opportunity. As soon as she would start orgasming, I would put my phone down and take a bathroom break, maybe drink some water, and come back in due time. And then we would start all over again."

"I don't believe this story one bit," Arun said with a disgusted look on his face.

"But it's true!" Neel exclaimed. "Why would I make something like this up?"

"Ten to fifteen orgasms a night? Every night?"

"I never said ten to fifteen orgasms. You can't have ten to fifteen orgasms in a night, every night! Of course, you can't! I said her one orgasm would sometimes last ten to fifteen minutes. And I know more about girls than you do," Neel said out loud with levity and smile.

Arun had gotten on his bike and started it. Neel got on his, and Niam hopped on behind him.

"I believe your story," Niam said to Neel. "What happened with the girl after this?"

"I don't know," Neel said. "I graduated and she later graduated, and we got busy and lost contact. I think she met a guy. She must be married or with someone by now. I should check her social media status. But during the times we were talking, it was intense. It was as close to love I've ever been. It was certainly very intimate. I discovered a lot about myself, too."

Niam liked Neel. Neel was an eternal optimist. His outlook on life was always tinted with rose-colored glasses. This optimism never failed to rub off on others around him. It was not so much that he was never ever sad or upset, but that he would never let things linger for too long. He actively sought pleasure, and actively avoided things that were bothersome. In many ways he and Arun were polar opposites. But they still got along well together. It never affected Neel that Arun disapproved of his lifestyle and life choices. In fact, it had quite the opposite effect. He once told Niam that he had taken it as a challenge to, as he said, upgrade and update this old rotary phone Arun to a 21st century smartphone Arun. Neel would often pester Arun to accompany him for city trips to bars and restaurants and to meet girls, until Arun would cave. Arun would keep his distance from girls, but he enjoyed the other things that Neel's companionship had to offer. And the companionship certainly opened him up. It made him more sociable and affable.

Neel was intelligent. Niam was certain he was more intelligent in their line of education and work than Arun and he were, and anyone else he knew of. He was not intellectual by any measure. His reading material was also mostly limited to what was useful for his work. His thought process was not overtly complicated, and he always tried to grab the simplest explanation or conclusion. This was the other part that Niam liked about Neel. He never demanded anyone open up and display their passions and strong opinions. A few times, however, Niam sensed a certain depth in his character, which was seemingly incongruous with this outward personality. It was as if his almost fanatical focus on the brighter side of life was not an innate, inborn personality, but a purposefully acquired trait. Niam noticed this the first time one evening. They were both sitting on the couch with Neel switching channels, trying to find something of common interest to watch. Arun was still at work. When Neel had switched through about thirty channels, stopping at each from anywhere between half-a-minute to a couple of minutes, he came across a documentary on the Cambodian genocide by the Khmer Rouge. He decided to watch it when Niam showed no signs of objections. Much to Niam's surprise, Neel watched the documentary with him till the end.

When it was done, Neel said, "There's a lot of evil in this world. What do you shed your tears for? What do you shed your tears on? Before you tell me, let's go get some beer and greasy food. I know just the place."

As they were leaving, he said, "Don't make me watch something like this again." He repeated this when they were eating *paneer* fritters over some bitter beer. Neel had made Niam pay for the food and drinks for seemingly forcing him to watch the documentary.

Another example of Neel's idiosyncratic nature was when Neel and Arun got into an argument in Niam's presence.

"What's the point of this all? It's so stupid," Neel said looking at the news on the TV screen. The main news was on a controversy over what a place of worship was before, and what it was now, and what it should be going forward.

"It's not stupid," Arun shot back. "This is a very serious discussion. Millions of people are very upset over this."

"That's my point," Neel replied. "What's the point of being upset over something as stupid as this? Just leave this be and move on."

"Why do you ask us to move on? Have you asked Turkey to move on and not create issues around that church there?" Arun raised his voice a little, making everyone raise their eyebrows.

"Why would I do something like this? Turkey won't listen to me, just like these folks on TV won't listen to me, and just like you won't listen to me, so there's that," Neel replied.

"What? You don't think these double standards you have for this country and for another are okay?" Arun asked.

"I do not know about double standards, but I do know raking up issues like these don't do anyone any good in the long run," Neel calmly replied. "You can say whatever you want, but religious arguments and fights are inherently so stupid. They are all about fighting over imaginary things. It's like asking who will win in a bout between Superman and the Hulk. It's a grammatically correct question for sure, but the very premise is nonsense."

Arun opened his mouth to say something but decided against it. "Whatever," is all he let out and marched to his room.

Later that evening, when Arun was not around, Neel said to Niam, "Some of the biggest problems in this world are created by people trying to create an imagined glorious past. I wish they would all just disappear and leave us alone with our work and parties."

For the vast majority of times, however, Neel displayed only a happy-go-lucky personality. These qualities, along with his looks, made Neel popular among women who were looking to have a good time or party with him.

Neel was content with his work, with his salary, with his roommates, and with the strings of short-term relationships and casual sex. While Arun entertained Niam with stories about his extended family, Neel would entertain him with stories of his sexual exploits. Neel was a womanizer and, per his claims, just about as good at it as needed to get the job done.

"It's all about the confidence and a don't care attitude," he once told Niam while trying to educate him on the art of picking up women. "They're drawn to it. They find it irresistible. Can't resist it."

"But if I show a don't care attitude, how will the woman realize I care?" Niam asked. He knew his deficiency when it came to all things romantic or flirtatious. He wanted to learn from the best, even a self-proclaimed one.

"There! That's the most important part. It's the crux of it all. You cannot seem to not care at all. If they feel that way, they'll move on to the next guy. You have to show you don't care to get them interested in you, but care enough for them to come back to you. It's tough to explain. Actually, it's about practice, and practice, and not being worried about rejections. It's the fear of rejections that does one in."

"He's one cocky bastard and that's not the only thing irritating about him," one woman had once mentioned to Niam when she was drunk. She had accompanied them both and a couple of others to a club for an evening of drinking and dancing. At the club Neel ran into a group of friends. For a while the woman and Niam found themselves sitting alone in a corner. "No one can stand that attitude for too long."

"But you two seem to be going strong," Niam said, feeling a little out of his depth.

"Look, don't get me wrong. He's not a bad guy. He's fun to be around in short bursts. He even pays for the drinks a lot of times. But he's too much into himself, too self-absorbed. In the beginning women see him as this fun-loving guy with a great career and great potential. But then it wears off very soon. I just hope he's able to get over this attitude of his. I like him and want the best for him."

As was his nature, Niam did not judge Neel. Like Arun, Neel was also a good roommate with his own set of quirks. He took care of what he owed on time, kept everyone entertained, didn't let things get too heavy, and kept the place very clean. In fact, he worked hard to keep it as spotless as possible, and the walls decorated with paraphernalia that, as he put it, a young guy should have. This included a long wall shelf with empty bottles of all the different beers and other drinks he had ever had, a cricket bat lying sideways on a few long nails, a road sign that appeared to have been pinched from a highway, but in reality was bought from a vendor in a street market, and a poster-sized image of a guitar and another with drums. He also had a set of party lights in a corner of the living room.

"Women like it," he had told Niam and Arun when he bought them. Much to their amazement, it turned out that he was not wrong. The few women who visited the apartment all admired his effort at the décor.

Niam left the apartment when Neel and Arun moved. The shelf along with the bottles was left there, the only reminder of the activity and camaraderie the apartment had experienced. Niam took a short-term lease with a colleague. This allowed him time enough to find a good place where Prisha and he could live after their marriage. The three former roommates kept in touch with each other over the duration of a few months. The first to lose touch was Arun, and happened gradually over time. Neel broke contact abruptly. He stopped taking calls or responding to messages. Niam tried to contact him through common acquaintances, but no one seemed to have any information about his whereabouts. A little disappointed, Niam got busy with his life and soon Neel and Arun were both relegated to a corner of his memory.

"Hello?" Niam spoke into the phone when Ella called. "Ella?" He didn't know why he was asking, he recognized her number.

"Yes, it's me. Hi Niam, how are you?" she responded.

"I am fine. How are you?"

"Fine, thank you," she said. "Did I call you at a good time? This is the only time I get to be by myself without anyone around."

"Yes, yes, it's a good time. How are things with you at home and work?"

Ella took up a good amount of time talking about her work. She harped on a demanding patient suffering from liver disorder because of excessive drinking and many others that caused her grief.

"You should hear him shout," she said. "He gets difficult.

He's got klazomania or something similar. When it gets too much, we need to hold him down and tranquilize him. But I like him when he's not shouting. Surprisingly so, he's a good conversationalist."

"I have a colleague who is an alcoholic, too," Niam announced, taking the momentary silence to get his words through. "He's an otherwise great guy. The one irritating thing about him is when he walks up to me early morning and breathes out on my face. He does it to confirm that his breath is not smelling of alcohol. I really don't like it. He carries a small bottle of whiskey with him all the time. One time in the evening we were playing ping-pong at our place of work before leaving for home, and..."

"Do you have a ping-pong table at work?" Ella interjected.

"Oh yes, and a small gym too, and a few other things," Niam responded.

"It must be nice working there."

"It's okay. I don't complain too much. I was saying we were playing ping-pong, and he was losing. He asked me to take a break for a minute. He reached into his bag on the floor, pulled out the whiskey bottle and took a couple of big swigs. Then damn it—he won! That's what gave him the energy. He's such an alcoholic. I shouldn't wonder if his liver is pickled too."

"That's sad," Ella said. She talked more about other patients and doctors and nurses. Before they ended the call, Ella said she would call the next day. When Niam looked at the call duration on his phone, he realized that they had talked for more than an hour. And he enjoyed the conversation. It was not very stressful on him because there were no non-verbal cues to pick up on or guard, and Ella did a larger part of the talking.

Ella called the next day as she promised.

"So, have you decided if you want to be my friend?" she asked.

"I don't know how to answer this," Niam said. "Why do you want to be my friend? Why not find someone else?"

"I liked talking to you yesterday. You seem caring and

59

engaging. It's not easy finding someone to talk to with those qualities."

"Then how about we continue talking? We don't need to answer any questions or define this right away, do we?" Niam suggested.

"I am fine with that, if you're okay with it," Ella responded.

This time they talked for over an hour and a half. She talked about her work again and her trivial likes and dislikes. Niam talked about his work and his roommates.

Over time, they fell into a routine. Ella called only during weekdays, and mostly Mondays to Thursdays. Weekends were family time for her, and friends' time for Niam. Their conversations also became longer—on some occasions as long as three hours or longer. Sometimes he would go silent, and she would talk at length about her dreams and hopes and aspirations. Many times, those dreams involved pursuing further education in nursing, and then working for a big hospital. She often talked about hospitals in Mumbai and the starting salaries they offered, or hospitals in the Gulf or Singapore. Occasionally she would go silent, and he would talk of his professional goals. This was the first time in Niam's life when he could talk without any pretense or expectations. He did not expect her to understand his line of work or how lofty or how silly his goals might sound, just like he did not understand hers. They just talked, and they just listened. They were both young. They both felt anything and everything was possible. They both believed anything and everything was possible. They were both validating themselves and the other in an environment where they were comfortable enough to know they would not be judged in expressing their hearts desires. Niam had not had this intense a connection with anyone else before, and would not have it with anyone after—including with Prisha.

"Have you talked about me with your roommates?" Ella once asked.

Niam took some time to answer. He did not want to lie, and yet, did not want to give an answer that could upset Ella.

"At the beginning I did," he replied, feeling a little awkward.

"Do you talk about me still?" she asked.

Niam had the feeling this was some kind of a test. "No, not at all actually. We're all so busy with our work and our lives," he replied.

"What about Arun. You said he's a bit of a radical. Does he say anything?"

"I suppose your relatives are somewhat conservative too."

"Yes, but's that different. They don't know I talk to you. But Arun does."

"Yeah, I guess so. Arun is a weirdo. I don't like his opinions. But he's a good guy. I would trust him to help me if I needed it. Neel, on the other hand, is not someone I can trust. It's not that he won't help. It's just that he's too engrossed in himself and will forget to come through."

"I don't like your friend Arun," Ella said after a pause. "What have people like me done to him? Nothing. We're leading our lives, we're doing our jobs, and we're contributing. Maybe we're contributing more than him. What does he do?"

"Listen, I don't really bother myself with such thoughts. And nor must you. We're roommates, and one day, we'll move out at some point. He'll go his separate way, and I will mine."

"But I am afraid he'll poison your mind against me, and then I'll lose my closest friend."

"I don't think so. If my mind could have been poisoned, it would have been by now. I wouldn't worry about it."

"I am glad you said this," Ella responded. "I have become so used to talking to you that there are days when I think my life would be completely empty and miserable if I didn't get to hear your voice. You're an addiction. I hope this turns out to be a good one."

"I feel connected to you too. Very strongly, in fact. I think we're both becoming addicted to each other," Niam replied, hardly believing that those words had tumbled from his mouth.

It was an addiction indeed. Come evenings, Mondays to Thursdays, Niam would become restless as he waited for Ella's call. During day times at work, or over weekends, his thoughts would wander toward her. Her voice was always in his head, conversing with him, asking him questions, answering his questions. He would often find himself making mental notes of what to say to her when they next talked. They even talked when he traveled for a couple of days for a job interview. Unfortunately, the interview wasn't successful. Under very different circumstances, if Ella had not come into his life, he would have been disappointed at not getting that job. But now, he acknowledged to himself, he was secretly relieved. Moving to another city for a new position would have meant a disruption in their phone conversations. They could still talk over the phone. However, being in different cities would have, in his mind, created an unsurmountable barrier. With both of them in Bangalore, there was still a small hope they would meet, he would get to see her, and the mystery would be solved.

Niam had not forgotten the conversation with Neel about phone sex from a few months back. He was tempted to try this with Ella, but he just wasn't sure how to broach the subject. He knew too that her time at Bangalore was fast coming to an end, and she would soon be leaving.

"Dude, that's stupid," Neel said when Niam mentioned her eventual leaving to him, and how it would cause him some heartache. "You both are complete fucking morons. First, how does her leaving even matter? It's a phone call. You can still talk wherever you are. And second, come on! You need to get her to meet you, and just do it, and just get it over with. All this crush and infatuation bullshit, just throw it out the window. At least get her to have phone sex. I am telling you from experience. It's going to be great. Have you even asked her about her figure?"

"I am not going to answer that!" Niam exclaimed.

"There. This is where your problem is. Here. Come here. I'll show you something. Come." Neel led him to his room.

In all this time living together, Niam realized this was the first time he had been in Neel's room. He had seen it multiple times from the outside when the door was open, but he had never had the opportunity to step into it. The room was immaculately arranged. The bed was perfectly made as if it had never been slept upon. The chair was in a perfect position by the side of the table as if it had never been sat upon. A closed high-end laptop, a single book on finance, a notepad, and an expensive looking pen on the notepad were placed in just the perfect way to give the impression that the table and the contents on its top had never been touched. Altogether, this made the room appear welcoming and more spacious than Niam's. In their three-bedroom apartment, Niam's and Neel's rooms were almost equal in size and layout. The floors were nearly square. The rooms were featureless, except for similar wardrobe with English Chestnut-stained wooden doors that contrasted well with the pastel yellow wall paint. The wardrobes were part of an extension into the wall opposite to the room entrance, and so did not occupy the limited room space. To the side of the wardrobe was a single window that provided ample natural light. Their two rooms were on the same side of the living room. To reach those rooms upon entering the apartment, one had to pass the small kitchen to the right, walk into the living room, and turn right. Directly opposite to their doors and across the living room was the balcony. This was a great setup for cross ventilation during warm evenings. It also helped to prevent the apartment from becoming too steamy from cooking. Arun's room was more private and larger, and to the side of the balcony. The way to it was through a narrow corridor to the left of the main door. For this difference, the contribution to the total rent was not equal. Niam and Neel paid thirty percent each, while Arun paid the remaining forty percent.

Once they were in his room, Neel made his way between the table and the bed toward the wardrobe and opened its door wide. Just like everything else with Neel, the interior too was very neatly arranged, with nothing out of place. He opened a drawer, and reaching his hand inside, pulled out a white matching bra and panty set. He held them out for Niam to see.

"See. Do you see? These belong to a girl I went out with a few weeks ago. I asked her to leave these with me for remembrance, and she did."

Niam looked at the underwear with confused emotions. "Are those even washed? Or have you been storing them like this since she took them off?"

"How does it even matter?" Neel said out loud. "How does it matter? The point here is sometimes you simply need to ask. This is where most guys lose it. They tremble at the very thought of asking. Hey, look. After I've talked to a girl for some time and we're touching each other and kind of fooling around, I'll just ask her if she wants to come to my place or go to her place. That's it. Done."

"Point taken. I need to be more assertive. Make sure you wash that underwear though."

Later that evening, when Ella called him, Niam did just that.

"Ella, listen, sometimes talking to you gets me excited. Does it excite you when you talk to me?"

"Absolutely," Ella said. "I am always excited to talk to you."

"Listen, do you think we should have phone sex? I mean, you said we cannot meet because of relatives and all. But how about phone sex?"

Ella went silent. Niam looked into his phone to confirm the call was still connected. "Hello?" he said. "Are you there?"

Ella responded. "I am here. I have to keep the phone down. There's someone knocking on my door. I'll call you tomorrow."

She did not call the next day, or the next. Then the weekend came along. This meant Niam was miserable for a grand total of five days. At one point he thought of taking out his anger at Neel and shouting at him, but changed his mind. Neel only gave a solicited advice. It was up to Niam to determine its appropriateness.

Much to Niam's relief, Ella called back on Monday. She apologized for not calling sooner. She said that her cousin had gotten engaged the previous week and things had simply gotten busy in the family. She promised to call back in a few days when she was sure they would not be disturbed.

She called him a week later.

"I have something to tell you," she said.

"What is it?" Niam asked.

"We won't be able to talk to each other for much longer."

"Why is that? Did I say something wrong?" Niam asked nervously.

"No, nothing like that. My family introduced me to a guy during my cousin's engagement party. He's working with his father on their family business. We two are to be engaged soon, and we're to be married after I am done with my training in two months' time."

Niam was always aware that their relationship had an expiry date. Sometimes, but not very often, he had wanted to end it himself. The long conversations on the phone with her came at the cost of the time he could have spent with his friends or at work or on other things. But he truly had become addicted to her voice, her tone, their small talk, him using her to vent out his frustrations with anything big or small, or to talk about his past, present, and future. She had never claimed ownership over him. She had never shown any signs of jealousy whenever he talked about being around women when he went out with Neel. Perhaps the absence of this made her have a vice-like grip on Niam. Possessing her was seemingly just within his grasp, but not quite it seemed. She could fully possess him, but didn't.

Two weeks of not conversing with her helped him in his effort to get a grip on his life. As days went by, he realized he missed the time with her less and less. Therefore, this news did not hit him very hard. Niam sensed this would probably be the last conversation they would have. They talked for some time about her future husband and her future personal and professional plans.

"Everything is now uncertain," she said. "I have talked to him, and he seems very supportive of my professional plans. I am not sure if his family is on the same page, though. His mother seems kind of old-fashioned and controlling. Maybe it's just my imagination. I'll figure it out."

"I wanted to apologize for that other day," Niam said when he got the chance.

"Oh? About what?" she asked.

"You know, the whole phone sex thing. Maybe I shouldn't have said that," Niam responded.

"Maybe you shouldn't have!" She let out a small laugh. "But we would have done it."

"Really?" Niam said.

"Maybe. I don't know. It's just that at that instant my aunt knocked on my door to tell me about my cousin's engagement. I told you that everything happened all of a sudden. I had no time to think about anything."

"Oh, well, that's just my luck," Niam said in a low voice. After a brief pause he stood up from the chair he was on. "There's one question I have to ask you again. You'll leave soon and we may never talk again. Can you tell me who gave you my number? When you first called, my friends told me this was a scam or prank call. I am glad I ignored them. At least for this reason I deserve to know the answer to this question. Maybe even a hint?"

"You really want to know?" she asked.

"I really want to know."

"If I tell you, do you promise to tell no one? Can you swear to tell no one? If you do, and if I find out you've broken the promise, I'll stop liking you forever."

"I really do. I'll keep it a secret," Niam responded.

"My friend at the hospital gave me your number. She said you're good-looking and a gentleman, and I should try to get to know you," Ella said. "Maybe now you know who."

"Who? I have no idea."

"You still can't guess? When she gave me your number she said you and her will be meeting soon. Her name is Nina."

Niam stared at Nina from the bus as she walked away for as long as he could. He took a seat by the window and stared out at the mass of people walking and bicycling. He stared into the cars passing by to glimpse at their occupants. He did not think of Nina and Ella until he looked at his phone and saw a missed call from Prisha. He wondered for a while if he should mention this strange meeting to her. He decided against it. It would be hard to explain walking around Paris with two attractive women. And it would be even harder to explain how he met them and what they talked about. He was convinced that howsoever this meeting may be labeled, it would be the first and the last. There was no point in telling her something he couldn't himself quite understand and something that would not be happening again.

The walk from the metro station to his apartment seemed like any other walk he had taken countless times before. On the way, he decided to stop by the local coffee shop. The owners of the place were an English couple who came to Paris for vacation about twenty-five years ago. They liked the city so much they decided to move to the capital permanently. They were fortunate with the timing, for a second time it turned out, because France was experiencing an economic downturn with falling real-estate prices. They were able to buy the coffee shop with their savings and a small loan, which had long since been paid off. They both knew a little French, were very friendly, and worked hard. The coffee shop soon became a local fixture, and became busy as the neighborhood grew and became crowded over the years.

Niam got to know Bertram and his wife Ida, the owners of the coffee shop, over a period of a couple of weeks of walking around the neighborhood with his notebook. The coffee shop was where he would stop by often on his way to or from the apartment, and write down notes from his observations and thoughts. Ida soon recognized him as a regular, non-French speaking customer, and introduced him to Bertram. The three quickly became good acquaintances. Niam would often try to time his visit to the coffee shop when Bertram and Ida were around, and not just the manager they had hired to help them run the place. During those times, Niam would usually be joined on the seat by one or the other or both. One reason they got along well was because of the language. Niam was one of only a handful of their customers with whom they could converse in English freely.

Over time, they opened up bit by bit. They asked Niam about his life and his family, and they told him about theirs. Bertram and Ida came from a town near Manchester that Niam couldn't recollect. The couple had met in school, fell in love, and later moved to Manchester University to study biology. At college they both realized they were not particularly interested in this field. Not wanting to drop out, they pushed each other to complete their education.

After graduation, Bertram found work at a department, store and Ida as a waitress at a busy restaurant. Within a year, Bertram became a shift manager at the same store. Shortly after, Ida became a manager at another restaurant. The income they were making together was decent enough to support a relatively comfortable life. However, they were always busy, and often had conflicting schedules. This meant they did not get to spend as much time with each other and with their friends as they wanted.

This led them to decide to move back to their small town. At that time, given how hectic their lives had become, this was where they felt their hearts belonged. They got married very soon after they moved. Wedded life was fairly okay in the beginning. The income they now made doing almost the same things was lower by a good margin. However, the cost of living was also low. Meeting up with friends and family was an almost daily occurrence, and going to Manchester for a day over a weekend was a once in a month or two event. Things were ticking along nicely.

Then in quick succession, Bertram's father and Ida's mother passed away, leaving them with inheritances of two small homes and some money from their savings.

The timing of the inheritances was fortuitous. Some time back, Manchester had been the scene of a markedly violent event. The Provisional Irish Republican Army had set of a massive explosion in downtown Manchester, which destroyed a big part of the city. In response, the city bounced back, and with a vengeance. Manchester saw a big surge in construction and economic activity. Some of this bustle had a spillover effect in the surroundings. The result was that Bertram and Ida were able to sell the two homes at good prices. With a good-sized financial safety net and secure jobs, they both decided to do what they had been wanting to do for a few years—they went to Paris on a later than intended honeymoon.

Bertram was uncharacteristically emotional as he sat down with Niam. Ida was behind the counter, busy rearranging things and talking to the workers and other customers.

"How are you doing?" he asked Niam.

"Doing well. How about yourself?" Niam asked.

"I am here. I am still here," he responded before going silent. Niam wasn't sure if he wanted him to pick up the conversation or if he wanted both to sit there silently. He decided it was more likely the former. He broke the silence. "I had the strangest day today. I don't know what to make of it."

"Oh yeah?"

"Yes. You will never guess. Some random woman approached me and talked to me and asked me to accompany her to a nearby park to meet another woman, where all three of us walked around a duck pond and talked about some random things I don't even remember," Niam said in almost a single breath.

"Oh, yeah? That sounds odd. How was it?"

"I don't know. It was weird," Niam responded. "I don't think I'll forget something like this ever."

"Yeah, I can sense that. You're a good lookin' guy. Why wouldn't the ladies be takin' an interest in you? Go for it." Bertram forced a thin smile on a drawn face accentuated by a full set of slightly curly, mostly unkempt, shoulder-length, light brown hair.

"Ha ha!" Niam exclaimed sarcastically in response.

"What are you two laughing at?" Ida joined them with a contrasting cheerful smile. Her dark pixie-cut hair was also in contrast to her husband's.

"Niam here says he spent time today in a park with two beautiful women," Bertram replied.

"Really?" Ida turned to look at Niam.

"Really." Niam looked at her. He told her what had happened.

"Now you be careful, alright," Ida said. "You don't want any trouble, do you? You're married with a beautiful wife and a lovely daughter. Don't be sneaking around."

Niam gasped. "Trust me, I have no intention of doing anything of the sort!" He looked at Bertram for confirmation. "Say, you look a little down and out today. What's up?"

"He's just feeling the blues." Ida turned toward her husband and ran her hand through his hair. "He's just missing England. And he's an old man now. I know he wishes he were younger. But I still love him regardless."

"I think we need to take a few weeks off and visit friends and family back home," Bertrand said. "But things have become busy here and we're needed."

"I can understand that," Niam said. "Maybe you can go separately. You go first and then Ida goes next, or the other way around."

"Maybe. We'll see. It's been a long time since we visited," Bertrand responded.

"Yes, it has," Ida said. "When's the last time we were there? Must have been like five or six years ago. We went there for my niece's wedding."

"Sounds about right," Bertrand said. "Listen," he turned toward Niam, "enjoy your time with your family as much as you can. I've missed watching my nephew and niece growing up. My brother, I can't stand. For that I am happy to not be there. But I miss the kids."

Ida had once mentioned to Niam their decision to not have kids of their own. They both liked children, but were not particularly keen on becoming parents themselves. "We love our freedom too," she said. "Besides, we thought that with so many people in this world already, overpopulation and whatnot, not having kids of our own would be our small, little way of helping the planet."

"How's your daughter doin'?" Bertrand asked Niam after the three of them were silent for a few seconds.

"She's doing very well. Getting ready for school in just a few months. We're excited." Niam smiled, his conversation with Nina and Ella now a distant memory.

"That's good," Ida said. "How old is she?"

"She's five, but she will be six very soon," Niam replied. "But we're not sure what to do. If she starts school here and we move back later, she's going to have a tough time adjusting. As things stand now, she can't speak well in our language. I suppose in a way it's all okay. Now that she's been exposed to different languages, she might pick up more languages as she grows. It can't be a bad thing knowing a few languages."

"You all talk to her in English at home?" Ida asked.

"Yes. It's the easiest. I don't know French, and I don't want to learn a new language. We're not going to be here forever. Prisha is picking up French slowly. She's better than me at learning new languages."

Their attention was distracted by a louder than normal sound from the wall-mounted television on the far wall. This is the norm followed by all news channels when announcing "breaking news. The news channel was in French, and Niam could not follow it well. He still looked at the report with interest. As soon as the sound, accompanied by poor graphics with something written in French, which Niam took to mean "breaking news" ended, a newscaster came on. The newscaster appeared to be in his early thirties, and had a sharp nose and eyes, and a prominent jawline. In all, his facial features demanded he be paid attention to even if you couldn't understand a word of what he was saying. This is precisely what Niam did.

"*Bonjour*," the newscaster said. "*Cette nouvelle vient d'arriver. Une hyène s'est échappée et rôde dans les rues de Paris. Chacun est invité à faire preuve de prudence. On nous annonce que cette hyène est très, très excitée.*"

The camera then moved to show some people running in panic. Niam looked at Bertrand and Ida. Bertrand and Ida looked at each other and then at Niam.

"What did he say?" Niam asked.

"I am not sure I understood it right," Bertrand replied. "Did you get what he said, Ida?"

"I believe he said there's a hyena on the loose on the streets of Paris, Bertie," she said, sounding surprised.

"I think that's what he said," Bertrand replied. "Did he say the hyena is very, very horny?"

"I think he said excited," Ida replied.

"No, I am pretty sure he meant horny." Bertrand frowned.

"I don't think so, dear. Why would they say something like this on the news?" Ida looked at him and then at Niam. Niam was still confused. He gave a quick shoulder shrug.

"I don't know," Bertrand replied and slowly moved his head. "He said we have a very horny hyena. How did it even get here?"

"Can you explain what he said?" Niam jumped in.

"I don't think I can," Bertrand said. "I don't fully understand. It looks like some hyena has escaped the zoo and is very excited or horny or something."

"How did it escape?" Niam asked.

"I don't know how it escaped. Animals escape from zoos all the time. I am more confused about this other thing the fellow said."

"What did he say?"

"That the hyena is very horny," Bertrand said.

"Excited, dear, excited," Ida said. "And maybe he should have said the hyena is afraid, which would make more sense."

"Maybe," Bertrand said. "I heard horny though. We should be finding out more when they give an update. I hope they catch it soon. We can't have a hyena running wild in Paris, horny or not."

Niam picked up his phone to check the time. He got up from his seat and adjusted his t-shirt.

"Alright. It's time for me to leave. It is getting late."

"Alright Niam, you take care," Ida said.

"Will do. And you two make plans for visiting England soon. It'll lift up his spirits," Niam said to Ida as he started walking.

"Will do." Bertrand smiled.

Niam walked at a slow pace to his apartment despite being late. He wasn't in much of a hurry. Prisha wouldn't be worried unless it was really late. They didn't have any particular plans for the rest of the day, so he could afford to take a bit longer without upsetting her.

People around him did not seem to share his lackadaisical attitude. Everyone seemed to be in a rush, some almost sprinting to get to their destination. Many were glancing around apprehensively, as if expecting something to jump at them. Niam noticed all that was going on but paid little heed. He was concerned about what he might run into while crossing the trench. He tried hard to remember what it was last time, but it escaped him. It was some kind of an animal for sure. Was it the hyena everyone seemed to be so worried about? Niam shook his head remembering that the animal had just escaped. So, it must have been something else. Was it something scary, something dangerous? It must have been, or why else would he be thinking about it? Or maybe not.

Niam's phone rang. This came as a welcome break. He did not want to think about anything too hard. He stopped and reached into his pocket to pull his phone out. It was Hamoon.

"Are you okay?" Hamoon sounded very concerned.

"I am okay. Why do you ask?" Niam was puzzled.

"Just asking. Good to know all is well. Where are you?"

"Me? I am very close to my apartment. I should be there very soon. Do you want to meet up this evening, or tomorrow, perhaps? They say it's going to be a nice day tomorrow."

"Heavens man! Why are you out? You'd better get back home right away! Didn't you hear the news?"

"What news?" Niam asked.

"About the hyena!" Hamoon exclaimed.

"What about it? It's just a hyena. They'll catch it. It's not a lion or a tiger or something. Just a single hyena. I've not even heard a cackle," Niam replied, surprised by his friend's anxious state.

"It's no ordinary hyena!" Hamoon shouted into the phone. "They say it's a very horny hyena. You better be careful. Get back home quickly. Run if you must."

"Alright, alright! Will do. You take care and let me know if you want to meet up," Niam said.

"Get home first. We'll talk later." Hamoon disconnected the call. Niam looked at the time on the phone and put it back into his pocket. He looked around in a full circle and saw people still rushing to wherever they felt they needed to rush to. Not feeling at all perplexed, he started his relaxed amble once again. He wasn't much bothered about the hyena. The trench was his main concern. He didn't like it. One had to climb down a hanging ladder, walk at least some distance in almost knee-deep muddy water, and then climb back up using another hanging ladder to reach his apartment building. This was not his idea of fun. Maybe, he thought, he could call Prisha and ask her to come meet him. Then all three of them—the daughter, Prisha, and he—could go to a nice restaurant for a good dinner, roam around the streets, and then together cross the trench to get back to the apartment. The trench was easier traversed together in good company than alone.

He, however, decided against it. One way or the other, the trench would have to be crossed. It would be better if he did it himself and didn't involve the others. He walked a short distance before making a right turn around a building. Up ahead, on this street was his apartment. It wasn't far, just about the length of two football fields.

Soon the despised trench was in front of him. People were still rushing around him, trying to save themselves. He stopped when he approached the ladder and looked down. He saw a woman climbing up and waited for her. When she reached the top rung, she reached out to hold a handle fixed to the ground to help lift herself up. She looked at Niam.

"*Bonjour,*" she said and smiled. She looked to be around the same age as Niam. She had bright eyes and curly light-colored hair. Those two features drew attention away from the rest of her face.

"*Bonjour,*" Niam said. He bent down a little and reached out to her with his hand.

"*Merci,*" she said and reached out to grab his hand. Niam helped pull her up. The woman was wearing a red jacket with a floral blouse and a black skirt. She had high heels on. They appeared to be red, but it was hard to tell because they were all muddy.

"*Merci,*" she said again, and started brushing her clothes

with her hand. Niam had nothing to say. He turned to climb down the ladder.

The woman looked at him and said, "*Faites attention. Il y a une hyène très excitée là-dedans.*"

Niam couldn't fully understand her, but as soon as he heard her mention the hyena, he took her message to be a general word of caution.

"*Merci,*" he replied and started his descent. He saw her looking at him until he was out of sight. He wondered why she was staring at him.

"I don't like this at all," he whispered to himself as he plunged into the mud at the bottom of the trench. Both his feet were ankle deep in the goo. He held onto the ladder and stared at the sky above. The day was still very bright, and the trench was well lit. This still didn't make it easy. After some struggle, he turned left and stared ahead toward the narrow path. "One foot at a time. One foot at a time," he told himself. He followed his good advice.

The trench took a sharp left turn in a few steps. Here the ground was dry. He took a sharp right turn barely five steps later. That's when Niam saw the hyena sitting on the ground and stopped. Both their jaws dropped when they saw each other.

Niam was no hyena expert. Looking at the spots on its torso, he assumed he was looking at a male spotted hyena. The hyena gave Niam a brief, intent stare and then looked away. Niam walked to the hyena slowly and sat down beside him.

For the longest time they looked around and not at each other—up at the sky, down at their feet and at the trench floor, and at its walls—all in silence.

"I think I should go," Niam looked at the hyena and spoke to him in English. He wasn't sure why, but he felt that English would be the appropriate language of communication here. "But I just don't want to walk through mud and climb a ladder again."

The hyena turned toward him and looked into his eyes. To

Niam, he seemed to be acknowledging his tribulations ahead. The hyena appeared to be weeping silently, with no sign of a cackle.

"Are you the horny hyena everyone's so scared of up there?" Niam asked. The hyena turned toward him and again looked into his eyes.

"Why are you horny? Did you lose your partner?" Niam thought the question to be appropriate.

The hyena hung his head and, with what appeared to be sadness, placed it on the ground. Then he lifted his head up and looked into Niam's eyes once again. Niam gingerly put his hand on the hyena's head and petted it. He stroked his back too. The hyena sighed, acknowledging the attention.

"You're not horny. You're sad and angry and hungry. No, not hungry. Lonely. You're no different than so many among us." He silently petted the hyena for a bit longer. "I wonder why they think you're horny."

After a few minutes of petting a great idea flashed into Niam's mind. "I know just the right answer!" Niam exclaimed. "I don't know why I didn't think of it sooner. Let me introduce you to two people I met today. They are really nice people, and I think they will love you. One's name is Nina. I have her number with me. The other is Ella. Maybe one of them or the other can take you in. Do you want to meet them?"

The hyena looked into Niam's eyes again. Niam took this as a cue. He patted the hyena's back lightly and stood up. "Come, let's go," he said. The hyena also stood up. Together, they walked back to where Niam had entered the trench. This time he found the trench floor to be very dry and hard, with no signs of mud anywhere. When they reached the ladder, Niam looked at the hyena wondering how he would scale it.

"We'll have to climb up. I can do it. Do you know how to climb a ladder? Maybe you go first and I push you if needed."

The hyena looked at Niam. He then stepped away from the ladder 'til his tail touched the opposite facing wall. Then in a quick succession of movements, he sprinted forward and leaped up into the air. With his front paws firmly gripping the trench wall, he pushed forward with his hind legs, and leaped again, and leaped out of the trench. Niam looked at the hyena's skills in awe.

"Alright then, give me a moment." As he climbed, he looked up at the hyena who was looking down at him as if mocking his inability to duplicate the feat. In response he took his time climbing the ladder. Once he had pulled himself up, he patted the hyena and turned to look around the street. The street had returned to normal. People were walking around as they usually did, and the road traffic looked normal too. Fortunately, no one seemed to be paying any attention to them.

"Just give me a minute," Niam said to the hyena. "Let me call Nina." He took out his phone and dialed the number Nina had called him from earlier in the morning.

"Niam?" He heard her voice.

"Yes," he replied.

"Do we need to meet? Are you with the hyena?"

"Yes," he replied again, surprised that she was aware of his new companion.

"Good. Then let's meet at the same place we first met this morning." Nina ended the call.

"Let's go!" Niam patted the hyena and started walking. "We'll need to take public transport. You okay with it?" The hyena did not object and started walking too. He showed no other reaction. "Let's stop briefly at this coffee shop nearby. I'll introduce you to an interesting couple. It shouldn't be long, and you'll like them too."

"Bertie! Bertie!" Ida shouted at her husband excitedly. She was outside the shop wiping a metal table and adjusting the chairs when she saw Niam and the hyena approaching them.

"What's the matter, dear?" Bertrand said when he stepped outside. She did not respond. He followed the direction she was staring at.

"My goodness. Now isn't that a sight for sore eyes?" he said with a dumbstruck expression.

"It is, dear, it is," Ida said with a big smile. "Come on in!" she said to Niam when he was close enough.

"Thank you. We won't be staying long. We have some distance to cover. I just thought I would bring my new friend here to meet you. I don't know if there'll be another chance. At least not any time soon, I think." Niam smiled and looked at the couple and then proudly down at the hyena.

They sat down at a table inside. The hyena sat on the floor between Niam and Bertrand.

"What would you like? And what would the hyena like? I am sorry, but does it have a name?" Ida asked.

"I am good, thanks. I think he is good too. Well, maybe I can have an espresso with some milk and sugar, if you don't mind," Niam said. "And my friend could perhaps have a croissant. I am not sure. We can try. Communication is not easy, but we're trying. Hopefully, soon I'll also learn his name."

"I am sure you'll work something out," Bertrand said.

Ida, in the meanwhile, had asked the waitress to bring the coffee and croissant.

"What's next?" he asked Niam after Ida turned back to them. "Will you take him to meet your family? I am guessing that your daughter will love him. His fur does look soft to touch."

"No, not at the moment," Niam replied. "I'll first take him to the two women I told you about. Or at least one of them. She's expecting me to bring him to her."

"Didn't I tell you to keep away from them? Why would you want to get in trouble?" Ida asked.

"Listen, I have no choice. I can't keep it in our tiny apartment. My daughter barely has a play area. Even if we make lots and lots of adjustments, he can't stay with us forever. Who knows where we'll be in a few months, or a couple of years. He is better off with people who I believe can take better care of it. I can't ask you two because you lead busy lives and are planning to visit England. The rest of Paris, even my friend Hamoon... You know Hamoon, right? What am I saying? You know him well. Even Hamoon has the misconception that he's a horny hyena."

"See! I told you. The news said he's a horny hyena." Bertrand turned to Ida beaming. She acknowledged him by simply nodding her head.

The three then silently turned their gaze toward the sitting hyena. In no time at all, the waitress brought a large croissant on a plate, just big enough to accommodate it, and set it on the table in front of Niam. Niam picked up the croissant in one hand, and broke a piece of it with the other. He bent down to put the piece on the floor in front of the hyena. The hyena lifted his head up, sniffed the piece, and with a quick action, grabbed it in his mouth, chewed on it twice and gulped it down. Then he looked up at Niam and the remaining croissant in his hand.

"I think he likes the croissant," Bertrand said.

"I think he does," Niam replied.

"You really should first take him to your daughter," Ida said. "She'll love to play with him."

"Maybe I can ask my wife to come by here," Niam said after a pause. He picked up his phone and tapped on Prisha's number.

"Prisha!" he exclaimed into the phone when he heard her voice. "Just to let you know, I am here at the coffee shop with the hyena... Yes, you heard it right. The hyena is with me. Bertrand and Ida are here too. Why don't you both join us?"

After his call, he set the phone down on the table. "They're coming."

"Good!" Ida said. "Now, if you'll excuse me, I have a few things to take care of behind the counter. Ah, here's your coffee."

80

The waitress placed the cup on the table. Niam put the remaining croissant piece in front of the hyena.

"Excuse me too," Bertrand said. "I've a few things to take care of while you wait for your family. I'll send over another croissant. Don't worry, it's on us."

"Thank you!" Niam replied and picked up the small cup.

Niam passed the next twenty or so minutes in silence, occasionally watching people outside going about their business, casually observing people who entered the coffee shop, smiling back at those who smiled at him and the hyena, smiling at Bertrand and Ida and the waitress working behind the counter and around the shop, and occasionally petting the hyena.

Hamoon called him when he was starting to get restless as he waited for Prisha and the daughter. "You're doing okay?" he asked Niam.

"Yup. Just sitting at the coffee shop, waiting for my family to show up," Niam responded.

"You're with the hyena, aren't you?"

"Yup."

"And it's not horny?"

"Nope, not at all. He seems pretty calm so far. Do you want to come see him before I leave him with someone I know?"

"I don't know." Hamoon sounded very hesitant. "What if he's very horny and takes a fancy to me?"

"Oh, come on!" Niam exclaimed. "Trust me. He's not. Now's your chance to see him. You may not get that chance later."

"I don't know," Hamoon said again, and paused. "How long are you there?"

"Not too long, I think," Niam said. "I am waiting for Prisha and my daughter. I suppose she'll play with the hyena for a bit first. I would say about an hour, maybe less."

"Okay, okay," Hamoon said. Niam could hear him take a deep breath, as if trying to make a tough decision. "Okay. I'll be there."

"Great! I am sure that you will both benefit from the experience," Niam replied and ended the call.

Just then Prisha and the daughter entered the shop. Niam turned to look at them. They both had a concerned look on their faces. In the case of the daughter, her eyes were also wide with excitement and curiosity.

"Here you are!" Niam gave a broad smile and stood up. The hyena also got onto his feet and gazed at them. Prisha stopped, as if trying to comprehend the situation. However, the daughter did not stop. She looked at Niam and then at the hyena, and with a shout of "Papa!" walked up to him. Niam picked her up in his arms.

"How's my daughter!" he asked, hugging her tightly.

"Good!" she replied, and looked down at the hyena.

"There's someone I want you to meet," Niam said to her. "You know who this is?" he asked her gently.

"It's the lost hyena. I love him. Can we keep him?"

By then Prisha had also walked up to stand by Niam's side. "No, we cannot," she responded sharply.

"Please?" The daughter looked at Niam with big, beseeching eyes.

"Your mother said it," Niam said. "But you know what, you can play with him for a while. Do you want to play with him?"

"Yes," she replied with a wide smile, exposing a couple of missing teeth. Niam gently put her down on the floor. He and Prisha watched carefully as the daughter stretched her hand out and ran her fingers along the hyena's back.

"His hair is so rough! He needs a good brush." She looked at Prisha. "Can we take him home so I can brush his hair? Please?"

"Listen," Prisha said softly, "why don't you play with him here a bit while your Papa and I talk?"

"Do you want coffee?" Niam asked Prisha. "And do you want something to drink or eat?" he asked the daughter.

"Juice. Can I have some juice, please?" the daughter asked.

"Now, what did I tell you about sugar?" Prisha jumped in. "You've had enough sugar for a day."

"It's okay," Niam said to Prisha. "Let her have a small juice drink just for today."

Prisha acquiesced with a sharp look at him. Niam turned to request Bertrand for a coffee each for Prisha and himself, and a glass of orange juice and a blueberry muffin for the daughter. While Bertrand got busy with the order, and Ida and the waitress took care of other customers and arranged things around the shop, Niam and Prisha sat down. They silently looked at the daughter sitting on the floor next to the hyena. She was smiling and petting him, and alternately looking at him and at her parents.

"What are you planning to do with him?" Prisha asked.

"I'll take him to someone I met this morning when I was walking around the city. She's agreed to take care of him," he whispered so that the daughter would not hear.

"That's very nice of her," Prisha said.

"Yes, it is. If not for her, I wouldn't know what to do. We don't have a big place."

"We don't. But we really should think of moving from here to a bigger place," Prisha said. "I like this apartment, and our friends are here, and everything is so close by. If it was just the two of us, then this is perfect. But since she appeared today, it's become very cramped."

"You're right. We should start looking. One of my colleagues moved further out recently. He mentioned something about the place being cheaper and safer with more open space. He said the schools there were also good."

"That's the most important. That and being safer. Those are the two most important things to consider," Prisha added. "Sarah said she likes her new neighborhood. We could try to find a place around where she is."

"Maybe. But it's too far. I don't want to spend two hours every day just commuting. I'll ask my colleague on Monday. I don't think he lives that far from work."

They again silently looked at the daughter. After a short while, Niam asked her, "How did you know the hyena was a boy and not a girl?"

She stopped talking in whispers to the hyena but continued petting it. "I don't know. I just guessed."

"You just guessed?" Niam asked.

"Yup."

"Do you like him?" he asked.

"Yup. He's so nice," she replied as the hyena lifted its head and rubbed it against her shoulder and arm.

The waitress brought their order and placed everything on the table. Niam handed the orange juice to the daughter. She took a small sip and held out the glass to the hyena. He brought his nose up to the top of the glass, sniffed, and pulled his head back. It was obvious that he did not like the smell.

"No? Okay then. It's all mine," the daughter said to the hyena and took another sip.

"Does she have a name?" Niam asked Prisha.

"Our daughter? No," Prisha replied.

"Should we think of a name for her?"

"Do we need to? I like to call her daughter."

"That's fine with me, but I am not sure if it's going to be okay at school. Her friends can't be calling her daughter too, can they?" Niam smiled.

"That's true." Prisha smiled too. "You think of a name for her. I am much too busy taking care of everything—cleaning the apartment, cooking, running after her, and working full-time. You take this responsibility. And you take the responsibility to find us a new home."

"I'll be on it from tomorrow. Don't you worry." Niam's smile broadened.

"I worry a lot. You always escape your responsibilities," Prisha said in a mock anger.

"I won't this time, I promise."

"You promise?" she asked, giving him a little smile.

"Yes, I do. By this time tomorrow I'll have a list of names from which you and she can choose. And I'll find us a great place to move into in just a couple of weeks."

"We'll see," Prisha said.

"We will." Niam let out a small laugh. He turned to the daughter. "Have you thought of a name for your new friend?"

She stopped petting the hyena and turned to Niam. "He has a name already, Papa," she said.

"Oh, he does?" Prisha asked. "How do you know?"

"He told me," she answered.

"When did he tell you his name? We didn't hear him speak?"

"I don't know? I asked his name, and he told me," she replied.

"What's his name?" Niam asked her.

"His name is Ajani," she said and took another sip of juice.

Niam and Prisha looked at each other. Prisha asked her, "So, what other things has your friend Ajani told you?"

"I don't know," she replied.

"You don't know? He's told you his name. Have you told him your name?" Prisha continued.

"I told him I don't have a name yet. I'll tell him when I have one," she said.

"What else?"

"He said he's missing his family. He says he's very happy to see me." She turned to Prisha. "He's very sad, Mama. Can we take him home and give him an ice cream?"

"We'll think about it," Prisha responded. "For now, finish your juice. And don't forget to eat your muffin." Prisha handed the muffin to her.

The daughter took a big bite of the muffin. She broke a piece off and offered it to Ajani. He gently took it in his mouth from her hand.

Niam and Prisha had their attention diverted when the door of the shop opened. This time it was Hamoon who entered with wide-open, fearful eyes, looking around for any lurking danger ready to pounce on him. He saw the four of them and stopped dead in his tracks.

"Hamoon! Come join us!" Niam exclaimed.

Hamoon did not answer. He walked gingerly toward them, all the while keeping an eye on the hyena. Only when he was close enough and sure enough that the animal had no ill-intentions toward him did he relax, but only somewhat. He said a curt hello to Niam and Prisha and sat down with them.

"Have you met our daughter?" Prisha asked Hamoon.

"Oh, is that your daughter?" Hamoon spoke for the first time since he entered. He took his eyes away from the hyena and, also for the first time, noticed the little girl sitting right next to the beast. "She is a very pretty child. What's your name?" he asked her.

The daughter looked at Hamoon and frowned. "I don't have one yet. Mama and Papa are working on it."

"Good, good. Make sure they pick up a nice one. You don't want them to pick a name that's not nice, do you? A bad name will stick with you for the rest of your life."

"No, I won't let them." And she let out a broad smile.

"How old are you?"

"I will be six very soon," she replied.

"You're going to be a big girl! Are you excited about all the gifts you'll get for your birthday?"

"Yes, I am!" She beamed again.

"I am glad you could make it so soon. I was concerned about the traffic," Niam said to Hamoon. "Do you want some coffee or anything?"

"Thanks. I'll get it," Hamoon replied. He got up from his seat and walked over to the counter. There he exchanged pleasantries with Bertrand and Ida and came back with a steaming cup of foaming chai tea latte. He sat down and looked at the daughter.

"How's your friend?" he asked her.

"He's good. His name is Ajani. He's very sad. Maybe he needs chocolate. Mama, can we get Ajani a chocolate?"

"No, we're not getting him anything for now," Prisha said. "Let him rest."

The daughter made a sullen face and turned to look at Ajani. She whispered something into his ears.

"When are you two going to pick out a name for her?" Hamoon asked Niam and Prisha.

"He promised to do it by tomorrow," Prisha answered. "And he promised to come up with a good one."

"Make sure he does!" Hamoon exclaimed. "Did I ever tell you about this guy I knew? His name was Scooby."

"Scooby, like Scooby-Doo?" Prisha asked.

"Yup, exactly like Scooby-Doo the cartoon character," Hamoon said.

"His name really was Scooby?" Niam asked. "It wasn't a nickname or something?"

"Nope, it really was Scooby." Niam smiled. "I didn't ever talk about him, did I?"

"Not that I can remember," Niam said.

"Scooby was this interesting dude I met a few years back in Atlanta. There was a restaurant with a bar not too far from my office at that time. I would frequently go there with others at my office during lunch, or sometimes for dinner when we were working late. It wasn't a great place, but it wasn't bad either. Scooby was a waiter there who would often serve us. He was a super skinny guy, but he was very quick and very strong. He could carry big orders easily without any effort. I got to know him slowly.

"Sometimes, when I would be there for dinner, I would sit at the bar and get a couple of drinks with my meal. Just a beer or two, nothing more. During those evenings, on a few occasions,

Scooby would be behind the bar helping the bartender. If the crowd was small, or the drink orders were mostly cocktails only the bartender could make, Scooby would have the opportunity to come over to chat. He was easy to talk to. On rare occasions he would be somewhat sullen and despondent. I first ascribed it to him working on three different jobs trying to make ends meet in Atlanta, which is just about as expensive a city as one can get. One job was at the restaurant. Another was at a smoke shop. The third was at a gas station convenience store. And these are not easy jobs. He told me he made good money, but it was still tough. Decent sleep was a luxury and a decent meal was very infrequent. I slowly prodded him on his jobs and on his life. Whenever he was in a good mood, he wouldn't talk much about himself. He would talk about cars and motorbikes and about different kinds and brands of alcohol. When he was not, that's when he would talk about himself.

"As Scooby grew more comfortable with me, those talks of his became darker. He told me that when he was born, his mother had decided to name him Michael. She asked his father to fill out the forms for this birth certificate while she recuperated at the hospital after a tough delivery. The afternoon he was supposed to fill out the form, his father got high on weed and alcohol while watching cartoon shows on TV. Scooby-Doo was on at the time, and this is how he ended up with the name Scooby. But his mother was not much better in this regard. Theirs was a small town, and addiction of one type or the other was rampant. There wasn't much else to do.

"Scooby didn't grow up in an overtly abusive home. He wasn't beaten or any such thing. His younger brother and sister also never faced any abuse. His parents would smoke weed a lot and drink as often and as much as possible, but they always tried to talk to their children with respect. It wasn't abuse the siblings faced, it was outright indifference. If they were sick, they were on their own, or had the occasional help from a diabetes and arthritis-stricken grandmother. If they had to go to school hungry because there was nothing in the kitchen, so be it. If they wanted to wear clean clothes to school, it was up to them to wash and dry them. If they wanted dinner, they had to find food.

"When he was mature enough, Scooby tried to take care of his younger siblings the best he could. Doing well in school was not an option for him. His life was set for hard manual labor helping his family. It wasn't a long life. He did help his brother become an electrical line worker and move out of the town. His sister died at the age of eleven when his father accidently shot her while under the influence. The sister could have been saved if she had received medical attention. Unfortunately, there was no one else in the house at the time, and their father was too drunk to realize what had happened. When he came to some semblance of sense and found his daughter had bled to death, he wrote a small note apologizing for his mistake and took his own life with the same gun.

"When Scooby was only seventeen, he was diagnosed with leukemia. It was a tough two-year struggle to recover. It wasn't just the fight to live that left him physiologically weak and mentally drained. It was also that he came to realize how being poor was a curse in every aspect. It was a fight to arrange for transport to doctors, it was sometimes, but not always, a fight to be treated with dignity at the medical facility, a fight to get the paperwork on time, a fight to be able to have a good diet at home, and a fight to not feel miserable at not having enough money for anything else and missing school. He was, however, young and strong. He survived.

"Once Scooby was up to it, he moved to Atlanta to stay with his brother. His brother had completed school during the time Scooby was battling cancer, and had joined a community college in Atlanta. Scooby worked that hard at those three jobs, I realized, to support not only himself, but also his brother's education."

"That's one tough life," Prisha said.

"Yup," Hamoon responded.

"I suppose I need to make sure I am paying full attention when I choose a name for her," Niam said.

"Yup," Hamoon again replied monosyllabically.

"What did you mean it wasn't a long life?" Niam asked. "What happened to him?"

"He died," Hamoon said and turned to look at the hyena. It seemed to him that the hyena was alert and looking at him, as if trying to understand what he was saying.

"He died?" Prisha asked. "How?"

"His leukemia came back. Last he told me, doctors were hopeful. But he was distressed about the prospect of going through all that he had gone through the first time. That was the last time I saw him. At first, I assumed he was not coming to work because he was undergoing treatment. A few months passed, and I enquired about his condition from another waiter who knew him and his brother. That waiter told me about Scooby's death. He had committed suicide. One day Scooby went back to his home town and shot himself with the same gun that had killed his sister and his father."

After a short moment of silence, Prisha said, "That's one tragic life."

"Yup," Hamoon responded again. "I suppose the gun still lives on." He took a long pause during which everyone at the table sat still absorbing his words. Hamoon turned to look at the hyena. "When I was young, life was full of possibilities. Now life is about hope. For some, even hope is a luxury."

"Now come on," Niam quipped, "The one and sure thing about life is that it will end. There's no need to get too gloomy over it."

"Actually, I am not gloomy. I am a bit disappointed with life. It's not that life has so much to offer, but that it has so little. This has been my realization. But let's leave all this. What are you planning to do with him?"

"Who? Ajani the hyena?" Niam asked.

"Who else?"

"I was thinking of leaving him with someone I know," Niam said.

"Who?"

"You don't know her,' Niam replied. "I met her this morning. Do you want to pet him? You can if you want. He won't mind."

"Are you sure?" Hamoon said with a skeptical voice as he looked at Ajani.

"I am sure." Niam smiled.

Hamoon quickly got up from his seat, and squatted very cautiously. Ajani looked at him with penetrating eyes, but otherwise showed no ill intent.

"He's a beautiful hyena," Hamoon said to the daughter.

"He's the best!" she exclaimed.

Hamoon drew out his hand and ran it over the animal's head and back. Ajani let out a low gurgling sound and stuck his neck out in an effort to encourage Hamoon to repeat what he did. Hamoon obliged.

"I like him," he said to Niam. "Would you be okay if I came with you to leave him with your new friend?"

"Absolutely! Be my guest!" Niam replied. "We'll leave once you're done. No, take your time. There's no hurry. I have a feeling this day will not be ending soon. We don't need to rush."

"Great!" Hamoon replied and picked up his tea.

"And if you don't mind, we'll take public transport. We all won't fit in a car anyway," Niam said.

"Sure," Hamoon replied. "Let me talk to Bertrand and ask him to keep an eye on my car. Hey Bertie..." And he got up with the tea cup in his hand to talk to Bertrand.

The five of them, Niam, Prisha, the daughter, Hamoon, and Ajani the hyena, stepped out of the coffee shop to start on a slow walk toward the metro station. The street had become busy, and the sidewalk was becoming packed. They were mostly ignored by most people. A few, though, gave them sideways glances, especially Ajani. The crowd, and at many places some of the shops and restaurants that had occupied parts of the sidewalk, prevented them from walking together. Soon, Niam and Hamoon were walking side-by-side, and Prisha and the daughter and Ajani were together in front. Prisha held the daughter's hand for most parts, who in turn kept a hand on Ajani.

"Don't be scared," Niam heard her say to Ajani once. He looked at her and kept up his pace. "We'll be on the train soon. You'll love it."

"What are you two talking about?" Niam asked.

"Nothing," she replied. "Ajani is afraid of the crowd. I told him that it's okay. He's not afraid anymore."

"Did he tell you he was afraid?"

"Yes, he told me he was afraid."

Niam looked at Hamoon. "I think she can communicate with the hyena. I don't know how, but how else would she know his name and what he's feeling?"

"It's possible," Hamoon replied.

A woman looking into her phone nearly collided with them. Hamoon turned to avoid the woman, but she continued her walk in complete disregard to her surroundings and him, and apparently completely oblivious to the accident she was about to cause. And while Hamoon's quick action saved her, his abrupt movement caused him to bump into a chair outside a restaurant.

"We need to do something about people on their phones all the time," Hamoon said after he put the chair back into its place. He and Niam turned to look at the woman as she disappeared into the crowd. She was still looking into her phone.

"We should," Niam said. "I think these phones and this round-the-clock digital connectivity is the reason why people are losing touch with their immediate surroundings and finding it difficult to live in the moment and with people who are physically in our presence."

"I agree!" Hamoon said. They turned back to face Prisha and the other two. The three of them had stopped when they heard the sound of Hamoon hitting the chair.

"Is everything alright?" Prisha asked.

"Everything's fine," Hamoon replied. "Some people should not be permitted to have a smartphone. They cannot handle it. They're not smart enough."

"Yes, I agree." Prisha giggled.

They restarted their effort of battling through the crowd.

"What were we talking about?" Hamoon asked Niam.

"I don't know. When?" Niam replied.

"Just before that woman with the phone almost ran us over."

"Yes. I remember now. I was saying that I think she can somehow communicate with the hyena. It's like they are psychically connected or something."

"It's possible," Hamoon said after a pause. "I wouldn't be surprised. Maybe you can ask her to talk to the hyena. You know. Ask her to ask him some questions."

"I should. I'll do it on the train. I hope it'll not be too packed," Niam said.

They were at the entrance to the train station in a few minutes. Niam walked to the automated ticket counter and looked into the small screen, and tapped it a few times. He turned around and looked at Prisha and Hamoon.

"What should I do for Ajani's ticket? I don't see an option for a hyena. Should I buy an adult or a child ticket for him?"

"That's a good question," Prisha said. "Maybe we should ask someone."

"Ajani says he's an adult," the daughter announced.

"That's good," Niam said. "But we should still be sure. We don't want your friend to get in trouble, do we?"

She looked at Ajani. "No," she agreed.

"Let me see if I can catch hold of someone and find out," Hamoon said. He walked toward the counter and talked to the man behind the windowpane. Hamoon had studied French when he was at school in Doha. By the time he went to college, he had forgotten most of it. When he learned he was to go to Paris for a project, he put in some effort to effort to revisit and brush up his French. His command over spoken lanaguage was very good. He also helped Niam pick up some very basic French. The reading and writing were what Hamoon still struggled with.

Hamoon did not appear satisfied with the man's response and walked toward them with a shrug of his shoulders. Before he could pass on what he had found out to Niam and Prisha, they were approached by an elderly woman. She was petite, perhaps no more than five feet tall. She appeared to be over seventy and proudly carried the collective weight of each and every year she had lived so far. Her makeup was immaculate, her hair was curly and dyed a shiny cinnamon brown color, and her full-sleeved shiny white blouse and long red skirt seemed to boldly project her love for life.

"*C'est la hyène excitée?*" She pointed toward Ajani while looking at Hamoon. Hamoon explained to her that this indeed was the hyena who was in the news a few hours back, but he was not horny. He told her his name was Ajani, and he was about to be taken to a new home.

"Oh, Ajani," she said to Niam and Prisha. "*Beau nom. Belle hyène. Bel enfant. Est-elle votre fille?*"

Hamoon interjected. He explained to the woman that this indeed was their daughter, and that they were not very good with French.

"Not a problem at all," she replied. "I know English very well. I said you have a beautiful daughter."

"Thank you!" Prisha said.

"Where are you taking the hyena?" she asked.

"We are taking him to someone I know. I wish we could

keep him and take care of him. But we can't as our house is too small," Niam said.

"God bless you for caring for him. And God bless the person who has agreed to take him in to make your life easier," she said. "As I always say, like almost everything in life, charity too is more satisfying if it is done with other people's money and effort. May I?" She stretched out her hand toward Ajani.

"Absolutely," Niam said. "He's very friendly."

She petted Ajani a few times. "Lovely animal. I hope he finds a good home. Are you all waiting for someone here?"

"No. We were trying to figure out what ticket to get for him," Hamoon said. "The man in the ticket office doesn't know and doesn't seem to be in the mood to help."

"People can be so unfriendly toward hyenas here," she said, and looked at Ajani. She petted him again. "*Belle hyène*," she repeated. "Here, I'll give you my pass." She reached into her designer bag, rummaged through its contents, and pulled out a smaller hand purse, and from that, she extracted her metro card. "Here." She held it out to Niam. "This will work. Keep it. Just be casual about it."

"Are you sure?" Niam asked. "You don't want to use it?"

"No, just take it," she said. "Actually, hold on." She pulled out her phone from her purse and tapped a number. She spoke into it very fast. Niam and Prisha couldn't catch the conversation. Hamoon apparently did because he kept on shaking his head. She removed the phone from her ear and said to Niam, "Can you tell me the place you're taking your hyena?"

Niam told her. She put the phone back to her ear and spoke into it. After a couple of sentences, she cut the call and put the phone back into her bag.

"You don't need to take the metro. Why don't you come with me? I'll drop you there in my car. My car is fairly big. I've asked the driver to pull up outside."

"This is very generous of you again. But are you sure?

Do you think your car will fit all six of us plus the driver?" Niam asked.

"It's not a problem at all!" she beamed. "It's a fairly big car. And your hyena can always sit on the floor or in the very back. It's better than taking the trouble of traveling with him on the metro. Besides, I've nothing important to do, and it's not every day I get to be around such a lovely hyena. This place you're going to is not too far from where I live. I will be grateful for the company."

The six of them walked through a huge crowd of people on their way to the station exit, and were soon back outside in bright sunlight. The weather had warmed considerably, partly because of the sun, and partly because of the crowd. The woman looked around and did not see her car. "It'll be here very soon. Give it a few minutes. The driver told me he's about two blocks away."

"Papa, I think he is getting scared again," the daughter said to Niam.

Niam looked at Ajani. He was looking wide-eyed around him at the throng of people rushing past them.

"Don't worry dear," the woman said. "The car is coming. Once we're in the car, it'll become quiet once again and the hyena will be calm."

She took the time they were waiting for the car to introduce herself. Her name was Delphine. In her younger years, she had been a successful musician with a few hit singles at the peak of her career. Later, she composed some songs for other artists, some of which also did very well. She made some money, opened a small music studio and a boutique, and married into a successful business family.

Those were tumultuous times in France, when the old world order was disappearing, and a new world order was spreading out some tenuous and some firm roots. Here, one generation was coming to terms with the losing of old glory and prestige, and a newer generation, which had grown up hearing stories of global dominance, was taking over. It was one manifestation of one of the longest continually running stories of humanity—of people who do not fully know the past, and of those who cannot overcome it.

Social movements and political movements have significant commonalities and oftentimes develop a symbiotic relationship. But they also differ in some critical ways. The former are more democratic and more chaotic, and often very difficult to control and guide, or even suppress. Political movements, on the other hand, are less democratic, with a relatively well-defined leadership and power dynamics. In Paris, and within the broader France, of the 1970s, American mass consumerism, speed, and efficiency were firmly on the march, and so was the associated culture and culinary habits. This did not come without the accompanying societal strains. The oil shock was a further significant impetus for socio-economic changes. And so too was the rise of Japan and the business philosophy of Kei-Haku-Tan-Sho and Kaizen, and the Kanban system that took the world of business by storm.

Against this dynamic backdrop, Delphine found her style of music ebbing. On the other hand, her husband's business took off spectacularly when he ventured into being a supplier for fast food restaurants, much to the chagrin of some of the older culinary connoisseurs in their family and circle of friends and acquaintances. She eventually decided to sell her own business and play second fiddle to her husband. This still turned out to be a demanding life, where her professional music goals were replaced with demands of social and professional gatherings and hobnobbing in support of the growth of her husband's business interests. It was when her husband passed away a few years back, and the running of the diverse, disparate businesses had been taken over by other family members, that she found herself thinking more and more about her prior life as a musician, and the possibility of venturing back into it.

Delphine's car was a spacious luxury SUV. Niam and Hamoon went to the very back row. The daughter, Prisha, and Delphine sat in the middle with Ajani on the floor sitting up straight and staring out through the front windshield. The driver was a man with sharp facial features and physique. He wore a perfectly ironed white shirt, black pants, and shiny black shoes. When he had stopped the car near where Delphine and the others were waiting, he stepped out to open the car door for Delphine.

"*Ce n'est pas nécessaire.*" She had waved at him and opened the door herself. "*Belle hyène,*" Delphine repeated as she petted Ajani when they were on their way. "Have you thought of a name for him?" she asked the daughter, forgetting that Hamoon had mentioned his name to her.

"His name is Ajani." The daughter smiled.

"That's a nice name," she responded. "Will you be sad when your papa gives him away?"

"Yes," the daughter said. "But mama says we don't have the space to keep him."

"It's not just space," Prisha spoke for the first time in a while. "We don't know where we'll be in a few months. It all depends on what happens with the project Niam, my husband, is working on."

"Yes, I can understand," Delphine said. "It's not easy with the uncertainty. I suppose you can still handle moving when you're young. At my age I become anxious when things are outside of what I'm used to."

"If you don't mind my asking," Prisha said, "why were you taking the metro when you have a car and a driver?"

"Not at all," she responded. "I've been trying to get back to making music for a few months. When you are old like I am, a feeling of helplessness can set in. You're not able to do things you could when you were young. You're not as agile or as strong, and you tire faster. People around you start dying one by one. My effort at not letting such feelings of gloom and helpless inevitability take over my life was by deciding to make the best songs I can possibly make to honor the remainder of my life. A great song connects the deepest parts of one's soul to the vibrations of the universe like nothing else can. The universe has many vibrations. This is also why each person is affected by many different songs, and not just one. I want to feel some of those connections with the universe, and some of those vibrations once again. I want to live those connections and vibrations once more. I don't want to simply wait for my end. My end should be the apotheosis of a triumph over melancholy. This is how I want to go.

"However, my voice is no longer what it was, obviously! And so, obviously, I cannot sing like before. I thought that I could perhaps still compose the way I used to. I tried very hard for a while, but I just couldn't rekindle that old spark. Nothing worthwhile came out of me. I figured that I had lost the creative touch because I had lost touch with people. When I was an active musician, I drew inspiration from the world around me—real people, their loves, their sorrows, their struggles. Decades of living a secluded, and often isolated life took that bit away from me. I am now seeking to get it back. I am jumping into the crowd and trying to become part of it. Every day, or as close to every day as I can, I take the metro to different parts of the city. There I simply amble through lanes and streets. My favorite part is running into street performers—singers, dancers, or musicians. I usually do this at times of the day when the crowd is small enough for me to be comfortable with. My driver here, Nabil, helps me out by picking me up from wherever I am."

Nabil glanced back briefly and smiled. He did not understand what Delphine had said. He knew French and Arabic, but very little English.

Nabil was Tunisian by birth. He was the second oldest of five sons and four daughters in a household that had seen good times and bad times. His father and an uncle ran a small Tunis-based travel agency for tourists. As a travel agency, their main focus was to work with some of the bigger travel agencies in Europe. Business was good when it was good, but it was seasonal and dependent on many geopolitical and economic factors over which they had no control.

Regularly hearing his father talk about the work at the agency, and watching tourists from across Europe, had sparked a desire in Nabil to go to Europe, and particularly to France, from an early age. His break came when his older brother joined his father in their business, and his next younger brother started helping out at the agency with odd jobs after school. This greatly reduced the family pressure and expectations on Nabil and gave him some flexibility to plan a different future for himself. He convinced his family to dig into their reserves and send him to France to get a degree in business. The hope, perhaps farfetched, was to have Nabil establish himself, and then the travel agency, in France. This way they would be less dependent on the whims of the bigger agencies they were partnering with. The unstable political climate within the country and the social and political challenges distressing the larger geographical area could negatively affect the agency's earnings at any time. This further helped cement Nabil's decision to go to Paris.

Nabil landed in Paris with awe and joined the university with dreamy eyes. Then in quick succession he fell in love with a fellow student, got her pregnant, accompanied her for abortion per her choice, married her a few weeks later, failed a few classes, went to his father's funeral, had an argument with his family because he let them down, had his financial support suspended, and had dropped out of the university because he now couldn't support himself as a full-time student.

Back in Paris, the young couple decided that Nabil's wife would finish up her education first while he supported them both by finding small work. Once she was done and hopefully working on a high-paying job, she would in turn support his education.

One gorgeous summer day in Paris, Nabil was somewhere between unhappy and outright miserable. Earlier in the morning, he had had a conversation with his family back home in Tunis. His favorite sister, the third sibling in the row, was to be married in a month. The family was still upset with him. He knew he would not receive a warm homecoming if he were to attend the marriage. But it was more than that. He simply did not have the money to travel.

Nabil sat remorsefully at a bus stop, hunched and reflecting on some of the poor choices he had made, while he waited for the bus to the Tunisian grocery store he was working at. At that store, Nabil was tasked with multiple exhausting things involving stocking, shelving, cleaning, and anything else asked of him. When Nabil looked up with a drawn face, he saw a well-dressed old woman walking on the sidewalk looking very lost. She would take a few steps, stop and look around, hesitatingly take a few steps more, stop, consider turning around but would decide against it, and repeat the process. On a whim, Nabil decided to approach her. He stood up, walked slowly toward her, and asked her if she was lost and would like him to help her. She joyfully agreed. He then helped her get on the bus he was taking. He got off with her about a block from where he was supposed to and helped walk her to the metro station. There she requested him to accompany her on the metro to her home so she wouldn't get lost again. She offered him a very generous compensation for his help. The amount was convincing enough for Nabil to call the grocery store and make an excuse he knew they wouldn't believe and would probably hold against him in future.

During their walk to the metro station, and then the ride on the metro, Nabil found himself opening up to her. She looked like a kindly old woman, one you would instinctively trust with your problems because she appeared to be genuinely interested in them. She appeared to be rich too, and Nabil found it very flattering that a rich Parisian would show an interest in listening to him. He therefore laid out his entire life in front of her. He had barely finished the monologue before their station, but she did not seem to mind not being able to get a word in.

Once they were out of the station, Nabil found himself in a very fancy part of the city he had never been to before. During his early days in Paris, Nabil had heard about the general area he was in, and about how it was populated by wealthy people. Now he saw it for the first time with his own eyes. He was mesmerized, and he told her so. When he asked her why she used public transport when she was rich enough to afford to live in a neighborhood like this, she said something similar to what she had said in the car to Niam and Prisha and Hamoon.

Delphine met Nabil on her second foray into the city by herself. She had not ventured too far from her residence the first time. This time she had felt bold enough to travel out farther. However, she had not realized how much she had forgotten about the city and public transport over the years, and she managed to get herself somewhat lost.

The two of them reached an intersection not far from the metro station. Delphine stopped and turned to look at Nabil. She instinctively trusted him, just like he trusted her enough to open up to her. She was, however, also a woman of tremendous experience in dealing with people, and rarely let her emotions guide her. This was her neighborhood, and she knew it very well. She would not risk Nabil walking to her home and knowing where she lived. She thanked him and reached into her purse and pulled out the amount she had promised him. Nabil's eyes lit up, which pleased her. She then went on a whim. She asked him if he would like to be her paid partner on her excursions into the city during his days off. This way, she explained, she would be more comfortable traveling farther out and even exploring places she would not feel secure venturing into by herself.

Thus started their camaraderie. They met a couple of times at the same metro station at designated times, discussed where they should go, and spent several hours exploring. In addition to the agreed upon payment, she also paid for Nabil's meals. After that she got paperwork done to formally employ him—and save on her taxes too.

Over a few months of this arrangement, Delphine got an opportunity to know Nabil's wife and a few friends, which also included two struggling singers and composers who supported themselves through street performances and on-and-off gigs at local bars. She considered this particularly fortuitous. Their songs inspired her to compose and experiment with her songs. The three even got into a loose partnership, where they would all help each other compose new songs. On occasions, she let them sing some of the songs she would write.

Therefore, when Delphine's driver declared his intention to retire, she did not take too long to offer Nabil the position. She offered him a salary significantly less than what her current driver received. Still, this amount was far larger than what he was making working at the grocery store and other odd jobs, including being her travel companion. This was the answer to his financial woes. He gratefully accepted the offer.

When Nabil started working for Delphine, his wife was in college, in her final year. She was hoping to land a good job in a few months, and then for Nabil to leave his job as a driver and get back into college. Nabil at times, however, vacillated. He was making good money and, like many young people in similar situations, finding it hard to justify spending some years to get a degree only to end up making a similar salary. But he knew he would do it. He would return to education not for his wife, but to be accepted back into his family in Tunisia. They had sent him to Paris to expand the family business, not to become a lowly driver. However, this did not mean he needed to rush to complete his degree. He planned to take his time. He would take classes at a slow pace while working for Delphine. Besides, he figured, if he continued to be nice to this old lady, she might not only increase his salary, but perhaps also support his education.

When the motely group of seven—Nabil the Tunisian and soon hoping to become French, Delphine the French Parisian, Niam and Prisha, Indians, Hamoon the Afghani-American, Niam's and Prisha's daughter of unknown origin, and Ajani the hyena, also of unknown origin—were driving through the busy streets of Paris to meet Nina, little did they know what lay ahead of them.

"I am glad to run into a fellow wanderer," Niam said to Delphine.

"So you too like to roam around Paris?" Delphine asked.

"Yes. I've been doing it for some time now. Though, my motivation is a bit different. I go around Paris and compile what I observe into articles for an online magazine."

"How interesting." Delphine turned slightly to look at Niam in the very back seat.

"This is how I met the person we're driving to meet," Niam continued. "I was walking around this morning when I ran into her. She seems like a person who can take good care of the hyena."

"I am happy to know this," Delphine said. "I wish I could take care of him. But I don't believe I have the capability to do so. Did you learn anything more about him? What was his name you said?"

"His name is Ajani," the daughter said.

"Good, good. Such a good name," Delphine said. "Anything else?"

"He says he likes this car. He was afraid of being on the street. I think he didn't want to go on the metro too," she added.

"He said all this to you?" Niam chimed in.

"Yes," she replied.

"But I didn't hear him speak," Niam said.

"I don't know. I just heard him."

"Can you maybe ask him a question for us?" Niam said. "I want to know more about Ajani."

The daughter looked at Ajani. Ajani removed his eyes from the road ahead to look at her.

"He says he'll be very happy to tell you," she said to her father.

Niam looked at Hamoon. Hamoon was sitting very still, pensively staring out the window. He appeared oblivious to the conversations going on in the car. Niam looked back at the daughter and Ajani.

When their eyes met, Ajani told him his story. He could hear his words clearly in his mind.

Ajani was born in a relatively large clan inhabiting a relatively large grassland. He was born with a silver spoon in his mouth. His mother was the matriarch, the alpha female of the clan. His father, though, like most male hyenas, was not important. His main role was to mate, and occasionally play with the cubs in the group if he was allowed this honor. He had joined the clan a few years before Ajani was born. This had not been easy. He had followed the clan from a distance for several days, and was let in only because he was submissive enough for the clan's taste. Ajani never much cared for his father. For him, his father was just another lowly clan member, who acted friendly toward him and deferential toward his mother.

Life was easy for Ajani as a cub. For many seasons, in fact, it was all fun and games. He drank his mother's milk for the longest time. She, in turn, had the top pickings after a hunt, and was therefore very healthy and produced quality milk. As the offspring of the matriarch, Ajani also received a good bit of affection and respect from other members. In the hyena world, where an overwhelming number of them die even before they reach maturity, this all proved propitious and contributed to his survival. And survive he did, and much more. He grew in size. He developed a shiny, radiant coat, which stood out among other cubs of similar age.

The first hunt he was truly a part of was the taking down of a pregnant zebra. It was a commotion like none other for Ajani. The sounds of the hunted and the hunters, and the tearing of flesh and crunching of bones, the smell of the pack and the meat and the dust around, were all imprinted in his memory. He was mesmerized, excited, and frozen all at once. During the hunt, instincts kicked in and he became part of the hysteria. At first the zebra stood her ground and then tried moving. But the clan was full of experienced hunters, with Ajani's mother being the best. The hyenas surrounded the zebra, giving her limited space to move. They took turns biting into her wherever opportunities presented themselves. Her hind legs received the most attention though. Ajani did his best to join in, but he was inexperienced. He mostly stayed on the side, observing. Then the zebra was brought down, and the clan pounced on her.

At first the zebra laid on her stomach to protect her most vulnerable parts. Unfortunately, this only prolonged her suffering. Eventually the biting and pushing was too much and she gave up and rolled onto her side. That's when the real feeding frenzy began. While she was still alive and braying in pain, the zebra's stomach was torn up and her fetus pulled out. A small group of hyenas took the fetus to the side. Ajani joined them and took his first bite of meat. The rest of the clan did short work on the mother. They left almost nothing behind by the time they were done. It was a good hunt for the pack. Everyone took part in the feeding, and no one went away hungry. Sometime later, as the clan rested, their stomachs full and their minds replaying their fortuitous day, Ajani filled his stomach with his mother's milk.

Soon after, Ajani started exploring the world around him on his own. He would leave the group and stroll some distance away, never too far to be out of earshot. He would chase small animals and birds, but often return with no success.

One day his wandering took him some distance farther than he was used to. As he was trying to make his way back, he found a carcass of an animal he had not seen before in a gully, being devoured by vultures. He gingerly walked up to the carcass and, much to the chagrin of the vultures, pulled it way. He tried to pull it up the steep wall of the gully, but it was too heavy for him. He tore into it and ate as much as he could. He tried to pull the remaining meat up the wall again. This time he managed to get halfway up before the carcass fell back. Dejectedly, he walked around the carcass, keeping an eye on the unhappy vultures. Just then he heard familiar sounds and looked up. He saw his mother with some other hyenas who had come looking for him. Together, they pulled up the carcass over the gully walls, and filled themselves on it. Then they walked back to the clan, with mother and son a few steps away from the group. Ajani did not know it yet, but his mother's affection toward him was going to decrease from this point on. His time with her, and with the clan, was coming to an end.

There were two dangerous hunts Ajani was to participate in before he left the pack. One was a lone male lion. This particular hunt ended in a disaster because not only did the lion escape but did so after killing one of their teammates and taking a big bite out of it. The other time involved a lioness who appeared to have become lost. This ended in failure too because the members of her pride heard Ajani's pack and the lioness's growling and came rushing to her help. The hyena pack had little choice but to run for their lives, with Ajani a whisker away from losing it.

Around this time, Ajani's wanderings had been taking him farther and farther away from the pack. His desire to move completely away had been growing in him. His mother was no longer paying him the attention he used to receive. His position in the pecking order was also being continually challenged. In short, his ties to the pack were stretching thinner by the day. It was only a matter of time before those snapped.

Ajani's break from his pack did not occur in the usual way for a male hyena. In fact, it occurred in a highly unusual, and most unique way. One fine warm day, on one of his routine wanderings away from the pack, he saw a shimmer of light some distance away among a canopy of trees. His curiosity got the better of him, and he approached cautiously.

As Ajani came closer, he could pick out distinct sounds he had never heard before. He lifted his nose up in the air to smell. The wind was gently blowing away from the source of the sounds, and all he could smell were the recognizable smells of the forest around him. The shimmering light was still there, beckoning him to satisfy his inquisitiveness. He brought his nose down to the ground and smelled around. Again, he found nothing out of his repertoire of known smells that had guided him thus far in his relatively short life. While keeping his eyes on the shimmer just a few steps away, he warily put his front paw on a soft patch of grass. Just then, in a fraction of a second, before he could comprehend, a soft *whoosh* sound reached his ears and he found himself helplessly bound in a net and lifted to hang low from a tree branch. He had walked into what he later came to know as a trap.

Ajani hung in the air for some time, with the ground below him tantalizingly close. He splayed his legs and twisted his torso to get some semblance of a grip. He was unsuccessful. Very soon the agitation and anxiousness wore him out. He gave up moving. Only his rapid heartbeat and his penetrating, excited eyes indicated that he was still in control of his senses. At one point he twisted his neck around and saw animals he had not seen before. He froze for a moment before panicking. He let out a distressed piercing loud giggle with the hope his pack would hear him and come to his aid. They did not hear him.

"Why, it's a beautiful hyena we have here," Ella declared.

"Aren't we lucky!" exclaimed Nina. "I was afraid it was going to take us days, if not weeks, of setting up the trap every day, and waiting and waiting. How wonderful, it didn't take us more than a couple of hours!"

"I was much more hopeful than you," said Ella. "I know there's a big pack not far away. This fine specimen must be one among them. Quick, let's take him away before we have a whole bunch of them around."

"There's nothing to worry about. They can't do anything to us."

"Yes, but they can still make things irritating," Ella responded. "And if we're distracted enough, they can pull the net apart and help him escape. We'll then have to restart this whole thing. The next time may indeed be days and weeks."

"You're right. Let's get a move on," Nina said.

Ajani felt a small sharp pain in his back. He felt calm very quickly after that. The exhaustion from the struggle caught up to him and he went into a drug-induced sleep.

It is incorrect to assume that Ajani did not have any concept of the human construct of time. It is true that he lived in the moment, was aware of the moment, and responded to external and internal stimuli in the moment. But like all sentient living beings, the moment was a function of past experiences, present provocations, and possible choices for future actions. The moment he woke up, however, he had no connection with any of his past experiences. He had never felt grogginess before. He let out a low giggle and tried to cover his head with his front paws. He then twisted and turned around to get rid of whatever it was that was weighing his head down. In doing so, he discovered that he could not fully move around. He found himself confined in a small kennel, just wide enough for him to turn around and stand up.

As the effect of the tranquilizer wore off, Ajani quickly felt much more in control of his senses. He stood on his feet and stared out of the cage. He saw things that once again did not make sense to him. He noticed smells he had smelled before, but he also noticed the scent of other things, similar, but different. He heard lots of unfamiliar sounds. This scared him. He cowered to the farthest end of the kennel he could reach and shook.

Later on, Ajani peered out of his kennel once again and found himself to be in a small room with two big open windows to allow ventilation and natural light to come in. He was alone when he woke up. But his complaining soon brought him company. From his position at the back of the kennel, Ajani could make out several footsteps moving randomly around him and in the room. He thought he heard two familiar voices he had recently heard—voices he did not like. But he wasn't certain. His agitated state of mind had made it impossible for him to focus on anything other than trying to sense where the next danger would come from.

"He's very worked up," Ella said. "We need to do something or else he'll have a heart attack and die."

"Poor hyena," Nina said. "Look, he's so scared. Don't be scared, hyena. We'll not harm you." She turned toward Ella and said, "What should we do? He may be dehydrated too. Maybe we should get him to sleep again? Maybe if we give him some chicken that'll calm him down?"

"Let's try it. I don't want to give him any more tranquilizers. We don't know how it can affect him. We need him alive till it's all done," Ella said.

Nina brought a small piece of chicken leg and pushed it into the kennel. Ajani stared at her and watched her every move with deep nervousness and growled. He was losing strength fast, but his hormones kept him focused. Soon the smell of flesh reached his nose, and deep-seated instincts arose. Surely, he surmised, if there's food, it can't be all bad. He needed to eat. He got up on his feet and warily moved forward. He smelled the chicken and gave his fears some rest. He tore into the piece and ate it all. He then looked out the kennel to see Nina looking at him.

"He likes it!" She smiled at Ella.

"Give him another piece," Ella said.

Nina pushed another piece in. Ajani growled again, but less agitatedly. He ate that piece too and looked at Nina again with expectations for more. She did not have anything else.

Giving him water was a logistical challenge. Ajani had woken up much before they had anticipated. Their plan was to take him out of the kennel while he was still asleep and tie him up to a post. This way, feeding him and caring for him would have been easier. They eventually decided to give him the small dose of the tranquilizer they had with them so they could achieve their goal.

Ajani was still in the same room when he next came back to his senses. This time, though, he was not in the kennel. He had a short leash around his neck. The other end of the leash was tied to an iron metal ring fixed to the wall. He was not happy to be tethered.

They were to have a daughter. It was certain. The stars were clear on it. The lines on his palm were clear on it. The stars were also clear on something else—the daughter was conceived at the wrong time. Venus and Mars together were in the wrong house. Niam and Prisha didn't know it at that time. They simply made love when they thought the time was right. They had been doing this for a few months. They would have done it for a few more before Prisha would start to worry. This month, however, things went just right. Except for the planets. Their daughter was to be born an epicurean of the sensual and sexual kind, perhaps even with poorly controlled animalistic desires when she came of age. She would be perfidious, lacking any sense or desire for contrition, and would bring infamy and dishonor upon her family, either through her words or her actions, or both. A devil is what she would turn out to be!

It was Ella who figured this out. Prisha and Niam had visited

111

her after they found out about Prisha's pregnancy. This was what everyone did for matters big or small—they went to Ella, and Ella guided them. When Prisha told her she was pregnant, Ella asked Prisha to approach her.

"Come here," she said. "Let me feel the baby."

Prisha moved to sit next to her. Ella gently placed her right-hand palm on her belly. She became silent and closed her eyes. When she opened them, she pulled her hand away and kept her palm face up. She asked Niam and Prisha to put their right-hand palms on her palms. They did. She closed her eyes again and clasped the three right hands tight with her left hand. She removed her hand about half a minute later and opened her eyes. She looked at Prisha.

"You are very blessed," she said to Prisha. "You will have a beautiful daughter."

Prisha looked at Niam and beamed.

"Indeed, she will be very pretty," Ella continued. "Here," she looked at Niam, "let me see your hand again."

Niam stretched out his right-hand palm. Ella held it and studied it very carefully. She turned his hand every which way. She ran her fingers over his lines. She gently placed her thumb over his various mounts. She rubbed her thumb over his plain of Mars and pressed down on his mount of Venus and inner and outer mounts of Mars. She wasn't very pleased with what she saw.

"Do you know when she was conceived?" She turned toward Prisha. "Just take a guess. There's no need to be accurate."

Prisha thought for a short while and told her, her best guess.

"I want you to come back to me tomorrow. Can you come tomorrow?" Ella asked them both.

"Is everything alright?" Prisha asked with some concern.

"Yes, yes," she replied. "Everything is just fine. I need to make a chart for your daughter. I will have more to tell you about her when I've had the chance to see the details."

Prisha smiled at her in appreciation for the extra distance Ella was going for her and Niam.

Ella prepared the chart that evening. She reviewed it carefully. She redid her calculations and reviewed the chart again. It was the same conclusion. She explained it to Nina.

"I've never seen a palm like his ever, Nina. Trifurcating lines. And the daughter. Well, that's even more bizarre."

"What do you make of it then?" Nina asked.

"I don't know what to make of it. His presence permeates everything. It's as if this is his world and we're all part of it. But the daughter is the most important one. She changes many things. But some drastic steps are needed here."

"Like what?" Nina asked softly.

"I have to think about it," Ella said. "It'll not be good if she grows up to be like this. Not good for her. Not good for her family."

"This world does not take too kindly to a woman's blemishes," Nina said.

"They're only so if you define them so," Ella added. "Defining them, branding them, controlling them, fighting against them, and fighting for them. Those things keep the world occupied. This is the external manifestation in all its myriad forms. And they keep attention away from internal failings and flaws. This keeps the world bearable."

"This may be true," Nina responded, "but I don't want to fix any systemic problems. I want to be a part of this society. And I think the couple do too. Why don't we help them if we can? You know I am always happy to help. This is what gives me the most happiness."

"I agree," Ella said. She didn't say anything further for a while.

The next day Prisha and Niam were shocked. The solution Ella had suggested involved a hyena.

"Why a hyena?" Prisha had asked.

"Because of what a hyena represents," Ella had responded. "The hyena's spirit will take away the faults of your daughter that come from her father's lines, afar from this world. She will grow up to be a beautiful woman who will make you proud."

Niam and Prisha were confused, but they wanted to do everything they possibly could for their daughter.

The first step to righting the inherent wrong was to name the hyena. After much deliberation, they collectively decided on the name, Ajani.

"It's a good name," Nina said.

"I think so too," Prisha replied.

"He will win us the struggle too," Ella chimed in.

Niam simply looked at them. He instinctively did not like hyenas. But he was here, staring at one, one who was, from now, to be called Ajani. He would have preferred to be with his brothers and cousins, and maybe even his wise uncle. However, he had been told strictly to be quiet or risk bringing ill-repute and shame to himself and his family. As bad as keeping a secret from his extended family was for him, this would be worse than anything he could fathom.

Ajani put up a good bit of struggle. He was born and raised in a jungle where danger was always around any corner one could see. His default position for anything new was a mix of fear and curiosity. In this small room where he was, fear was much heavier than curiosity. The room now contained four people, and the faces of all four of them were glowing brightly from the heat and light from the fire at the center of the room. There was no other source of light. Everyone was sitting around in a circle, around the fire. Ajani was still tied to the wall on a short leash. On his right, at some distance away for her own safety, was Ella, and on his left was Nina. Niam and Prisha were facing him from the other side of the fire. He could barely make them out. The fire, the bright burning light, the cracking sounds of burning wood, the smoke, the smell, they collectively flooded all his senses. He growled. He cackled. He did not know what to make of it. But he knew it wasn't good, whatever it was. He felt an unbearable need to defend and attack. His heartbeat was strong enough for him to hear. At one point it became unbearable, and he stood up. He paced from side-to-side, with his mouth open and saliva dripping from his tongue. He walked back toward the wall and turned around to face the fire again.

"Poor Ajani," Nina said with a look of deep concern. "It'll all be okay very soon. Please don't die."

"He will die, and very soon," Ella said.

"I know, I know," Nina said. "I don't want him to die before we are done. Look at him. He is so agitated. Should we give him the tranquilizer again? He could have a heart attack if don't do something."

"He'll have a heart attack if we give him any more of that tranquilizer," Ella responded.

"But, but there is something we can do, isn't there?" Nina asked pleadingly.

"Let's finish this ceremony quickly and remove him from his misery. This is the best we can do," Ella said.

They both looked at Ajani, and then at Prisha and Niam. Prisha and Niam were watching the proceedings expressionlessly.

Ella went through an elaborate but short ritual. It involved lots of incantations, throwing things into the fire, and rolling her head in every which way she could. A large part of it involved pointing to Niam, calling out his name, and then pointing to Ajani, and calling out his name. Nina's role was to sprinkle small amounts of water on the fire and at Ajani and Niam, and occasionally to throw woodchips at the fire to keep it burning bright. She would sometimes look at Ajani with a gloomy face, frown with deep concern at his state, and go back to her role. At times, she tried to tell Ella to speed things up. Ajani, she felt, would not survive longer than a few more minutes. He was now sitting very still and staring at the fire. His heart was beating even stronger than before, his growl was even deeper, and his drool looked even more ominous as it hung from his open mouth as it dripped in large globules onto the floor.

Ella was doing things as fast as she could, but this had to be done right, or not at all. The chants had to be perfect, the pace had to be perfect, and the knife had to be plunged into the neck at just the perfect time. That time was quickly upon them. In one quick motion, Ella stood up, rushed over to Ajani with a small dagger, plunged it into his neck, and rushed back.

Ajani let out a loud growl this time and jumped up. He fought against the pain, and the chain leash holding him in place.

"Poor hyena. Poor Ajani," Nina cried out loud. "It's going to be alright. It's going to be okay. Just sit down and try to relax."

Ajani did not sit. The dagger had missed the vital mark by a small distance. But that only prolonged his excruciating pain and suffering. As blood gushed out from around the dagger, he gathered his strength, and gave the leash one last big pull. The leash came loose from the wall, and the thrust propelled him forward onto and across the fire. He paid scant attention to the heat, or anything in his immediate surroundings. He jumped, as if jumping would leave the pain behind. He landed on Niam and dug his teeth into his shoulders.

Ajani and Niam landed on the floor, with Ajani's teeth buried into Niam's shoulder, their eyes meeting each other in fear and pain.

"Do something!" Nina looked at Ella. Prisha shouted something too. Ella sprinted to Ajani, pulled out the dagger, and plunged it back in. Ajani's teeth dug in deeper into Niam's shoulders. Ajani's spirit—not the spirit of an anthropomorphic devil or a deviant, but the spirit of a living breathing being doing only what nature shaped it to do—merged with Niam's. His body too dissolved into him. Only his blood was left on Niam's shirt.

"I don't think this went right," Nina said, somewhat nonchalantly.

"I think it went very well!" Ella let out a small victorious laugh. "We did not want the daughter to grow up to be known as a slut or a whore, and she won't. If you think about it, it's been a great success. My solution worked and no great harm has been done!"

Ajani floated through and with an amorphous sense of being. In instants he covered eons. In eons he covered instants. In a single step he covered unfathomable distances, where unfathomable distances were no more than single steps. Human and hyena had fused into a shatterproof, indestructible bond, the like of which had always existed, and had always been acknowledged in whispers and in roars, where one side is treated hagiographically and the other with traducement.

The thing with history is that it is all true. Everything about it is true. Even the truth is true. Even the falsehood is true. Every point in history, in time and in space, is a culmination of everything that precedes it. The daughter was a culmination of the entirety before her, even the good parts, even the bad parts. Including Niam. Including Ajani.

Ajani was not the culmination of anything though. He was the accompaniment. He told Niam everything. He told him because he knew all. He had seen it all and experienced it all and been part of it all. Niam, however, was only human. He saw only some and understood even less. This was partly because there were countless pivotal moments, and partly because there were countless culminations of unnoticeable, overlooked minutia. Everything was simply permutations and combinations of multitude of ripples across space and time, converging and diverging at all points.

Niam decided to focus only on some. For a long time, he

only heard snippets of Ajani's words. His attention was finding it difficult to place strong anchors. Ajani's vocalization was making it even more challenging. His pitch would at times be low, and at times be high. At times he would giggle loudly, and at times he would growl low. But he was always raspy, giving the impression of a lustful wantonness directed outward and carried by every sound, particularly his howling screams.

"There's a difference between authority and power, and power and glory. That's an effective leader."

A loud giggle.

Sometime later when Niam's attention returned, "What is plausible versus what is believable?"

A growl. A long period of inattentiveness.

"Who is the bigger villain in history? Genghis Khan or Inalchuq? Or are they both just players like many others?"

Another growl.

"Ban Chao's dealings with the Kushans, now isn't that something? A thousand years before Genghis Khan."

Niam's attention swam away for a while.

"A thousand years before Ban Chao, right? The Iron Age? More cruel weapons? Defined humans for two thousand years. Then what? Replaced with gun powder, whose effects are still being played out. What next a thousand years from now? What fates?"

Niam was lost for a long time. Ajani, the hyena, was lost with him. They swam on the ripples, their movements perfectly synchronized, performing an elegant dance of a repetition of disjuncture, and intertwining. Niam tried to lose Ajani, but Ajani refused to let go. Ajani moved away, and Niam felt a tug on the thread that connected them, the thread that was in Niam all this while.

Ajani taught him the ways of the hyenas. He taught him how to hunt. Together they caught a fawn. Niam held it by the neck to try to break it, while Ajani tore into its stomach. They didn't have much time to enjoy the feast, though. The commotion caught the attention of lions. The two of them had to acquiesce to the demands of superior strength. They ran, and they galloped, as fast as they could. In the safety of a thicker foliage far away from the bully lions, Ajani and Niam sat down to take deep breaths. Then they laughed together. Heartily. They were a symbiotic team, critical for each other. Niam engraved their names on a tree trunk, just below a carving of the two of them holding hands. In the drawing, Ajani stood on his hind legs. Then Niam sang a song to celebrate their togetherness. Ajani listened to it with rapt attention before closing his eyes to take a nap.

Ajani was there too when the daughter was born. He saw that little, defenseless, fledgling thing in Niam's arm, and felt a love like no other. This wasn't the love he had for his mother. In those dynamics, he was the larger recipient of affection. In this situation, however, he was the selfless giver of affection. It was more than affection. It was also protection and care—an overwhelming need to be responsible—feelings he could not fully reciprocate toward his mother. But he did understand her better than before.

The daughter became the most important thing for Ajani. He would spend hours watching her cooing on the bed, watching her sleeping, watching her smiling when he moved his paws across her face and over her eyes. He dreamt of her too. Of her growing old enough to be able to sit on his back as he raced across the forest. He dreamt of her growing old enough to be able to walk with him through the forest. He dreamt of teaching her everything he knew, of passing all his collected wisdom to her, of her being always by his side, and he by hers. Prisha was important too. After all, she was the reason the daughter was there. Both were important to him. They were Ajani's purpose. The infinitely vast universe may seemingly not care for Ajani, or Niam, or Prisha, or the daughter. Their existence may seemingly not make even an infinitesimal difference to the universe. But it was still okay with Ajani. It mattered to him. This was all that he cared about. And the universe should care. He was part of the universe, no matter how insignificant. The universe will care because he cares. The universe will care through him.

The daughter fortunately died quickly and suffered only briefly. Prisha suffered through the brutality for much longer. She suffered the brutality meted out to her physical self by bad hungry lions who were accompanied by a pack of bad hyenas. After that, she suffered much more watching the daughter being flung alive into a fire set by the lions. Later she suffered physical brutality once again as the lions tore into her with leisure and left some for the hyenas. It stopped when she too died. Her body, like the daughter, was flung into the fire.

Niam, like the other men, had been shot first. Their skulls were systematically smashed to ensure their death. Niam survived because of sheer luck. First, his critical organs were not hit. One bullet passed through his shoulder, and another grazed his rib. Then his dead cousin fell over him in a way that when the bad lions went around smashing skulls, his head was badly scraped but not broken.

When Niam came around, he was greeted with smoke and silence. He pushed his dead cousin aside and stood up. He felt dizzy and fell over. Next when he got on his feet, it was with slow deliberate steps. He looked around and saw a heap of dead bodies. He felt nothing. He saw his brother with eyes open and staring into the ground. He turned him over and ran his hand over his eyelids to close them. He felt nothing. He saw his cousins and friends. All were dead. There was nothing to feel. He knew what he would find, the horrors he would see if he went toward where the homes were. This is where the thick smoke was coming from.

Ajani said nothing too. He had seen it all, been part of it

all, for ever and ever. He had reveled in bloodbaths numberless times, ripping into bodies, rending flesh, crushing bones, and basking in the smell of burning flesh. But this time it was different. The daughter was involved. His purpose was to protect her. He had failed. Maybe this was just a bad dream. Maybe she was still alive, somehow a miraculous escape just like Niam's? Should he look for her?

Niam knew better. Prisha was dead. The daughter was dead. What was there to see? Nothing would bring them back. But Ajani was insistent. He had to look. He had to be truly sure.

And he did look. He saw the half-burnt body of the daughter. One side of her face, the side facing up, was still bright and unburnt. The bottom part had sunk into the slightly smoldering dark ash. From his angle of view, this part of her face appeared to be practically indistinguishable from the residue. He found no reason to turn her on her back to look at her whole face. Her eye on the side facing him was open, staring into the nothingness to which she had returned under acutely abhorrent conditions. Maybe she had cried. It was hard to say. The unburnt parts of her lips were drawn into an expressionless thin line. However, in the stillness of the surroundings, this part of the face was howling out very loud for protection. But no one came to her aid. Ajani had failed her completely.

Ajani growled and growled some more. He felt an anger unlike anything he had ever felt before. He wanted to catch a bad lion and rip it apart. Then he wanted to catch another one and do the same. And the next and the next, till there were no more bad lions. He wanted to do the same with bad hyenas, all of them. However, this anger within him came not from a place of strength, but from a place of extreme helplessness, hopelessness, and impotence. He could not protect her. He wasn't there when she lay there burning in the fire. He was responsible. And the only way to correct it would be to kill as many bad lions and hyenas as he could. Niam, however, was more circumspect. He still felt nothing, not even emptiness. He had decisions to make, work to do, and to grieve. In exactly that order. In his still hazy brain, he had to decide if he was going to start collecting all the bodies, to make it easier to take care of them when people would eventually show up, or to walk half a day for the nearest help just in case word had not reached there already.

Fortunately, he did not have to make any of those execrable decisions. They were made for him. In his delirious and physically weak state, he could not remain on his feet for long. He saw a shattered clay pot lying not too far away. He trudged toward it, hoping it would have a small amount of water. Once he reached the broken pot, he stood to stare into it for a short while. He tried to figure out why he had made his way to this pot in the first place. He saw the early morning light dance on the surface of the very small amount of water at the bottom and remembered. He fell on his knees, lifted the pot, and gulped down the water. When he finished off every single drop, he cast the pot away with a jerk of the same shoulder that was hit with the bullet. A tremendous sharp pain emanated from there. He fell on the ground and lost consciousness.

A few hours later, Ajani found himself to be among a group of good lions and good hyenas. They had heard about the attack and had rushed to drive the bad lions and bad hyenas away. The good hyenas took Ajani with them in the back of a jeep. The last he saw was a group of good lions and good hyenas working to collect all the bodies and laying them in rows.

Once Ajani was healed, he joined the good hyenas. He frequently went with them and the good lions to hunt for bad lions and bad hyenas. He was one of the most ferocious among them. Every kill was a kill for the daughter. And for Prisha. The more ferocious the kill, the more salutary it felt for his body and for his mind. It wasn't cathartic in any way. The wounds were too deep. But those forays made him feel, when most of the time he did not feel.

He didn't attack women and girls. He sat those out and just watched from a distance, and sometimes for a good few hours. Fellow good hyenas made fun of him. They taunted him, called him gay, and called him impotent. He wasn't gay. But he knew he was impotent. Thoughts of Prisha still often filled him with yearning, and his body reacted and ached. However, he did not act on these with anyone. He was impotent. He had failed. His task was to protect, and he did not. He wasn't vicariously experiencing what the good lions and good hyenas were doing to the girls and women. He didn't care. They were simply taking revenge on his behalf in a way they thought best. They were not impotent—he was.

Ajani found himself without any purpose when the good hyenas won. There was no one to take out his anger on, to take revenge on. The good hyenas and the bad hyenas were now walking together, eating together, living together. Having a half-empty stomach for days, however, forced him to find some work. He worked briefly as a security guard for a hotel in the evenings, and as a porter at the local bulk goods market during the days. The hard physical labor would tire his body. It kept his mind from thinking. At last, he could sleep like a log for the whole night. Thoughts of the daughter, of Prisha, of the extended family receded somewhat. This helped him heal a bit. He started talking to people more. He even made some friends he would occasionally eat and drink with.

In the beginning he only heard small gossips and tidbits. They would be about someone or the other from the wholesale market leaving for Europe for work and sending huge sums of money back home to their families. The amounts of money people whispered about sounded incredulous to Ajani. One evening, as he prepared to leave his work at the hotel, he ran into a waiter who also worked there, and one whom he had befriended. The waiter stood in the back alley of the hotel, as he usually did over short breaks, smoking.

"I'll not be working here for long. Maybe a day more, maybe a week, but not much longer," he told Ajani as he exhaled the smoke.

"Why is that?" Ajani asked. "Found a better job?"

"Not here. There's nothing here. It's tough here to even afford a loaf of bread. How can one support an entire family? No. I am leaving for France. My brother is working at a restaurant in Marseilles. He is living a very good life there. Making lots of money. He wants me to join him. Says he can easily find me work. He paid this guy to take me to France. I'll leave as soon as I hear from him. My bag is packed and ready. I am just waiting for a signal from him."

The waiter was gone three days later.

Ajani decided to depart too. He didn't want to leave for the money. Money wasn't anything to him but a means to buy food and some clothes. He had no material desires. He wanted to leave to escape his dark thoughts, and everything around him that reminded him of his recent past. He didn't have much money to pay a trafficker, though. He would have to do this on his own. This was not a comfortable thought. However, it was better than being where he presently was. Hushed and not so hushed talks about Europe around him had led him to believe that this magical place could provide him with the ultimate escape, one he truly desired but could not clearly characterize.

It took a few days to reach his decision. The next few days were spent planning for his trip. It was going to be a long, long trip, one unlike anything that had been done before. He broadly knew the lay of the land, but not the details. He looked at a continent-scale map that was on display at the hotel he worked at, and studied it in all the details it provided. He roughly determined the direction he had to take. The day before he was to leave, he collected some empty bottles and filled them with water. He also bought bread enough to last him a few days. For the rest of the journey, whatever the duration may be, he would try to live off the land. He was a hyena, after all. He just needed that part to come out.

Ajani left before the break of dawn. A few dogs barked at him, but they went silent when he growled at them. He had decided on taking this direction and didn't give it a second thought. His backpack was unusually light—three medium-sized bottles of water, bread, an extra pair of new expensive and comfortable shoes he had bought from his savings, two changes of clothes, and all the Euros he could obtain after converting the rest of his savings from an unscrupulous currency exchanger.

Ajani was soon on the outskirts of the town, and as day broke, he left the road he was on. Much to his disappointment, the road went in the opposite direction to what he wanted to take. His route was over a hilly barren terrain. For anyone else, this course would be extremely demotivating, if not outrightly deterring. Ajani, though, didn't think much of it, and took it. Soon the city was out of sight, and the calmness of the barren land settled around him. His inner hyena opened its eyes and stirred. This was his territory. He knew jungles, he knew wilderness. Ajani did not stop, not even to take small breaks to rest his tired legs. The undulating hills slowly took him higher up in elevation, and the sun beat down on him. He took small sips of water and even smaller bites of the bread. But he did not stop. As evening approached, he stopped climbing and started to descend. In front of him, beyond the hills, he saw a vast picturesque plain as far as the eyes could see.

Ajani rested in the cool of the night. He started again early in the morning, and was soon on the grassland. Things would be easier for a while. He picked up the pace.

Ajani walked across a topography of interspersed grasslands and hills for a few days. He walked with many animals that were grazing on the grass. Once he came across an active kill and walked around the feeding lions. When the last water bottle was empty, and the last morsel of bread gone, his feral instincts took over. The land provided what he needed.

The land changed to semi desert and then merged into a vast desert. The sun became unbearable during the days. This did not deter him. He met up with a caravan of camel riders at a village he had stopped at to rest and to plan the desert crossing. He joined the caravan. The caravan moved mostly at nights when it was cooler, with men riding camels and Ajani walking by their side. The days were spent in tents away from the heat. Twice, the caravan stopped at small oasis for overnight stays. Ajani continued sticking with them. The clear star-filled night sky over the desert, with the milky-way galaxy stretching from end to end, kept his spirits up. But the pain, dull as it had become, refused to go away. His heart still hurt, his impotence still stung.

Many days later, too many for Ajani to have kept track off, the caravan reached its destination—a big village connected with the outside world by a single road. Ajani walked along the road for days, stopping at small villages on the way to fill water and buy food. He did this until he reached Tunisia.

Ajani had figured out that Tunisia was the best option for the next leg of his travel. It wasn't perfect. But it was good enough. It was better than Algeria or Morocco, and certainly better than Libya. He walked for a couple of more days and reached Tunis. There he spent the next few months contemplating.

One reason for the long sojourn in Tunis was because Ajani needed to plan for the journey over the sea. He wasn't a water creature. He was a land being. Crossing a huge body of water was not natural to him, while traversing the great distance he had over land was. The second was that he was short on money. He could live off the land, sleep under the stars, but instincts told him he would need some money when he reached France. He needed to find some work and save.

Ajani eventually found work with a janitorial services company catering to the business district. One of the offices they worked for was a travel agency, *Le Meilleur de la Tunisie.*

This was very propitious for Ajani. He used his sociable hyena nature to befriend some of the staff there. He learned about different yachts and ships and the routes they took around the sea. He learned about the best weather to be in the water. He learned something about the time it took to reach the coast of France. He also learned that the owner of the travel agency was a man by the name of Tarik.

Tarik took a liking to Ajani. Ajani's quiet steely look, and his wild giggle that came less than often but did come, gave the impression that he did not belong to the work he was doing. One day Tarik asked him to help with cleaning and other odd jobs at his home. They were expecting a large gathering of guests for his sister's wedding, and needed all the reliable help they could get. A few days later when they met at the agency after the wedding, Tarik paid Ajani for his services. As small talk, he asked Ajani about his future plans.

"I am saving money to go to France," Ajani replied.

"Don't go there," Tarik said. "Take my advice. Nothing good can come from it. France is a trap. My brother, Nabil, is in Paris. He has fallen into hard times, all because of his fault. He is cut off from his family, from his friends, from everyone. It's all because of a French woman. Someone like you should be thinking of building something over here, not destroying everything over there. Remember too that here you are one of us. You may be different in many ways, but you're still one of us. You fit in. There, over there, you don't fit in. You'll always be an outsider there, never one of them."

Ajani simply smiled and did not respond. Tarik looked at him and said, "I don't know what the pull of that place is. It's not good. I know you'll not take my advice. Before you leave for France, whenever it is, do me a favor. Meet me first. I'll give you my brother's address. If you can, just check on him to make sure he's doing okay. You don't have to talk to him or anything. Just take a look and give me a call. Our mother will be happy to know. Do this for her if you can."

There was not much for Ajani to say. He nodded and thanked Tarik for the money.

A month later, Ajani decided to leave. He had saved enough, he thought, and learned enough about the route he had chosen. There was nothing new to learn. He met Tarik the day before he was to depart.

"So, you've decided to ignore my advice," Tarik said, as he handed Ajani his brother's address. "I knew it. It's the pull of that place. Indeed, it's not good. But there's nothing one can do when God wills it. Just try to stay safe."

Early next morning, Ajani reached the shore. The sun was just breaking out over the horizon on the east, and the sea was relatively calm. Ajani dipped one paw in the water, and then the next. He took a deep breath and dove straight into the sea. He was swimming surprisingly well.

Ajani swam for considerable hours. It was a lonely swim, and he liked it. The farther he swam, the better he felt. He was leaving everything behind. It would be a new beginning. He would still be impotent. He would still be carrying the weight of his past. But just like the travel across vast distances to reach Tunisia and the swim across the sea he was now undertaking helped him focus his thoughts on something else, so too would the efforts to adjust to a new life on a new continent. Perhaps, eventually, his psyche and his impotency would be healed too.

He kept swimming with broad, powerful, purposeful strokes. The vast open sea provided no distractions. The sun beat hard on him over a perfectly clear sky but couldn't stop him. He was so focused that he felt little hunger. He only felt the need to eat something whenever he took short breaks. It wasn't difficult finding food. He was a hyena after all, a scavenger by nature. He knew how to locate carcasses. And he was in the right place for them. There was no dearth of corpses floating around him. Even better, these cadavers were all boneless. Their bones had long been removed when they were alive—pulled out, beaten out—the bodies left to move as blobs. Therefore, as carcasses, they were easy to chew, easy to digest, and left little to be discarded as waste or memory.

It was when the sun had settled in the west, and the stars had come out to keep him company that Ajani encountered some rough weather. He tried to maintain the trajectory he was set on, but the waves kept pushing him off course to the east. For some time, Ajani gave up fighting the weather to conserve his strength, and let the waves take him. When the winds and waves calmed down, Ajani picked up his strokes once again. However, he had misjudged the distance by which he had been pushed off course. The sun rose again in the east, and Ajani continued swimming. He saw land late afternoon. As he came closer, he also saw impressive buildings and big yachts. He sighed in relief. However, he didn't know it, but he had not reached Marseille. He had reached Monaco.

Ajani touched the hard rocks that formed a formidable steep wall separating the sea from the land. Over the wall perched an impressive looking palace He had arrived. This was the culmination of months of intense efforts. Now all he had to do was climb the rocks, and he would be in Marseille. From there he could take any number of public transport options available and reach Paris. But Ajani did not feel any overwhelming emotions he thought he ought to have felt. At most he felt a detached, indifferent curiosity about the castle and its beyond. For a brief while, as he was swimming toward the rocks, he had harbored the hope, false he knew, but nonetheless a hope, that he would be cured as soon as he touched land. It did not happen. He still felt damaged. He still felt impotent.

Ajani remained in the water for some time. He had no pressing demands on his time, nothing in particular that he needed

129

to accomplish, nowhere in particular that he needed to go. He could afford to spend time gathering his strength, rejuvenating his sore muscles, planning the course ahead. He soon realized he could procrastinate no further. He would need to take the next step if he was not to spend another night in the water. He started to climb the wall.

The climb wasn't very difficult. The smooth walls of the palace did not appear to provide any place to grip and hold. The rocks next to the wall, though, had ample. He reached the top in little time, and found himself lost among a throng of tourists.

Ajani enjoyed the company. He was, after all, social. However, his life had also taught him to be impartial to associations. He was comfortable being alone too. This time, though, he was relishing being surrounded by such a big crowd after being in the sea for nearly two days all by himself, all alone. He couldn't help a little smile on his face. Perhaps life was going to be okay. Ajani giggled.

This is when he noticed everyone around start to stare at him. At first, he did not pay much attention. However, the stares became deeper and more obvious. Then he heard whispers and stopped. He lifted his ears. The whispers became louder.

"*Hyène impuissante.*" He heard.

"*Là! Hyène impuissante!*" He heard again. And again. The whispers to his ears became a loud chorus. The stares, to his eyes, became denunciatory and accusatory. The crowd all around him began to appear intimidating, frightening and closing in on him. Ajani's ears moved forward and back. He became discombobulated. He stood frozen for a while, looking around and looking down. Then he slowly moved. At first it was just a few steps, barely perceptible, even to himself. The cautious steps then became more obvious and more deliberate. He turned around, and with a burst of energy, ran across the palace compound and down the hill, until he was in the city. He did not stop there. He ran on the road and around bends and curves. Shortly he approached Monte Carlo casino. There he encountered an even bigger crowd. This time it wasn't whispers he heard.

"*Là! Hyène impuissante!*" The crowd seemed to bellow almost in unison.

Ajani ran faster. Everywhere he looked, he thought he saw people stop what they were doing to glare at him. He rushed away from the casino area. The exertion caught up to Ajani suddenly. He felt delirious and disoriented. He turned onto a street that seemed somewhat less crowded. He tried to dash through it, hoping to get away from the city as fast as possible and as quickly as possible. But his body simply gave up, and he collapsed. Before everything around him turned dark and he fainted, he looked up to see a dark tainted glass door to a small outlet beside a grocery store. The door had the words "Tarot Card Reader, Palmist, Mind-Healer" written across it.

"Nina, is that you?" Ella asked when she heard the door open.

"Yes, it's me. Is everything alright?" Nina asked.

"Yes, yes, everything is fine. Come on here."

"You left me a voicemail, but you never mentioned why you wanted me to come," Nina said as she entered the inner door to Ella's small office space at the end of a poorly lit narrow passageway. She found Ella sitting in her usual dark brown faux leather chair behind a large and heavy-looking wooden table. Behind her was a small window that had not been opened in a while, if ever, because it was missing a handle to open it. The window, though, did provide ample natural light during the day. This was, for many visitors, a sharp and welcome contrast to the passageway. Nina was one such visitor. The desk was very clean and organized. On one side were three different tarot-decks. On another corner was, to a first impression, a crystal ball. But it was not. It was simply a table-lamp. On a side of the wall was an impressive wooden mahogany almirah, one half of it open bookshelves, and the other half had a door at the top and drawers at the bottom. The bookshelves held some books on the occult, small decorative items, a photo frame with two portraits of Ella, and an artificial rubber plant on the top shelf. Nina did not know what was behind the door or in the drawers, and was never interested in knowing. She had once seen Ella put a Ouija board in one of the drawers, and she assumed that section of the almirah was filled with paraphernalia of Ella's trade.

Nina walked to the desk and took one of the three chairs facing Ella. She looked at her. Ella looked back with a thin smile but did not say anything.

"What am I missing? Why did you call me?" Nina asked.

"Look behind you," Ella said.

Nina turned around to look at the door she had entered the office from. When she had walked in first, she had failed to notice a furry animal curled up on the floor by the side of the door. Nina looked at it with wide eyes, and then squinted them because she wasn't certain what she was looking at.

"Is that a dog? Did you get a dog?" Nina asked after she turned back to Ella.

"No, it's not a dog," Ella replied.

"Thank God! For a second I thought you got yourself an ugly looking dog. It's fairly big for a pet, though, whatever it is. What is it?" Nina asked.

"Guess," Ella said. Her smile broadened.

"You know I am not good at guessing. What is it?" Nina asked again with a slight plead.

"It's a hyena!" Ella exclaimed.

Nina took a deep breath. She stared into Ella's eyes and took another deep breath.

"A hyena?"

"Yes, a hyena!"

"Is it the same hyena they were all talking about yesterday?

They said it was an impotent hyena," Nina spoke as she turned around to look at the hyena.

"It's the one!" Ella's smile deepened. "Guess what! I opened the front door to leave for the day, and what do I see? I see this beautiful creature on the ground, passed out. And I mean really passed out." She made a gesture by sticking her tongue out and to the side of her mouth and reclined back on her chair with her hands stretched out and her eyes closed. "I couldn't leave this poor creature lying there by itself, could I?"

"No, you couldn't," Nina said with her eyes wide open and mouth agape. "Then what? You brought it in? Why didn't you call me yesterday? I could have helped you."

"I thought about it. Then I said to myself, 'Why bother her. She must be out having a good time. It's Saturday evening.'"

Nina let out a small laugh. "That's true!" she said. "I was indeed having a great time. I can feel the headache pounding. Still, I would have come."

She turned back to look carefully at the hyena. It was curled up and not moving. "Is he alright now?" she asked.

"He seems to be okay," Ella said. "Just exhausted. I put some water in his mouth after I brought him in. He woke up, walked around the room a little, and went back to sleep. I left him here with some water in a bowl. When I came back this morning, I found him still sleeping. I know he had woken up during the night because the bowl was nearly empty."

"Poor hyena," Nina uttered. "It must have been such an ordeal for him yesterday. It's one thing to know you're impotent. It's another for everyone to call you such on the streets."

Ella looked at Nina. "We are all impotent. Some realize it and some do not. Some are better at masking it and some are not. Some accept it quickly and some need time."

"It could be true," Nina said. "I think you're right. Everyone in this world is trying to deal with their impotence. Maybe that's what life is simply all about, a struggle to deal with impotence from birth to death. But it would still feel horrible to be called out in public like that and exposed. Did you try feeding him? Perhaps giving him more water?"

"I'll let him sleep for as long as he wants," Ella replied. "He needs rest. He appears to have traveled over considerable distances and overcome severe hurdles to reach here. The world happens to those on the move. That world can be overwhelming at its best. A day or two more of rest will nourish his weary body and soul."

"He's a beautiful hyena," Nina said after a long pause.

"Didn't you just call him ugly?" Ella said.

"I called him an ugly *dog*, as if he were a dog." Nina smiled. "But he's not a dog. He's a hyena, and as a hyena, he's beautiful."

"How many hyenas have you come across?" Ella grinned.

"I've come across a few. I've come across a few," Nina replied, a bit defensively, and with her arms crossed. "Say," and she uncrossed her arms, "have you decided what you'll do with him once he's fully awake and well-rested? Are you going to keep him?"

"I don't think I will," Ella replied. "I don't know what I'll do with him. Maybe he'll just leave by himself. He'll decide to go wherever he was going to before he showed up here."

"But wouldn't this be a problem? I mean, it could again be a repeat of yesterday for this poor, beautiful hyena. And we know how that went after the commotion for this poor, poor, beautiful hyena."

Ella and Nina talked at some length. Just before noon, they determined they were hungry. They left for a Thai restaurant they frequented whenever Nina showed up. There, over a dish of Red Curry for Ella and Pad Thai for Nina, and a glass of red wine each, they tried to settle on what they should do with the hyena.

"His name is Ajani," Nina told Ella. They were back at the office, where they found Ajani awake but sitting in the same place they'd left him.

"How do you know?" Ella asked.

"I just know," she replied, and then gave a small grin to show off and put her hands on her hips. "Now don't you go around thinking of me as just some alcoholic schlub or worse. Maybe my years of education and training in semiotics and linguistics have made me very perceptive to Hyena-talk. Or maybe, you never know, I may even have some kind of a mental connection with him." The latter was meant to hit a spot with Ella, albeit jocularly, and it did just that.

"You?" Ella looked at her. "You have a connection with him? You, the one who thought he was ugly! This is not fair. I should have had the connection. I took him in and took care of him. Why should you have it?"

"First," Nina shrugged her shoulders, "how would I know how I have this connection? And second, I never called him ugly, okay. He's not ugly for a hyena."

"Alright, alright," Ella went behind the desk to sit on her big chair, "maybe he has a connection with you and not with me for a reason. We'll figure it out later if we get the chance. Is there anything else he's been telling you?"

"Yeah," Nina said. Ella looked at her for a few seconds, expecting her to say something more. Nina remained silent while looking at her pensively.

"Tell me then?" she asked when she could not take the silence anymore.

"Tell you what?" Nina asked in return.

"What more did he tell you besides his name?"

"He told me everything. I don't think you'll like it. We might need to change our plans, if you had formed any," Nina said.

"No plans. At least nothing decided. Why don't you tell me what he's been telling you?"

Nina conveyed Ajani's story to Ella as Ajani had conveyed to her. It took her well over three-quarters of an hour. She left out no details. When she would be uncertain about something, or would miss out any parts, Ajani would tell her. Once she was done, she pushed back on her reclining chair and closed her eyes. Ella looked at her and then swung her chair to look out the window.

"He's very strong, very, very strong," Ella said, still looking out the window and away from Nina.

"Yes, he is for sure," Nina responded. "Many facing even a fraction of what he's faced would contemplate suicide."

"Suicides are for humans." Ella reacted with a shrug of her shoulders. She slowly looked straight up by bending her neck backwards to stretch. She kept her head in that position for a few seconds and brought it back down slowly. "Animals don't commit suicide. Never. Only humans. This is because we can use words to express ourselves and what we're going through, and we can convince ourselves that taking our own lives is an option. Soliloquy of the trenchant, unforgiving, loquacious kind. Nothing good comes from it. Animals do not do this, and don't even have the ability to. This is why there are animals raised and killed for food or medicine or clothes in the most pitiful, deplorable, and heartbreaking conditions. And yet, they all still want to live. You don't hear of them committing suicide."

Nina did not respond to this. They both remained silent for several minutes before sitting and indulging in small talk. A short time later, they decided to step out for coffee. They sat outside at the coffee shop next door. It was a somewhat warm afternoon, but was pleasant enough.

"Are you sure you still want to help him?" Nina asked. "This doesn't look easy to me at all. Do you think you can?"

"For sure it's not easy! And for sure I think I want to help him. You know me! I'll not deny that I am sometimes about putting on a show, if that's even what you want to call it. Whatever gets me to make a decent living without putting in too much effort is my goal. Rarely do you get something serious and seriously worthwhile, something to test my skills, to sharpen them.

Why lose such opportunities? Who knows where this effort will take us!"

"I agree," Nina said. "But still. This is not going to be easy. Do you think you'll be able to retrace his path to when he was pure?"

"We'll trace some path for sure!" Ella said with a wide grin. "We will just have to see where it takes us!"

"What now, then?" Nina asked. "We just wait for him to show up?"

"Yup. This is another of his versions. Shouldn't be too long now."

"I hope so! I can't wait. And while we're waiting, why don't you help me?" Nina chuckled.

"Help you? No, not that again! There's nothing I can do about it, you know it. You're trying to find a perfect man to marry. There's literally no one in the whole world who fits your definition of perfection. And why do you want to marry a perfect man? What will you do for the rest of your life with nothing to work on?" Ella smiled.

"You leave that to me! By the way, how is he? Do you think you can make him fall for me?"

"Him? He's married. Of course, I can try to make him fall for you. I've just the right formula for this. But, but, what's the point in falling for a married guy?" Ella said. "You can have fun with someone like that and fill up your time with company. I get that. And you know me. I don't care much for what society calls moral or amoral. The hypocrisy surrounding those is desiccated, overflowing with hackneyed arguments. All I am saying is that anything more serious can create unnecessary problems."

"I know, I know," Nina said softly with a serious expression. "You know me too. I like my morals. They're mine. They belong to me. They are good company. And I have a feeling my morals like me too. Sometimes they leave me for extended periods. But they always come back. Always."

They both went silent for a few short minutes while they worked on their coffee and gazed at traffic and people passing by. Once their drinks were done, they simply nodded to each other and got up to go back to Ella's office.

Nina stopped at the door when Ella gripped the handle to open it.

"Why don't you go in? I'll be right back. I've got to meet my travel agent. It shouldn't be too long," Nina said.

"Is this about your trip to America? What's happening there?" Ella asked. She put her right foot as a door stopper, while still holding the handle.

"Nothing actually," Nina sounded a little disappointed. "The tickets are still too expensive. Maybe I shouldn't go."

"But isn't the university paying for it? I thought they did, didn't they?"

"No, they're very cheap. They might do it for professors. They couldn't care any less for us students. Fortunately, they're covering the cost for conference registration and some additional amount for meals and incidentals. Unfortunately, nothing more. I'll go if the travel agent can find me a good cheap ticket. Since this would be my first time to America, I don't want to spend all my money to just go to the conference and come back. What's the point? I want to travel around and visit as many places as I can. I want to see Las Vegas, and New York, and Los Angeles. I don't know when I'll be there next, if ever."

"You're right. If you can, then go," Ella said. "Why don't you call up your travel agent, though?"

"Nah!" Nina said with a slightly drawn face. "I just don't seem to be getting the service I want over the phone. I think if I drop into his office and sit right across from him and refuse to budge, he'll take me more seriously and actually put in the effort to search for the best tickets."

"I hope so!" Ella exclaimed. "Just be careful with the drive. It's a bit of traffic out there."

138

"I will be," Nina declared with a smile. "It's not going to be bad. About half-an-hour going, half an hour coming, and half-an-hour there. Easy."

"Wonderful! Then we can even have dinner together today!" Ella said gleefully and clasped her hand. She still held the door slightly ajar with her foot.

"At that new seafood place you've been talking about?" Nina asked.

"If that's what you want."

"Absolutely! Aren't we so completely simpatico? This is why I love you. I'll be back before you even know it! Don't go about creating problems before I am back. We'll create them together," Nina said as she turned around and walked away.

Ella looked at her for a second, then went into her office.

Book II
Anomie

"My problem with these pesky child achievers is how their very presence makes you feel that your life is truly worthless," Nina said to Ella. "I hate them."

"I agree." Ella smiled.

"You do, right?" Nina almost shouted. "I am there for my tickets, and possibly even some tour packages, and in walks this guy's nine-year-old son into the office. This son is supposed to be this genius or something, and that's how he introduced him to me. He supposedly knows all the capital cities of all the countries. Isn't this such a useless thing to know? How's it even going to help his boy when he grows up?"

"All the capital cities in the world?" Ella looked at her with a mock squint of her eyes.

"Yup. All the cities!" Nina continued. "This guy asks me to test his son. So, I ask him the capital of Zambia, and he says, Lusaka. I ask him Zimbabwe, and he says Harare. And I pretend to be impressed. He says he's going to get his son's name in the record books. And I pretend to be even more impressed."

"I feel sorry for the son," Ella said. "It must be tough memorizing all that information. And if something changes, a country disappears or appears, you've got to memorize it all over again."

"Isn't that right!" Nina uttered. "What a waste of time."

"True," Ella said. "But I think it's perhaps better than being on your smartphone all the time. I hate it when people are on their phones all the time. They can't even have a normal conversation with a person sitting right next to them."

"I know, right!" Nina shouted. "The worst thing is when two or three people are sitting together, and all of them are on their phones. I see them and I am like, 'What's wrong with you people? Can't you just talk to each other? Are you that bored with people?'"

"These smartphones are evil, I can tell you that," Ella said. "They don't solve boredom but exacerbate it. They are the wrong answer to boredom. But I must say I am impressed that you know the capitals of Zambia and Zimbabwe!"

"Oh that? It's nothing big, you know that. Part of my research is focused on linguistics of some of the languages in Botswana, and I work with some people there. All these countries are close."

"I never realized they were neighbors," Ella said. "But then, I've no reason to be aware of such facts like you do. But, at the end of it all, did you get the tickets you wanted?"

"Now, that's the other sad, unfortunate, catastrophic, whatever you want to call it, part." Nina raised both shoulders and gave a sullen look. "Tickets are so expensive! Nothing good is available. I've given up all hope."

"Don't feel so dejected. I am sure something will work out soon."

"I've got to fix up everything by next week or give up on my plans. So yes, I am upset," Nina said.

"Don't be. Look at the brighter side. At least he walked in with his wife. We didn't have to wait for too long."

"I guess so," Nina said. She looked at the slumped figures of Niam and Prisha. "What now? When do we work on this?"

"Why not right now?" Ella said. "Why wait?"

"I don't mind," Nina responded. "You're the one who's got to do the bulk of the work. I'll just be sitting in that corner there," she pointed to the corner of the room close to the slumbering body of Ajani, "and reading this magazine while I wait."

"What's this magazine?" Ella asked while she pulled out a drawer in the almirah and picked up a small wooden box.

"I don't know. It seems pretty stupid. I picked it up from the travel agent's office. It has an article on," she looked down at the cover of the magazine, "*10 Easy Ways to Get Your Man Excited About You*. I had started reading it when I was waiting for him to help me with my tickets. I brought it along so I can finish it. It's very dumb, but I feel compelled to finish it and see if I learn anything new."

"Good for you!" Ella smiled, seemingly uninterested in what Nina had just said. "Don't get too lost in the magazine. You're the one he talks to, not me. I may need your help."

"I'm here. Do whatever thing you do. Take your time. Since it's almost certain I am not going to the conference, I'll be sulking for the next few days, if not longer. That corner looks good enough for doing just that."

Ella let out a small laugh. "Be my guest," she said, and opened the wooden box she had put on the table.

The procedure for the most part went as well as Ella had wanted. This was the first time for her, and she was glad that, so far, nothing unexpected had popped up. In just a few more minutes the hyena would be in a better place and better able to blend and fit in. Nina had not been needed till now, and if things went as they had been going, she would not be needed. They would soon be heading over for dinner. All in all, this was looking to be a fruitful day, a productive day, a day she helped someone, and also helped herself develop a new skill. This day wouldn't make her any money. But it was still a day she could be proud of.

Ella was counting her chickens when she should have been focusing more on her surrounds. Nina was engrossed in the magazine. Prisha was still sitting drooped in the chair with her eyes closed and hands hanging loosely by her side. Niam was not in a much different state. Only, he was on the floor with his back against the wall, with one hand on Ajani. Ajani, though, was stirring. His movements were subtle, but they would have been obvious to anyone paying attention. Then, in one big jerk, Ajani stood up and shook his body. He looked down and saw the slumped figure of Niam. He knew him. He knew Niam well.

He turned to look at Prisha. He knew her too. He also knew Ella and Nina. He saw Ella busy with something on the table. He looked at Nina sitting in a corner. She was the only one who noticed him over a magazine she was holding with both hands.

Nina saw Ajani gnashing his teeth. His eyes were now focused, and his body was taut, as if ready to spring. She realized there was the possibility of trouble, but couldn't decide on what to do. She could not bring herself to have Ella pause. There was no knowing what could happen. There was also no knowing what could happen if Ajani did something.

Ajani did not do anything for some time. He was too overwhelmed with trying to find his bearings. He thought he had left everything behind, Niam and Prisha, included. Now they were here with him in this small room. Then he realized that the daughter was missing. But why would she be here? She was dead, half-burnt, all because of his impotence.

Ajani would have sat back down to brood and reminisce over the daughter. However, Ella's incantations were reverberating across the room as low decibel noise. The noise seemed to seep into his very soul. Ella's words were agitating him and stimulating him. He felt the tips of his hair all over his body leak out and release the feelings of inadequacy and powerlessness that had been his constant companion for as long as he could now remember. In their place was an empty cauldron that was slowly heating up. It was being heated by the same incantations, the same noise. The cauldron was waiting to be filled up with something. That something had to be singed, had to be whipped, had to be cooked, and then had to fill the empty space inside of him in its entirety. He was, he realized, more tired of being miserable than from all the efforts he had put into trying to run away from that misery. He would no longer need to run away from it. He was no longer miserable. He was no longer impotent.

But what was he going to be now, now that he was no longer his old self? He did not know. This started to cause a great deal of consternation in him. It is one thing to know you are no longer your old self. It is another to not know what your new self will be like. Ajani let out a low growl. He moved his neck very slowly to examine every part of the room, trying to find a replacement for his old self. He saw Niam, now lying on the floor near his feet. He looked pathetic. There was no form, no beauty, and no exquisiteness in the prostrate body. What was the point of this lifeform? Live every day only to fight against its shortcomings, until there are no more days left to fight? Then leave a burden for others to fight the same fights in the guise of a legacy, or even more pathetically, a lack of one? For all the pitiful fights, for all the efforts, for the farce and the tragedies, does it even fundamentally matter whether such a despicable lifeform exists or not? How dare such a lifeform define him, Ajani? Defile him? Treat him only as an afterthought?

Ajani let out another growl. He looked at Nina. She was watching him with sharp eyes. He did not bother about her. In one quick motion, he lunged at Niam and dug his teeth into his shoulder.

Nina reacted instinctively. She ran toward Ajani, with the magazine still in her hand, only now rolled up.

"You! Leave him. That's a very bad hyena! Bad hyena!" she shouted as she hit Ajani with the magazine. "Ella, do something."

Ella looked up from the box. "Oh, God!" she said and rushed around the table toward the three of them. She didn't think much as she grabbed a very small dagger from the box. She didn't think much again as she plunged the dagger into Ajani's heart, missing the critical part by just a few short centimeters. "Bad hyena!" she too said as she did so.

Ajani felt the sharp pain. He howled very loudly and grabbed the magazine from Nina's hand with his powerful bite. Ella pulled out the dagger and plunged it back again. This time it was on the spot. Ajani opened his jaws wide, and closed them around Niam's shoulder, with the magazine stuck in his mouth.

"I don't think this was how it was supposed to go," Nina said to Ella after she had had a chance to catch her breath.

"I guess not," Ella muttered. Her hand was stuck on the dagger, which was stuck in Ajani. She was still trying to process what had happened. She stared at the blood flowing onto the floor and onto her hand. "What a mess to clean up," was the only coherent thought that came to her mind.

"I guess at least someone will get a chance to go to America after all, just not me," Nina said.

"I guess so," Ella said in a monotone voice.

"And I guess at the very least he'll not be called impotent anymore," Nina continued.

"I guess so," Ella again responded monotonically. She lifted her head to look at Nina.

"I hope he can fit in," Nina almost whispered to Ella.

"Depends on where you're trying to fit him into," Ella said very softly.

When part of a mass migration, show comportment befitting your status as a diminutive member of the throng. Fit in. Do not stand out. You are no different. Nobody is. The journey is a communal effort. Everyone behaves in a way expected of them. This is the only way to make it, to reduce your chances of getting lost, being left behind, dying.

These were the words reverberating in Ajani's head as he woke up. He looked around. There was excitement in the crisp air. Ajani wasn't used to the cold, and would have been somewhat miserable if not for all the hair on his body. And something else too. He felt different inside. He wasn't filled with self-pity anymore, and didn't feel like a pipsqueak. In fact, there wasn't even a vestige of this old feeling, his constant companion, until very recently, anymore. It was as if such a feeling never existed in him, was alien to him. In its place he felt invigorated, excited, thrilled. And something more. Something he hadn't felt before perhaps, at least in a way that defined his existence. He felt aroused.

Ajani's newfound feelings notwithstanding, it still was colder than he would have preferred. Thankfully the flurry and flutter, quite literally, of activity around him helped to distract him from being too uncomfortable. He realized what was happening. He was going to be part of something big. He was going to be part of a horde. He was going to be participating in one of the greatest migration events ever. Something told him that he would be able to make it. Those around him, though, would not. But the journey would still happen. The migration would still happen. It would still be the horde, a living horde, where individuals are lost just like cells in a body, to be replaced by new individuals, new cells. But the journey continues. Ajani was to be part of the great deluge of exodus by butterflies across borders known only to humans, and for them too only recently. On their journey, these butterflies would be traversing not borders, but intermittent nebulous, shapeless, tenebrous zones of human activities not known to their ancestors, and zones where they knew better how to navigate through. This exodus was to be multi-generational, where one generation is only guided by the desire to make it possible for the other generation to make it through.

The one problem, though, as Ajani saw it, was to be able to fit in, to blend in, with the horde. How could he do so if he could not fly? Maybe he could run, while the rest flew?

During the migration, Ajani trotted, trekked, and sometimes trudged, but he did not run. This was because he needed to match his pace with everyone around him. They were all taking their time. Their movement was deliberate and purposeful as a statistical average. But for large parts, individual movement was also meandering and exploratory. Ajani did not mind this at all. He was in no hurry to be anywhere else other than to be with the horde. When he walked, he would be completely encircled with an explosion of colors and designs of immensely intricate details on wings. These wings danced a collective dance with a cadence that pulsed and undulated across his immediate surroundings. At times he felt overawed, his senses saturated, with different designs containing infinite hues and shades, and displaying hypnotic motions. But he never felt lost. He had long realized that even though the universe was cruelly and heartlessly indifferent to everything, including its very own existence, this shouldn't prevent him from being appreciative of the many things about it and of so much in it. Big goals and little markers had served him well so far, and would continue to do so in the future, or so he hoped. This specific journey of his not only had a goal but also came with uncountable little markers all around him.

At some point along his journey, Ajani crossed from Canada to the U.S.A.

Ajani had to make a great effort to cross the border. His companions flew right over it because they could. He, on the other hand, was stuck to the ground, and could not simply go through the barrier that seemed to block his path. He watched them, members of his horde, fly gently away from him over the barrier. Just a short while ago he was completely covered by them, almost invisible to a cursory glance from a distance. And now, he was there for the world to see in his entirety. He could have felt naked, despondent even, but he did not. It was quite the opposite. His was a state of profound felicity. A world of possibilities awaited him, just within his reach. He simply needed to have patience and to apply himself. He took a careful gander at his surroundings. The barrier looked intimidating. But so did many things he had overcome thus far. This wasn't going to stop him. He sat down on the ground and decided to think. He did not want to take very long, or else he would lose his horde. Completing the rest of the journey, any journey, alone was no longer what he wanted to do.

A long while later, Ajani still sat thinking. The barrier loomed large before him, and seemed to become larger and larger as time passed. It still did not seem insurmountable. Nothing was. The large barrier was nothing but the penultimate hurdle before he reached his destination. All he needed was a bit of contrivance, maybe to discover an inimitable skill he had but was not aware of, to solve this problem. After all, this was just an innate, internal barrier, an implicit reflection of an internalized sclerotic world he had once traversed. This barrier was simply the contrail of what he had left behind. It would be overcome, he had no doubt.

Ajani thought some more. Then a small trace of doubt crept in. Maybe a barrier is not always internal. It is possible for it to be external, perhaps even explicitly and overtly so. Maybe it was deliberately set up to ensconce from some version of reality. If that's the case, then chiseling away at it with a hammer was going to be pointless. This could take forever. He needed to strafe it, or use a wrecking ball, or anything unrefined. But he didn't want to choose such an option. And even if he decided to, he simply neither possessed the means to do so at this moment, nor was he willing to expend his energy to gather those means. This was turning out to be a very vexing dilemma indeed, something that would require further pondering over. He stood up to pace in a wide circle. After several tiring rounds, both clockwise and counterclockwise, when still no agreeable solution was forthcoming, Ajani sat down on the ground once again. He realized that while he was full of confidence, what he was lacking was perspicacity.

Ajani sat for a long time. The sun went down, and it became dark very quickly. The stars lit up the sky and the ground even though a few clouds tried hard to cover the stunning display. Ajani started counting those stars to take his attention away from the problem consuming him, to give his overworked mind a rest. He started his count slowly across the sky, moving his gaze along a straight path from the west and brought it to the east. He was about to go from the east to west, but his concentration was distracted by the rising moon. The moon appeared huge as it broke free from the grips of the eastern horizon. In time its size would diminish as it rose, but in that instant, it overwhelmed the entire sky.

Ajani stared at the moon as a welcome break from staring at the barrier. In the sharp, soft moonlight that lit up the landscape, he thought he saw a silhouette of something close to the ground and moving. The distance was too large to make out what this thing was, but the bright moonlight vivified its slow motion in an otherwise still, tranquil landscape. Ajani kept his eyes on that thing. His body became taut with anticipation. Then that thing stopped and stood up. It was a human child, short, and clumsy in its movement. It awkwardly walked on its feet for a short distance, but then decided to crawl instead. This baby appeared to be a good, fast crawler, with a decidedly deliberate sense of direction. The direction was toward Ajani. In record time, the baby had crawled close enough, and Ajani could make out who it was. It was the daughter.

When the daughter saw Ajani, she stopped, and again got up on her feet. She covered the short distance between the two cumbersomely and slowly. She reached out to him with her small hands and touched his nose. She then ran her hand up his nose and to his head and smiled.

"Thank you for coming. Thank you for being with me. I am sorry," Ajani said. His eyes teared up.

The daughter looked into his eyes, and gently wiped away a tear with a finger. She smiled. She was still too young to say anything coherently, and only made a few babbling sounds.

"I know. This opportunity to say a few last words, to apologize, to seek redemption, is an opportunity vouchsafed to no one, certainly not a lowly hyena like myself," Ajani continued. "I know there was nothing I could have done. Absolutely nothing. All this while, all this time, I, like so many, did not want to go back into the past to change it. I just wanted to go back to tell you how sorry I am. I am sorry for not being capable enough to change the outcome. Now that you are here, once again I am sorry. Don't forgive me. If you do, I am afraid I will move on. I don't want to simply move on. I want this sense and this feeling to remain in me for as long as I live."

The daughter sat down next to Ajani. She kept a hand on his head. Ajani moved his neck forward and dried his eyes against her blue colored dress.

They remained like this for a long time. The daughter eventually let out a yawn, rubbed her eyes, laid her back against Ajani and went to sleep. Ajani remained awake. The moon was now high in the sky, much smaller and much less prominent. Its light still shone on the barrier.

When the eastern horizon began to show signs of luminosity, the daughter woke up. She sat quietly for a short while as Ajani looked at her. As the sky became brighter and the stars began to fade away one at a time, the daughter got on her hands and knees, and without looking back, crawled away at an unhurried pace. Ajani kept his eyes on her until he could no longer make her out from the landscape. He returned his attention to the barrier. Crossing it would now be easy. He knew what to do. He had to simply re-realize that he was opposite to what he was before. The world may still be as gruesomely the same as it was, and perhaps will always be, but he wasn't the same impotent self. He wasn't very clear on what he was now. He would figure it out later, or better yet, let the world figure it out for him. For now, he was going to rejoin the horde and ask for help.

The butterflies came back when they heard Ajani call for help. Crossing borders for those who can fly is always easy. The butterflies flew right over it. Ajani saw them and let out a loud giggle. In response, the butterflies fluttered their wings harder. They reached him and surrounded him. Many flew around him, and some sat on him. Ajani stood up and calmly walked toward the barrier. The butterflies moved with him. Once they reached the barrier, the butterfly horde arranged themselves on it to form one thin patch from the bottom to the top. Ajani looked at the patch, then turned back to look at the landscape where he had met the daughter. He did not dwell much. He stepped back a few feet, and then with a rush of energy, rushed forward toward the barrier. When he was close enough, he leaped up. He used the butterflies for grip and leaped again. In a couple of more leaps, he was near the top of the barrier. Then, with a final burst, he leaped up high and was over the barrier. He landed in the middle of the busy, bustling Las Vegas Strip.

More than any other place in the world, the famed Las Vegas Strip is the one place where one can be a vicious looking hyena, or super horny, or, in the case of Ajani, both, and fit in perfectly. Here a horny hyena can walk one end of the strip to the other and back, take one's time to be awestruck by the carnival-like atmosphere from noon-to-noon, be mesmerized by the lighting, stop by water-fountain shows at regular intervals, gawk at people, some drunk, some stoned, and so many just blissfully walking, watch some make a fool of themselves, make a perfect fool of oneself at any time by doing things a horny hyena could be expected to do, and still blend in perfectly well.

Ajani did just that for a long, long time. All day, and all night. He would start his walk on the famous boulevard from near where the big casinos start. He would go north, taking in the sounds and the bright dazzling lights of the sin city. When he would reach the end, he would simply cross the road and walk back south. Sure, the glitz on the street glossed over the pain, the exploitations, the suffering, the broken dreams, the shattered aspirations—a whole lot of wretchedness—but he found a freedom there that he had not found anywhere else. He had survived wretchedness for the longest he could remember, he had escaped it. He knew it, he understood it very intimately. At least to Ajani, the Las Vegas Strip did not pretend that misery and despair and exploitation did not exist. There was no way not to see it all around. All that the Las Vegas Strip did, and the genius of the Strip, was to make it feel okay to indulge in decadence in spite of the misery, and even add, irreproachably by others and by self, to that exploitation.

Another aspect that made Ajani smitten with this place was the insight he gained here, and then put it into practice. He realized he simply needed to ignore what people thought of him. People had mocked him and taunted him for what he was before, and were still ridiculing him for what he was now. His instincts told him that no matter how he changed, and by how much, he would still be made fun of. This had nothing to do with what he felt internally and what he projected externally. It had to do simply with how people are. Here, on the Las Vegas Strip, even during the busiest and most crowded of times, among a mass of humanity pushing and shoving, sometimes for every single step, he felt strong enough to ignore everything and everyone. Whenever he did so, he would feel a surge of tranquility, a feeling of being, of an existence detached from the world, in sharp contrast to the crowd around him. On such occasions, only the pushing and shoving, and occasional looks and less occasional whispers of "horny hyena" would be the gossamer connecting him with the more mundane and more veridical reality.

Whispers, even the very soft ones, are louder than silence. They travel far and wide too, much farther than loud voices. Loud voices are prone to faster attenuation. Such voices may excite their immediate surroundings, but it is the soft whispers that carry the message outwards. They are the ones that carry the songs and the stories, the myths and the eulogies, the hopes and the devastations, the light and the darkness. It is when many whispers combine to produce a fringe pattern of euphony and cacophony, that giant waves appear, and change happens.

Whispers are easier to combine in a confined space, such as the Las Vegas Strip. The so-called tunnel effect then carries the waves fast through the Strip from one end to the other.

It was toward evening on that fateful day when Ajani decided to take a short break in his amble through the Las Vegas Boulevard. He stopped by at the water fountain show in front of the majestically towering Bellagio. The show was to begin in a few minutes, and the crowd had started to gather. People were pushing themselves into every possible nook that could provide them with the best possible view. Ajani did not feel the need to bother with this commotion. He had seen the show innumerable times. The first few times had mesmerized him, but the novelty had worn off. He still enjoyed the show whenever he watched it, but now it wasn't something he felt the need to rush and butt and shove through the crowd for. This time he stayed under a tree away from the balustrade where people had gathered and were standing shoulder-to-shoulder. When the show started, Ajani watched those people and, through the gaps between them and above their collective heads, the water fountains perform an intricate and elaborate dance to loud music. He found himself once more absorbed by the scenery, and as with so many other times, simultaneously losing touch with his very immediate surroundings.

"Are you liking the show?" Ajani's attention was broken when he heard those words close to his ears. His first instinct was to ignore them. They may have not been directed at him. This may simply be a conversation among two people who happened to be standing close to him.

"I hate it, I tell you. I've seen it so many times. Each time it gets worse and worse. But I still watch it, I tell you. I don't know why, but I still do. Maybe it's because I hate myself, I tell you. And why wouldn't I? Look at me. Why wouldn't I?"

In spite of himself, Ajani turned to look. He saw a ragamuffin with a balding head and a thick, unkempt dark beard. A pothead, Ajani thought.

"Not a pothead," the man replied. "I can tell you that. I am a little high right now for sure, but I am not a pothead."

Ajani gave a slight nod and returned his attention back to the show. It would end soon, and he did not want to miss the finale. To him, the finale was always the best part. This was when all different fountains would come together to reach the pinnacle of the buildup to a crescendo, meant to enthrall the audience and nothing less.

"Say, you're the horny hyena they talk about, aren't you?" The man did not take the subtle cue. Ajani turned back and gave him a hard cold look. The look did not fail to convey the message. It did not, however, bring about the intended response. Maybe, Ajani thought, his stare did not evince strong enough his distaste for communicating with anyone, particularly a pothead.

"Again, not a pothead," the man said a little testily. "Why do you keep on thinking I am one. For the love of everything that's holy or wants to be holy in this world, I am not a pothead."

The show came to an end, and the crowd began to disperse.

"Listen," the man continued, unperturbed by the show's end or Ajani's non-verbal unfriendly display of displeasure, "my less than presentable garb is not the result of a conscious choice but the vicissitudes of my fate."

He was silent for a few seconds. Ajani thought it best to remain silent too and slowly walk away. He did not want to encourage this man any further.

"If I were you," the man continued, "I would not walk. I would run. And this is precisely what I'll be doing once I am done talking to you. I'll be running, and running as fast as I can, I tell you, and not looking back until I've reached the end of the world. And I'll still keep on running. They are here, and they'll catch me and you. It is only a matter of time."

Ajani looked up to study this man's face carefully. He looked deep into his eyes, as if trying to reach into him to verify the veracity of what he was saying.

"You know I am telling the truth. They're here. I was running from them and then I saw you, and I asked myself, 'maybe I should warn him? Or maybe not?' I told myself 'I shouldn't. Let them catch this hyena.' If they go after you, it'll increase the chances of saving myself. They'll show less interest in pursuing me. They're here because of you anyway. You're the horny hyena. The whispers have reached them. Now, they'll not let you go. They are the Foreign Legion. A horny hyena among their ranks will do wonders for them."

Ajani's demeanor still did not register any expression. The man's expression did not show any change.

"But in the end," he blurted out, and his eyes went from a glassy defiance to a steely boldness, "I said to myself, 'this isn't right. No, Sir. Not right. Not by me. I can't let this hyena suffer. The Foreign Legion is not the place for him. The Legion's done enough. No more of it.' That's why I took a break from running to come by to warn you. Once it's chewed you up, it'll come after me, and then someone else, and then another. I can't fight it. It's like fighting against history. I am just a single man down on his luck. The most I can do is try to help a fellow traveler escape for as long as possible. I will do it myself till the very end."

Ajani moved his eyes around rapidly, trying to catch any out-of-place movements among the crowd. He believed this man's story and began to be worried for his safety. The Foreign Legion will catch him with the same gracelessness and coldness as an old cartoon antagonist dogcatcher reserves for a cartoon dog, and perhaps worse. This would be the good part. His situation will only go precipitously downhill from there. The Legion will drag him by a tight chain around his neck through the Las Vegas Boulevard to who knows where. There, he will be shaped up and shipped out back to do what he had risked his life to leave behind and forget—fight bad hyenas and lions. He couldn't do that anymore. He was no longer that Ajani.

"Get the hell out of here! Do it while you can," the man yelled loudly. A few people slowed to look at him briefly. They noticed a crazy looking man trying to converse with a hyena. They readily dismissed his outburst, and carried on with their main aim of enjoying the evening with all that the Strip has to offer.

Ajani now didn't think twice. He dashed through the street faster than he thought he could. The crowd made it difficult to pick up a good pace, but it also protected him. The Legion would find it difficult to identify him among the throng of people that filled the place.

Ajani wasn't thinking much about his destination. He didn't have one. At this time, he was simply trying to get away from the Strip. The Strip was busy now, and would be busy for many hours to come. However, at some point, the crowd would thin out. He would be easier to spot then. He would also be easier to corner and capture. His only real option was to go as far away as possible from here, and as quickly as possible.

Ajani soon came to a major intersection. The only way to reach the other side was by an overpass. He, like so many others around him, climbed up the steps. Once he reached the top, he looked around for a view. That's when he saw them. The Foreign Legionnaires, numerous, all on fine-looking white horses. The horses were trotting, with scant regards to the people they were pushing aside. The riders were looking carefully at each and every face. Ajani knew they were looking for him. With a petrified face, he moved back, trying to disappear in the crowd, hoping he had not been seen. In doing so he lost his balance and rolled down the steps. Near the bottom step, he hit his head hard. He hit it one more time on the very last step, but did not feel it. He had lost consciousness by then.

Ajani woke up with a dull throbbing pain on one side of his head. He hated himself. He looked around and found his movements hampered by the pain. He could make out a small well-lit room.

He hated it. The room had a small cabinet in a corner, dull blue in color, and below it, a small shelf, with a tap and a sink at the very end. He hated that too. It occurred to him that he was in a clinic. He put his head back down on the treatment table he was lying on, and closed his eyes. Despite the pain, he slept again.

The next time he woke up, his pain was gone but a heaviness in his temple remained. As he gathered his strength, Ajani realized he was not alone. There was a shadow of someone on his face. He lifted his head with some effort to get a better look. He saw an old looking man, clean shaven, with marked wrinkles and saggy skin around the jaw. The face had some sharp features too, including a prominent nose and bright eyes and a kind, gentle smile. A receding hairline further made the face more prominent and his look tenderer. Ajani knew the look. He had met people like him—those who had suffered enough through bad times in the past to feel a strong compulsion to show their gratitude for the good times they were finally living in. If this was a Foreign Legion facility he was in, Ajani felt he could at least get a few moments of sympathy in the company of this man before being stripped off any vestige of hope. These were the kind of people one could freely commiserate with.

"Hello," the old man spoke tenderly, his voice matching his facial demeanor, "my name is Sayyid. You are in a facility to help those in need like you. You are safe here."

Ajani did not bother with the truthfulness of what Sayyid said. The enormity of the accumulated exhaustion from his interminable walk on the Las Vegas Strip, the cumulative fatigue from each whisper, and the recent mad dash to escape the Foreign Legion had gotten to him. His head fell back on the treatment table, and he fell back into a long dreamless sleep.

Sayyid checked on Ajani a few times over the course of the next couple of days. Their communication was mostly single-sided. Ajani may have been seeking security despite the gung-ho persona he was projecting—quite the opposite to his previous life when he sought action while projecting something entirely different. Sayyid was looking for affirmation for his self-reasoned conclusions to his life-arch. As such he had more to say. He believed that the trials and tribulations in his life were expressly for the purpose of leading him to this moment, the moment when he could devote his life to actively helping those who needed help. As age advances, people start thinking about retirement. Sayyid, on the other hand, decided, at the insistence of his son, to study for and take the medical licensure exam. This way, he reasoned, he could get back to the real passion he had long had to leave behind—to be a doctor. He cleared the exam on the first attempt. However, before he could make the next move, he was diagnosed with a brain tumor.

"That was something," Sayyid said. "My wife had been insisting for a few years that I get my annual checkup. When I cleared the exam, I decided to go to a physician. This was not because I wanted to, but so that I could get her to stop nagging me. Everything in the exam came out great. My blood report was normal, my heart was normal, everything. I put my report right in front of her face and told her not to bother me with this again. She looked at the report in detail. When she was done, she politely asked for the results from my hearing test. For a while she and my son had been complaining that they often had to be loud to get my attention. I told her I didn't get my hearing checked because the doctor never asked me to. She insisted I get it. We even had a big argument over that. She was adamant though, and called up a hearing specialist herself to make an appointment for me.

"I ended up visiting a hearing specialist the next day. She checked me and immediately ordered an MRI for my head. The doctor didn't explain why, but said she wanted to be sure there's nothing to worry about. An hour later, I was at an MRI facility. Another hour later, as soon as the radiologist saw my report, he asked me to check in for immediate surgery. It turned out that I had a big tumor, benign thankfully, on the left side of my head. They didn't want to let me go back home because they feared I could have a life-threatening seizure at any time. It was a big operation. It took over twenty-four hours and required a team of four doctors—two neurosurgeons and two ENT specialists—who took turns removing that tumor, slice by slice.

"I recuperated quickly. That was completely unexpected, too. I was told to be ready for a lengthy and painful few months. I was told I would never be wholly back to normal. But I was. In a month I had recovered. It was all thanks to my physiotherapist, this man by the name of Ramakant. A brilliant and gifted individual. He looked at me, and looked at my reports, and said, 'We'll get you fixed. Trust yourself.' He pushed me and made me push myself. It's because of him that I am standing here on my feet. I owe him a lot. Not so much to the doctors. I am a doctor myself. I could understand a good bit of what they would discuss about my condition. I did not appreciate their attitude. Compared to Ramakant, they were outright lackadaisical. Ramakant is a good man. He's the one good friend I have in this country. I know a lot of people, but Ramakant is someone I consider a friend. 'If you ever need my help, if you even think that I can be helpful, I'll be upset if you don't call me,' I tell him whenever we talk."

Sayyid talked some more a day later. "Once I recovered, I decided I'd had enough of pursuing my passion. Life is fickle. One morning you leave your home upset with your wife, and in the evening you're getting ready for a major surgery from which you may never emerge. I'd had enough of running and trying to look out for myself and my family. I'd done so in some desperate conditions, and I have been justly rewarded for it. Very justly indeed. It was time to give back. Ramakant introduced me to this organization. He had been associated with it for some time as a volunteer. I decided this was for me too.

"Ramakant could have been a good doctor, I think. He likes the medical profession. But he told me he had very little

162

respect for them and was happy being a physiotherapist. Here, he could make a good living and still be associated with the profession. I don't blame him. He's had limited interactions with doctors, most of them not very great. One pediatrician, he once mentioned, had a minor argument with him on creationism versus evolution when he'd taken his child to him. Another, he said, had mockingly asked him if he believed in many gods, and then went into a tirade on virginal birth. I tried to explain to him that a doctor is just like any other person you run into. There's no need to raise or lower your expectations. I told him a few things I've experienced in my life. Even in this country, I've had some unflattering experiences. Once a cab driver who was taking me to the airport for my flight to Detroit, asked me if there were lots of blacks in Michigan. Another time, a little boy at a zoo—couldn't have been more than three or four or five years old—was trying to get into a narrow tube for kids to look at some animals. He came out flustered and said to his mother, who was standing not too far from me, 'Mom, there are some kids blocking my way. They're all black.' The mother looked at me with her hand on her mouth. Maybe she was embarrassed, or maybe she felt guilty that I'd heard it. Maybe dinner table conversations at their home are interesting. Who knows. I simply walked away. There was nothing to say.

"Just the other day, I think last week, I met this man who's a landowner somewhere. We got around to talking about all the interesting technological changes happening with crop growing and harvesting. Toward the end of the conversation he said, 'When we have all those technologies developed, Jose won't need to come here no more. We can say goodbye to Jose!'

"What I tried to explain to Ramakant, now I say to you too—people are people. Some are bad, but you'll also find enough good people. You'll find good and smart doctors too, lots of them, maybe even most of them. It's not a good thing to form an opinion based on just a few."

Ajani was feeling better within a day of being there. Sayyid asked him to remain in the facility for a couple of more days to fully recuperate. Ajani did not mind. This was the first time in his life when he did not have anything to do besides remain lying. He also harbored the hope that the Foreign Legion would lose interest in pursuing him by the time he was out back on the street. This break also gave him some time to think about his next steps. Maybe, he thought, he could go down south and try to meet up with the butterfly horde. Who knows, maybe he could go farther, cross the Panama Canal, and lose himself in the Amazon. Wouldn't that be nice? Or maybe continue going down farther, eventually reach the ocean and then, perhaps, cross it to disappear in the icy wilderness of Antarctica, never to be found again. But it would be cold, very cold. He had not enjoyed the weather up in Canada. Antarctica would be a thousand times worse.

Sayyid had wanted Ajani to remain in the facility for a few more days, not only because he wanted to see him well, but also for a selfish motive. Sayyid had a lot to say about his life, but rarely found anyone willing to listen for too long. Ajani appeared very attentive. He would nod, move his ears around, sometimes look up at him with a jerk when he said anything to surprise him, and then go back to lying down. But he would almost always have his eyes focused on him. Sayyid liked him.

"I like you," he said to Ajani. "You are one decent hyena. I don't know why people think you are that kind of a hyena, the bad one. I know you're not. I can try to help you if you let me. I've told you so much about myself. You can tell me something about you if you are comfortable doing so. Maybe it can help me help you. Of course, it's up to you."

Ajani wasn't very thrilled about taking Sayyid up on his offer. Where would he even begin? What would he even say? Did he even need any sympathy? Maybe, he thought, he did when he had arrived here. He was in a very vulnerable state then. But now, when he had regained his strength and had some tentative options to choose from for his next steps, he did not feel lost and defenseless. He decided to take his time and select his words carefully if he was to let Sayyid know anything more about him.

He did not need to tell Sayyid much.

"I know you. I know those like you," Sayyid said. "You're running away from something, right? You don't have to say it. You may be laconic on the surface, but it's obvious to anyone who spends any time with you that you have a lot to say."

Ajani lifted his head with a jerk, looked carefully at Sayyid, and slowly brought it back on the table. He had begun to like Sayyid's calm, soft voice. There was something soothing and therapeutic about it. This was one thing he would miss above all else when he was back outside and on the move.

"I can even guess what it is." Sayyid smiled. This had the effect of stretching his face just enough to reduce some of the wrinkles and bring his bulbous nose into attention. "You're running away from dying in pointless wars and for empty glories." He looked at Ajani for confirmation. He got it from a slight movement in his eyes. "I once ran away with my family from one too. If I hadn't, I might have lost my life, or my family, or both. But there are no good options. Once you start running, you're not allowed to stop that easily. I ran for a long time. I am now at peace. You'll find it too. Have faith."

Ajani did not respond. Experience over the past few days informed him that Sayyid would quickly fill any silence. He wasn't mistaken.

"Listen, I've just had an idea. Go to Paris. Paris is the one place the Foreign Legion cannot reach you. They're not allowed to be in Paris. You'll be safe there. My son is also in Paris, working for some big computer company. I don't know much about what he does, but he's doing well. His name is Hamoon. I'll talk to him when I get a chance. He's very busy, but maybe he can give you some advice on Paris."

Ajani was immediately taken with the idea. Paris may work

out for him. Getting there, however, was not going to be so easy. Sayyid sensed his puzzlement. "It might not be so difficult to get to Paris, you know," he said. "If you get back on the Las Vegas Strip, something will work out. I am sure of it. It's only in completely Godless places that miracles happen."

Ajani managed to get to Paris through a convoluted route. This included first a long, exposed walk along the Las Vegas Boulevard. There, he was seen by the horse-riding members of the Foreign Legion. They chased after him through the main street, back streets, and through many casinos.

"Look at that horny hyena," was only what he heard around him as he pushed people to make his escape. None came to his aid. But it didn't matter. After his stay under the care of Sayyid, he had become hopeful, but also more circumspect on expectations from people. He was going to struggle through this by himself. He would remain defiant to the end before any Foreign Legionnaire could catch and conscript him. It was natural for anyone to be timorous in the situation he was in, but not him.

Pushing and bumping into people and things bruised him a bit. But he made good progress, and managed to put a good distance between himself and the Foreign Legionnaires. He soon arrived at the famed casino, Paris Paris, a landmark on the Strip, but a casino he had not cared about much before. It was, he had felt, a poor ersatz of a poor ersatz of his idea of what Paris was like. However, it would serve the purpose. It would protect him from his bête noire.

Niam had uncharacteristically lost attention to his surroundings while the car made its way through the busy streets and Ajani related his story. When he finally looked at others, he could not determine any change in them. They were seemingly oblivious to whatever the hyena had been saying. Only he was privy to this hyena's words, besides his daughter.

"You're saying," Niam said this in his head, "you entered Paris Paris, the casino, and then something happened, and you found yourself in the real Paris?"

Ajani responded in the affirmative.

"What happened?" Niam asked.

"She happened?" Niam asked, silently again, and looked at the daughter. She was looking at him, smiling. "How did she get you here?"

Niam did not need to wait for an explicit, verbal answer. Changes in Ajani's facial expression and the daughter's smile made it obvious. She had made everything possible. At turns and at twists, at crossroads, it was the daughter, his daughter, who made the journey possible, who lit up the path. The car ride they were undertaking was also her doing. This was her journey, her odyssey. And Ajani's pilgrimage, if he could make it to the end. Niam was only a conduit. Later that day, Nina had told him something about this too, and something more.

"They spent a good deal of time at the casino trying to put a value on life," she had said. "It's not easy, you know, trying to find out how much a life is worth. To me, if you ask me, it's probably impossible, or close to it. I admire them for attempting it though. How many hyenas are equal to a human life? I don't know the answer to this. How many lions? There are so many people who take a very cavalier attitude toward this. It shouldn't be this way. We need to know. Maybe there is some other scale to measure the importance of a life. Maybe some kind of an absolute scale. An ant can be, say, a one on that scale, a tree can be a thousand, a human can be a gazillion maybe. We can even subdivide among humans, something like a gazillion-point-one for a baby, and a gazillion-point-two for a teenager, and so on. I find this very fascinating, but also too ponderous and weighty for my fickle mind to solve. But that's me. However, this may not

167

be unworkable for Ajani and the daughter. It may be a challenging and laborious exercise, but those two together are the ones who have the best chance to solve this problem."

"Did they figure it out?" Niam had asked.

"Not yet, if I am not mistaken. The work and discussion were so intense that it created the same hole that's now taken your wife, and helped them get here to the real Paris, though. So, there's definitely something that happened. I can only hope it's just a matter of time. Think of how big an accomplishment this will be, to be able to assign a number to each and every life, a number that lets us know how relatively important it is, how worthy, or maybe unworthy, it is. That would be something! Once you have associated numbers, you can do some serious advanced calculations and know the true cost of doing or not doing something."

Niam had not responded.

The group met Nina at the same location from earlier in the day where Niam and Nina had first met her.

"My entire day today has basically been about journeys between coffee shops," Niam said to Prisha when they had stepped out of the car and onto the pavement. Nabil and Delphine stood next to the car, taking in the surroundings. Nabil had the precise muted smug look of a driver who had wadded through the busy streets of Paris with some level of finesse. He threw occasional glances at Delphine and at the patisserie, with the hope that his employer would offer to buy him something. His employer, Delphine, though was unaware of this. She was busy looking around. She was in a neighborhood she lat visited in her youth. It had changed much, but had still retained its upscale image. Hamoon, Ajani, and the daughter were together as a group, standing between Niam and Prisha, and Delphine and Nabil.

"Does that mean it has been good so far, or boring?" Prisha looked at Niam. He was looking at the shop when he turned to her.

"Not boring, no, certainly not boring," he said with a thin smile. "Tiring for sure, but not boring. Maybe I can have another coffee."

At that moment, Nina stepped out of the shop holding a cup with a brown frothy drink in one hand, and her phone in the other. She looked exactly as she looked when she and Niam had parted at the bus stop. She stopped momentarily to look at all seven of them. Her eyes rested on Ajani and the daughter a little longer, and then her face broke out in a broad bright smile.

"Why don't all of you come inside? It's much cooler in there. Let me buy you something. Isn't that Ajani the hyena? He's so beautiful! And you?" She looked at the daughter. "Aren't you the pretty one? What's your name?"

The daughter looked at Nina and broke into a glowing smile. "I don't have one yet. My dad promised to find me a good one by tomorrow," she replied demurely.

"Oh, how silly of me!" Nina exclaimed. "Of course, of course!" She momentarily paused and extended her arm toward the daughter. "Come, let's go in. It's hot out here. I'll get you something cold and nice. That is, if your mom permits."

Nina looked at Prisha. Prisha simply shrugged her shoulders, but maintained a blank expression.

Soon they were seated around two small tables that Niam and Nabil had pushed close together. Ajani remained on his feet between Nina and the daughter, near the far corner where casual eyes could either mistake him for a dog or miss him altogether. Nina kept a hand on his back and intermittently petted him. This motley group was the crowd at the shop. There was a steady stream of people who were dropping in the shop and leaving after being taken care of by two young women behind the counter. These women exuded an aura of no-nonsense efficiency in whatever they were doing, handling customer orders, idly chat with them, and even having the occasional chit-chat between the two of them. No action of theirs seemed to be extraneous.

By contrast, the group seemed boisterous. The small talk was lively and loud. Delphine was the most curious among them, and insisted on hearing everything about the neighborhood that Nina could remember. She told her about the changes that had been taking place in front of her eyes, while Delphine talked about its layout from a few decades ago. She turned toward Nabil occasionally to recount her forays through this locality and detail the transpired transformations. This she did in French, because this was the language that connected them. It was also clear to others that Delphine shared a bond with Nabil and felt the need for him to be there, more than anyone else, to appreciate her life's journey.

"A life's journey," Ella said to Niam sometime later when they met, "is more often than not a good journey where those important phases have been covered—ignoring and disregarding death, then putting in efforts to avoid and overcome it, and then finally accepting its inevitability. And even then, in that acceptance, seeking to live beyond it as a legacy or a memory."

In the patisserie, Hamoon quickly finished off his single shot espresso. He then took a nibble of a thin cinnamon biscuit. He wasn't in the mood for anything in particular. However, he also did not want to let go of the offer for a free anything from Nina. At first, he had thought of ordering something small but expensive, maybe, and he toyed with the idea in his head for a bit, a frappe perhaps. But he didn't know Nina, and didn't want to come across as inconsiderate. He settled for the espresso. Once he was done, he put his empty cup on the table a little hard. This had the effect of diverting everyone's attention away from Delphine to him.

"My friend and colleague here, Hamoon," Niam said to Nina, "is from United States. We're both working on the same project."

170

"How nice," Nina said. "I've always wanted to visit the U.S. I've just not had an opportunity so far. I want to see New York and Las Vegas. Maybe soon."

Hamoon looked at her with bright eyes. "I love Las Vegas! You should absolutely go there at least once in your lifetime. My father moved there sometime back, and I rush to visit him whenever I can. I think that's what all old parents and grandparents should do if they can—move to some big-time touristy place. This is a sure way to have your kids and grandkids visit you regularly, and have regular family gatherings! I'm just kidding. I love my dad. I'll visit him all the time even if he decides to move to some crazy cold place like North Dakota, or some crazy hot and dead place deep in Arizona!"

Niam, Prisha, Nina, and Delphine joined Hamoon in letting out a collective small laugh. Nabil smiled. He realized that something mildly funny had been said. He understood Las Vegas and New York, but nothing else.

"I've been to the United States a few times," Delphine said. "It was nice. I liked it. But call me what you like, I prefer France any time over any place else."

"Maybe it's because you were born here and you've lived your entire life here," Hamoon said.

"I agree with you." Nina looked at Delphine with wide eyes. She kept her cup of frappe gently on the table and moved her shoulders and neck ever so slightly, as if she was trying to collect some weight to bring to what she was going to say. "I cannot think of myself being anywhere other than France. It could be because of what Hamoon said, I was born here, and I've lived here for my entire life too. Not as long as yours, certainly, but still long enough. I like to believe that I love France because it's the most, best, perfect place in the world. We have everything, the weather, the wine, and the people. And we have deep roots in culture. In music. In everything. Now, don't get me wrong. I don't think it's all perfect. After all, what is culture but customs ossified. I don't

171

like the ossified part. And I know too the one thing common to all old cultures is a misplaced, synthetic pride. Maybe I carry that pride in me too. Maybe we all do. On balance, however, I'll still take it. This is where I feel, and I know, I belong."

Hamoon looked at them, and looked down at his empty cup.

They sat there for over an hour. The sun outside, perched high up in the same position it had been for many hours, still blazed its heat in the form of sharp pointy rays. These rays were targeting everyone and everything mercilessly, with no sign of relief any time soon. The shop was cool, but the outside traversed the physical and snaked its way into the collective psyche of everyone inside. Everyone shared stories from their lives, minus the daughter and Ajani. Nabil's were collectively conveyed by Nabil, Delphine, and Nina, for the benefit of Niam and Prisha. His stories from the Sahara were apt for the occasion, and so were Prisha's on the weather extremities she had experienced in India. For most parts, however, everyone had something to share about the changing weather and an uncertain future.

Once everyone had finished their drinks and had shared all their stories and all their opinions they wanted to share, the attention turned to the reason they were all there in the first place—the hyena in the room.

Delphine was the first to brooch the topic. "Is it really you who has offered to take care of this animal?" she addressed Nina.

"Yes, she is the one I told you about," Niam responded. He turned toward Nina to address her, "Thank you for agreeing to take him in at such a short notice. I wouldn't have known what to do if it were not for you. Our apartment is fairly small for an animal this size. Actually, for any size. But it's not just the size. We simply don't know how to look after him."

Nina didn't respond to Niam. She petted Ajani slowly and deliberately. Ajani, for his part, moved closer to Nina. He moved his head down and pushed his nose slightly into the daughter as a mark of affection and protection. He then walked around the group leisurely, pushing his nose into everyone until he was back by Nina's side.

"If we're done, then perhaps we should leave," Nina said. "It'll be a long trek. Do you think you'll be able to do it?" she addressed Delphine.

"Oh, don't you worry about me, young lady," Delphine replied with a self-assured defiance. "I've many a trek left in me yet. Don't you write us old people off!"

"That's not my intention at all." Nina smiled. "I just don't want you to be in any difficulty. I'll be very happy if you can be with us, of course!"

"And I wouldn't miss it for anything!" Delphine responded and stood up. On cue everyone else did the same. They made their way out of the shop in a single file led by Nina. She stepped out and held the door open. She was joined by Ajani behind her, followed by Delphine, Nabil, Hamoon, the daughter, Prisha, and lastly, Niam.

"There. We will take Ajani, our hyena there," Nina said, and pointed in the direction that she and Niam had taken earlier in the day to meet Ella. Niam took the daughter's hand and stepped forward. Ajani walked by his side. The rest followed them.

"You know what to do, right?" Nina called Niam from behind.

"No, I don't." Niam stopped and turned to face her. "I know how to pass through a trench. I am not sure about this."

"This is certainly not going to be a trench, I can tell you that." Nina smiled. "But it's going to be okay. We are all together in this with you. Don't forget that. It'll make it easier."

Niam moved his gaze from Nina to Prisha. Prisha silently stepped forward and held the other hand of the daughter. Niam turned and started back on his walk.

"Do you know where we're going?" Prisha asked Niam.

Niam looked at the daughter, who looked up at him. They

exchanged smiles. Niam looked up at Prisha. There wasn't a smile there.

"I know where we'll finally be," he replied. "We are to meet someone by the name of Ella. It's the way to meet her that might be a bit of a challenge. Will you be okay with all this?"

"I'll be okay. And I'll be with you. Don't you worry," Prisha replied, and turned to look at passing vehicles on the road.

Niam turned to Ajani. Their eyes met. Niam returned his gaze to the path ahead.

The sidewalk they were on was not nearly as congested as the sidewalk they were on a few hours earlier when they were trying to reach the metro. The few people they came across left them a wide berth. The walk, therefore, wasn't difficult.

"I love your blouse! It's very lovely," Nina said to Delphine.

"Thank you!" Delphine replied. "I like your top too. We are matching in white today! Isn't that a coincidence?"

"It indeed is." Nina smiled.

"Though," Delphine continued, "your clothes suit you so much better than my clothes suit me. It's all about the age. You're young. When you're young, everything looks good on you. At my age, I have to be very selective. I miss those days when I could wear whatever I wanted. Unfortunately, they're not coming back."

"Do you know where we're going exactly?" Hamoon asked when Delphine and Nina became quiet.

"Why, we're going on a trek!" Delphine exclaimed. "I thought you knew that already."

"I do, I do," Hamoon replied. "It's just that I am confused about the whole thing."

"There's no need to be confused," Nina said. "Think of it this way—we don't always need a deep, solid reason to do something. We simply do it. We do it because if we don't, we would be wasting our time on something else. If you're not coming with us, how will you spend the remainder of your Saturday afternoon and evening? Watch TV? Spend time and money at a restaurant you don't much care about? Get drunk? You might as well be here."

"Some people would consider the other options as good options too for a Saturday evening."

"Yes, you're right," Nina responded. "My point is, again, we don't have to focus on the why, and just enjoy the moment. We don't need to worry about why the eight of us are here together. We are here and we're going on a trek!"

"I guess that's good enough for me!" Hamoon exclaimed.

"Me too!" Delphine joined him.

A few paces later, they turned a corner to their right and stopped. In front of them, not more than half a kilometer away, rose a majestic, intimidating hill, the peak of which seemed to pierce the sky.

When they had marveled long enough at the peak, Delphine spoke, "Let us all take inspiration from Hannibal and conquer the hill. We can do it! If I think I can do it, so can all you youngsters."

"I think I can do it too," Hamoon said. "I can think whatever I want. But it doesn't mean I can actually do it."

"Come on!" Delphine touched his shoulder. "Don't be a sourpuss. We just decided to focus only on enjoying the moment. The moment calls for a climb up the hill, and so we'll do it."

"This hill looks very much like the hill I used to climb a few years back," Niam said. "If there was a temple at the peak, I would have thought of the two to be identical. It used to be fun climbing that hill. But it was steep, I'll tell you that. If you're not in good shape, you might not be able to climb this."

"We'll be fine, I think," Nina said. "We'll take the less steep path. It'll be longer, but it should be okay."

Nabil leaned slightly toward Delphine and said something to her in Arabic, followed by French. Delphine turned toward the group.

"Nabil tells me about this saying, in his country, 'Your aim determines what you can achieve,'" she said. "I say we aim for the peak, and nothing less!"

There was a short pause during which every adult human looked at each other, and then at the daughter and Ajani.

"What about them? Can they do it?" Hamoon asked. "What do you think?"

There was a pause again. Then Niam kneeled in front of the daughter.

"We're going to need to go up that hill you see there. Then we're going to come down the other side. That's where Ajani needs to go. It's not going to be easy. Do you want to do it?" he asked her softly, as he ran a finger through her hair.

She looked into Niam's eyes and spoke without a hint of hesitation. "Yes, I want to do it. And Ajani too. He says he doesn't care if he's on this side of the big hill or the other side. If you want to take him there, he's okay with it. He also says that you do not need to worry about him."

Niam kept still for a moment, trying to figure out what to say. He stood up and turned to the group. "They'll be okay," he said to them. "Let's go."

To say the views from the summit were astounding was an understatement. Breathtaking was also an understatement. The destination had absolutely made up for their tough journey, beyond everyone's wildest expectations. And the journey had been painstakingly tough. They had gained height very slowly. The path up was narrow. It zigzagged along the face of the hill, the turns getting shorter and sharper as the altitude increased. It wasn't difficult in the beginning. At times the path appeared almost flat. They were all smiling and chatting away, and watching the view of Paris slowly appearing to them in all its vastness as they gained height.

But soon enough, things started to become treacherous.

It began with small rocks on their path, which they did not mind. They simply walked around them or over them. Those rocks, however, soon gave way to large boulders that completely blocked their paths.

"There's no way around this," Nina said when they came across the first big boulder. "We have no choice. We'll have to climb it."

"I think I can," Hamoon said.

"I think I can too," Niam said. "And I am sure Nabil can too. But I can't see how the rest of them can climb it."

"I think she can help," Nina said and looked at Delphine. "If there's one thing I know in life, it is that songs carry us when nothing else can."

Everyone turned to look at Delphine. She smiled, and her face became radiant. She started singing. The song was in French, the melody immensely upbeat and infectious. It roused everyone up. Nabil hauled himself over the boulder. He reached down and grabbed Delphine by her hands to pull her up. Niam offered his palms, and Delphine stepped on them. Niam and Nabil, working together, quickly pulled her up on the boulder. Once on the top, Delphine, who had not stopped singing, sang louder. This was now her stage, the one she was seeking after a gap of many decades, and there was a crowd, an audience. And the crowd was genuinely excited by her singing. Ajani stepped back and swiftly sprang forward to jump on the boulder. Prisha and the daughter and Nina needed some help. But they were all soon standing on the boulder, greatly enthused.

They continued on their journey after coming down the boulder on the other side. They found other big boulders at regular intervals, and Delphine sang different songs at each one. The temperature had also started to decrease ever so slightly as their height increased. These two factors made it easier to overcome those boulders.

As tough as the climb was, they did eventually reach the top.

"I've climbed many peaks in my long life," Delphine said. They were standing on a very flat platform that was just a few feet below the almost sharp tip of the hilltop, and ran all the way around it. "This has to be the most magical of them all."

"Or the most realistic of them all," Nina said. She gripped the railing as she stared far away toward the horizon. "The world is often so full of magic that reality can sometimes be very refreshing."

"But it is a magical peak," Prisha said. She was standing next to Nina and Delphine. "I can feel it. It's in the air. It's all around us."

Nabil said something to Delphine, and she translated it to English for the group, "The world always appears enchanting to those who are elevated enough."

"It indeed does." Hamoon smiled and broke away from the group to walk around the platform.

"The magic up here," Nina said softly to Niam when others too had dispersed, "are only three. Nothing more. The daughter is one. The hyena is the second. And the third is the ability for an individual to see what they want to see down below, blissfully ignorant of what you see. You see what is. You see non-existence creeping in from every direction, trying to trap you into staying put, making any meaningful movement on any path seem ultimately pointless. But you already sensed this. You can see it clearly too now, can't you?"

"I can indeed." Niam turned to face Nina. The daughter and Ajani stepped almost in unison to stand beside Niam. Niam reached out to take the daughter's hand. The air carried the soft sound of Delphine singing a song, again in French.

"She sings for herself," Nina said to Niam. Niam nodded his head slightly, a gesture that suggested he heard her but nothing more. Nina wasn't discouraged and continued, "All her life, she sang for others. Climbing up, too, she sang for others. Now, she sings for herself."

Niam still did not show he paid attention to what she said. "I wonder what they are all seeing?" he asked.

"Them?" Nina turned around a full circle. "Do you want to know? Why?"

"I don't want to know," Niam replied. "It would be interesting. Nothing more."

Nina stared at his face for a moment. She moved her jaws slightly, as if hesitating. This was followed by a slight twitch in her eyes. It seemed to signal an end to the hesitation.

"I don't exactly know what they're seeing. If you want, I can tell you my best guess. It's nothing too interesting, for sure. People are not really that interesting."

"You might as well, since we're here." Niam smiled. "We have to kill time till everyone's had their fill of the view, and we can begin our climb down to meet Ella."

"Aah, yes, we need to meet Ella! And we need to take care of the hyena. The excitement of the climb had almost made me forget why we're here in the first place!" Nina told him as she petted the hyena.

Nabil saw a desert stretching out to meet the horizon in a blaze of shimmering, blinding light. The light made the horizon invisible, and the sand dunes hard to look at. There was life there, for sure. At least he thought he was sure. Occasionally, the light would give way, just a little, and something, or someone, would break through. He liked that. No desert should be completely lifeless, barren. There is only so much one can be in awe of desolation before it becomes too much to bear. There must be an anchor, and there must be a sail. One holds you, and one guides you. One grounds you, protects you from unforgiving dust storms, and one glides you over endless undulating sand dunes.

He missed his family.

The seeds for his dreams and ambitions may have been

planted by his world. However, he realized, he had cultivated them, watered them, protected them, and when they were ready enough, he had unveiled them for his world. Those dreams were his sails. They brought him here. They brought him here, high enough to be able to look down and see. To see his family, his anchor. Deadweight. Pulling him down. Still giving him the grounding he needs, the protection, the safety. Sails set you loose, the speed animates and galvanizes the senses, but they also drive you directly headlong into sandstorms.

Nabil was conflicted. This was to be his fate.

Hamoon wasn't conflicted. This was to be his fate.

Hamoon looked down and saw only the urban sprawl of Atlanta from horizon to horizon. The buildings and open spaces, all merging into a giant continuum, teaming with life, movement, intensity. He was part of it. He may only be a tiny flash of light in it, but he was a flash of light with an assumed punch. He had an oversized fighting spirit in a fight to be relevant. The fight for relevancy was his anchor and his sail. That fight was his sense of belonging. He had nothing else to fall back on, nowhere else to belong. He didn't really choose to be in Atlanta. In actuality, he hadn't really chosen to be anywhere throughout his life. Those choices were made for him. Now that they were made, and they brought him here, his life was going to be led in that knowledge. He felt great about it. It rejuvenated him. He was a citizen of the world. He belonged here, there, everywhere, and nowhere.

Nowhere is what Delphine saw when she looked down. And she didn't mind it one bit. She welcomed it. People had hurled themselves through space to be here, some in ways that could be construed to be unfathomable. In the nowhere she saw, she made out a few complex patterns of crisscrosses of paths—paths that were traversed upon, created, recreated by those she was sharing this platform, perched so high up that she saw nowhere way down below. Delphine had not had to launch herself into space to be here. She had launched herself in time. She traveled time when others traveled distances. Or was it time that had hurled itself toward her while she remained stationary? Either way, there was movement, change. She was a participant in it. A very minor one, for sure. But so are most of those who travel in space. Lots of travel in space is suffering, lots of travel in time is suffering too. She was fortunate, indeed very fortunate, that her travel was not attached to suffering at any point. So were Niam's and Prisha's.

"She's right, you know," Niam said to Nina. The breeze around them was gentle enough to move a single strand of hair, but nothing more. "If that's what she's seeing and thinking."

"As far as I can tell," Nina replied, and moved her hair from her face.

"I should be honest with myself," Niam continued, seemingly ignoring Nina. "I would be suffering from some sort of a cognitive dissonance if I cannot even see and acknowledge how privileged my life has been."

"People don't suffer because they cannot see or cannot acknowledge," Nina said. "Ask anyone, ask me, ask anyone you see, anyone who's got a comfortable bed and good food, and they'll acknowledge, if they're truthful, that they're privileged. It's not that. It's about how they feel. They don't feel privileged."

"A single life..." Niam tried to get in a few words, but wasn't successful.

"And the constant judging that goes around," Nina continued. "That judging is the result of this feeling of not being privileged, and constantly wanting to. No one has a right to judge anyone. People take it as a right. But sorry, what were you saying?"

Niam did not waste a moment. "I was saying that a single life is a very complex, complicated composition," he said. "A collective, on the other hand, is somewhat simpler. Simpler to understand, simpler to predict."

"That may be true," Nina said. "I've always felt something

like this. For example, every interaction I've ever had, no matter how small or how significant, has left an emotional mark on me, like a signature. My mind carries the collective weight of all that baggage. Even a simple exchange of greetings with a grocery store worker leaves something in me. I may forget about it completely from my conscious mind, but it has affected me, left a small indent in my psyche. Bigger interactions leave heavier, deeper marks. My point is, who may affect me and how, who I may affect and how, what may affect me and how, are not easy to understand and predict, if at all. Even for me, if I think about it."

Niam did not have anything to add to this. He silently turned to the daughter and Ajani, and then turned to look over and down the hill. He slowly moved his gaze toward the horizon as he tried to make out the people and individual small features. However, he was too high up to do so. He was soon joined by Prisha, who made a complete circle around the hilltop.

"When do you want to climb down?" she asked.

"Soon, I suppose," Niam replied. "Let's wait until everyone is ready."

"If you don't make a move, no one else will. You know that," Prisha said.

"I know, I know. It's just that getting here was so demanding and arduous that I don't want to force anyone to suffer any further until they're all well rested and ready. Exhaustion can make the most docile, sweet-tempered person an irascible powder keg."

"Alright, maybe I can go around and gather everyone," Prisha said. "Gently, of course. I don't want anyone to get too explosive."

Niam did not respond, but smiled. Prisha stepped around him to gather the others.

"You didn't tell me what she, and the daughter, and the hyena saw?" he asked Nina once Prisha was a few steps away.

"I can't tell you what she saw. It's all blurred. Very hazy. I wish I could. I am keen to know too. But I simply cannot," Nina said.

"It's okay. What about the two of these?"

"You mean the daughter and Ajani? They only focus on you. They are not bothered with what's around them and below them. They don't need to care about anything more, do they?"

Delphine was the first to disappear into non-existence. She was the oldest in the group. Therefore, her disappearance into non-existence followed an understanding of what the natural order must be.

After Prisha had gathered everyone around Niam, they talked and smiled and laughed a lot. It had been tough coming up. Going down would not be easy. They took their time to gather their strengths and pull themselves and each other up for the journey ahead. Niam joined them in their merriment and took great efforts to hide his concerns. Non-existence was gaining around them, little-by-little. They had to quickly make their way to Ella before all was lost.

The descent was similar to the ascent. The path was similarly narrow, with steps and slopes zigzagging across the face of the hill. Fortunately, this time, they did not come across a single boulder, not even a big rock. It was just the path. On it, they walked in a single file, with Nina leading the way, followed by Niam, the daughter, Ajani, Prisha, Hamoon, Delphine, and finally Nabil. Nabil was taking a very protective attitude toward Delphine, never keeping more than an arm's distance between them. In short time, they both had lost some distance with the rest since Delphine was walking slowly. But they were still keeping up well, and not far behind. The entire group had begun their walk with laughter and jokes. Those soon gave way to mentions of 'careful,' 'easy there,' 'go slow here,' and 'mind your steps,' and a solemn, intense mood took over everyone. Delphine began humming a song.

"She sings for herself again," Nina said softly to Niam. "I can't make out the lyrics, but it seems to be a pastiche of some famous songs I can't quite remember." She turned her attention back on the path ahead. "Do you see it?" she asked Niam, softly again, without looking back.

Niam glanced back. "Yes. It's getting close. It's getting close to her. What should we do? What can I do?"

Nina stopped and turned around. On cue, everyone stopped. Niam turned around too, toward Delphine. Everyone did the same. Nabil first thought the group was staring at him, perhaps because he had done something wrong. He realized they were looking at Delphine.

Delphine had stopped too. She couldn't see it. But she felt it very strongly. She could fight it, give it all her best, or she could accept it. She chose the former. She would stand still, not move, and let this thing come to her. Then she would let this thing know who she thought she really was. She started singing with force. Her singing reached a crescendo. The passion in her voice reverberated up and down the hill and moved everyone, even those who did not comprehend what her song was about. It didn't matter. The emotive fervency of her voice, of her facial expression, were enough to understand. Delphine saw Paris in its entirety. All the lights, all the glory, all the beauty. She stood still. Paris came to her. It surrounded her, overwhelmed her senses. She did not relent and continued singing. Paris became ever larger, and she became smaller and smaller. She was now in her arrondissement. That too became very big and very overwhelming. She was now in her home. And then, as Niam saw it, it happened. Non-existence rolled up to Delphine's feet and around her. It began its crawl up her legs. Delphine realized it. She looked down in dismay. With a pleading look, she looked up at Niam and Ajani and the daughter, and then with saddened eyes, her right hand stretched out toward them. But there was no acceptance yet. There was a fighting spirit still in her. She took a deep breath and started singing again. Niam saw non-existence, now waist high. Very soon it would completely engulf her. Delphine stopped her singing. There was nothing more she could do. She turned to Nabil and pushed him back.

"*Au revoir,*" she said to him, her eyes moist. Nabil watched, agape. He could not see what Niam was seeing, and he could not feel what Delphine was feeling.

Delphine turned to Niam. "Goodbye," she said with a voice barely loud enough to reach him. Then she pointed to the daughter. "Remember," she said again to Niam, this time louder, with a final burst of energy, "children are a conduit for unrequited dreams from one generation to the other."

And then, before she could add anything more, non-existence consumed her completely. A long lifetime of all her memories and all her experiences and all her emotions merged into the collective whole, where they became a miniscule part of a miniscule part. They were bereft of any individuality, indistinguishable, not attributable.

Everyone watched in bewilderment for a while. Nabil was the most frantic. He raised his hands and moved them around, over his head and face. His facial expressions were diverse, but all were some versions of desperation. He calmed down eventually.

Hamoon was the first to move. He strode to Niam.

"Did you just see that?" he said. "What happened? She's dead, right? Right?"

Niam did not respond immediately but kept looking at the spot Delphine was last seen. "Come, let's keep walking," he eventually said to Hamoon. "There's no reason to remain here, standing."

"But..." Hamoon tried to say.

Niam interrupted him. "Let's just go. There is nothing we can do here. Come."

Niam turned to face the path ahead. Nina followed, as did the rest. Nabil took a few shallow breaths and looked at the spot Delphine had stood. He walked around it gingerly, and turned back to glance at it again. Then with a final sigh, he too moved on with the rest.

"She's dead, right?" Hamoon was now walking right behind Niam. Nina was still leading the group.

"Non-existent," Niam said.

"I don't understand. To me it means dead. I feel all shaken up. I truly do. Right to my core. She was here one instant and now she isn't. Just gone. Sometimes I don't think about the dead at all. Even if I think about them, I dismiss them. I couldn't be bothered any less. But sometimes the dead affect me very deeply and very viscerally. I mean they were here one moment and next they are not. I feel sad, feel a deep sense of loss for the world, and for the dead."

"She is not dead," Niam said a bit more assertively this time. "She is non-existent. The dead can still overarch the ones living and the ones to be living. She will not. That's the difference."

Hamoon decided to stay quiet.

The next one to go was Nabil. For Nabil it started with a deep feeling of great bereavement. He tried to control it for a while, focusing instead on the narrow path and his steps. But it grew stronger. He gripped his heart. He was too young to have a heart attack. He took care of himself. He ate well, exercised, and slept well. It couldn't be a heart attack. He started to panic. The feeling of being alone, being left alone, was now too strong to ignore. The loneliness was crushing.

Nabil let out a loud cry. Everyone stopped to look at him. Niam watched again helplessly as non-existence crawled up all around and all over Nabil. He was completely in its grip. Nabil shouted something in French, but there was nothing he could do to stop the inevitable.

"What did he say?" Niam asked Nina.

"He said he's being crushed under the enormous weight of sand," Nina replied.

Niam took a step toward Nabil. Nina reached out to touch his shoulder. "There's nothing you can do for him," she said.

Niam turned and looked helplessly at Nina. "Surely there's something we can do?" he asked.

"Nothing," she replied, looking deep into his eyes.

Niam looked back at Nabil. He watched as Nabil was being squeezed and stretched, like a noodle. Others didn't see that. Nabil didn't see it. Others saw Nabil shouting with his arms flailing. But to Niam, it was clear. Non-existence had turned him into a long, thin strand of nothing. Nabil passed through a pinhole and emerged on the other side as an entangled jumbled mess of an infinitesimal yarn. In less than even a blink of an eye, even that yarn was gone, covered over completely by sand.

"Is he, what you called, non-existent too?" Hamoon asked Niam a moment later with a worried voice. He ran his hand through his hair.

"He was fated to be non-existent from birth. He just met his fate," Niam replied.

"Come, let's go. There is nothing we can do here," Nina said, and started walking. Hamoon stood there, with his hands on his waist. Prisha walked up to Niam and took his hand. With her other hand, she held the daughter. The daughter put her hand on Ajani, together making a chain. They restarted their descent in silence. When they were a few steps away, Hamoon raised his chin to look up at the sky. He shrugged his shoulders and followed the group.

Hamoon was the next to go.

For Hamoon it wasn't anything dire or distressing, like it had been for Delphine and Nabil. One instant he was walking at the very end of the group, hacking his way through air overburdened with melancholy. The next instant he was overcome with ecstasy. He let out a loud laugh, causing everyone to stop and turn.

Niam watched it again, the nebulous cloud of non-existence surrounding Hamoon. It seemed more determined this time, more resolute. Hamoon felt the determination. There was nothing he could do, or wanted to do.

"Is this the non-existence you talked about?" he asked Niam.

"It is. Unfortunately, it is," Niam replied. He turned to Nina with beseeching eyes.

"There is still nothing you can do about it. I am sorry," Nina replied with a tender, sympathetic expression.

"It's okay," Hamoon said to Niam when he turned around to face him. "If this is non-existence, then I am perfectly okay with it. It's actually very uplifting."

Niam could see through the nebula. He saw Hamoon stretching like Nabil did. But Hamoon became longer, much, much longer. And instead of passing through a pinhole, he rose up toward the sky and toward the far away horizon. On the horizon was Atlanta, the city glowing under its own lights. Hamoon, or whatever it was at this point since Niam could no longer see any distinguishing features associated with Hamoon, untangled upon Atlanta slowly. This was now an extremely thin thread, like a ring. The ring glowed too as it slowly descended on the city. Niam froze, mesmerized with the spectacle. He waited apprehensively and with revulsion at what he knew was inescapable. Then very quickly, before Niam could even take a deep breath to prepare for it, the circle fell upon the highway loop that encircled the city. The ring's glow merged with the city lights. It disappeared, and was only a distant memory.

"You've lost your friend," Prisha said. She couldn't think of anything else to say.

"I suppose it was inevitable too," Niam said. "Let's go. We still have a good distance to cover."

They walked in complete silence for a while. Once they were close to the halfway point of their descent, the temperature became markedly warmer. The path also became wider and less steep. The walk became easier. But it also became more precarious for Niam. He could see non-existence surrounding them, closing in and trying to take them. He became more fearful. He did not want to lose anyone else. But how do you fight something that surrounds you from all sides and is completely impervious to any weapon?

"Maybe you do not fight it. You accept it," Nina said to Niam.

They had taken a break from the walk. For a while Niam and Prisha stood arm-in-arm, close together, reassuring themselves through their touch. They smiled at the daughter and Ajani, both on the ground. Ajani's head rested on the daughter's legs as she sat cross-legged.

"Do you think we'll be able to make it down soon?" Prisha had asked.

"I think so. Look, it's not too far now," Niam had responded as he pointed below.

"It's not me I am worried about, you know that," Prisha had said. "It's her. If something happens to her, I don't know what I'll do. Nothing will happen to her, right?"

"Nothing will happen to her, for sure," Niam had said as he squeezed her hand lightly.

Prisha did not say anything further. She sat down cross-legged next to the daughter. Niam moved back a few steps till he was standing next to Nina. He told her about non-existence surrounding them, and his overwhelming desire to fight it to make it go away.

"I cannot accept it," he said to Nina when she suggested he do otherwise. "What if it does something to them?"

"It will not, as long as you are here. Don't worry," Nina replied with a thin smile.

"And what if I am not here?" Niam looked at her.

"When you're not here, it's no longer your worry, is it?" Nina replied with a broader smile.

Niam continued looking at her, trying to formulate a coherent sentence. Nina realized his anguish.

"Look," she said, "it's my responsibility to guide you through this. Didn't I tell you earlier in the day before you got on the bus? Let me worry about this. I'll help you through this. It won't affect them because it knows they are the ones who really matter to you. We'll be down soon, and in the park. I think Ella is there already, waiting for you and Ajani."

Nina took charge after that. Not only did she walk ahead of the group, as she had been doing all along, but she also forwent her near silence. She became outright garrulous, like an over enthused tourist guide wanting to make extra on tips.

"Watch out!" she shouted occasionally as they left the path to traverse through and around small shrubs and big boulders, and big shrubs and small boulders.

Prisha couldn't fathom why Nina was doing this. She followed her silently because she trusted Niam. Niam could see what Nina was trying to do. She was trying to find a way through non-existence. She was feeling for any gaps, any openings in the thick fog that surrounded them. All the while, she was relentlessly pushing and calculating, trying to determine the path that would cause the least apprehension or panic. Sometimes their steps took them back a few paces along the path. Sometimes, they took them up beyond the path and around back. And sometimes, they cut across down to meet the path at another point. This wasn't difficult for Niam and Prisha. But with the daughter it was another story. She didn't show it, but her short height made for a different walking gait, one not particularly conducive to trekking on ill or non-defined paths on a hilly terrain.

"I am worried about her," Prisha shouted to Niam. "How much longer are we doing this? I am afraid she cannot go much further," she called and stopped so they could rest.

Niam looked at Nina for guidance.

"We can't stop for too long now. We need to keep moving," Nina said to him gently. "It is gaining on us. I am afraid it may soon become too thick for me to handle. The more we delay, the more the danger increases."

190

Niam helplessly turned toward Prisha. "We need to carry on," he said. "Maybe we can take turns carrying her."

"It's okay. You don't need to worry about me," the daughter interjected. "Ajani will help. He says he will. He says he wants me to sit on his back."

"It's not safe, dear," Prisha replied. She had taken a moment to let what the daughter had said play in her mind.

"Ajani says not to worry. He will take very good care of me," the daughter said. "Please. Can I please sit on his back?"

It was Prisha's turn to look at Niam helplessly. Niam simply shrugged his shoulders.

"Okay," Prisha said, with a weak conviction. "But only if you're careful."

"Yay!" the daughter exclaimed and pushed herself on Ajani's back. Ajani let out a small whoop to show his pleasure.

"I don't like this. Keep an eye on them," Prisha said to Niam.

The walk became much easier now. Ajani kept by the side of Prisha, as if he understood that she needed a constant reassurance that the daughter was safe. The daughter now had a near constant smile on her face, which helped Prisha in controlling her anxiety.

"It's not too far now," Nina said out loud. "I hope," she added rather softly to Niam.

"I know," Niam said. "I can barely see anything beyond a few meters. It's gotten very thick."

"Don't worry about it," Nina said. "I meant it when I asked you to simply accept it. The way to fight non-existence is not to fight it, but to simply keep moving."

"How'll moving help here? I don't understand."

"Because when you're moving, you're not thinking about it. Accept it and move. Don't fight it, don't think about it."

"Is that what you've been doing all along? Simply moving? While all this time I thought you knew what you were doing, knew exactly where you were going?"

"Maybe. But I am moving. And I've brought us all here and covered a considerable distance with no problems. I see it approach us, trying to encompass us, and I look around. I try to see an opening. Once I see it, I take it. And I hope it works. It has worked so far. You're all still here."

Niam looked at her, but didn't respond. He was eager to get done with this. This eagerness was not because he was exhausted or, he also realized and felt a pang of guilt, because he was worried so much about Prisha or the daughter. He was worried about them in a general sense of course. He was worried that they could fall and hurt themselves walking down, or they could roll and tumble down the hill and be seriously injured, or something else might befall them. But he wasn't worried about non-existence affecting them. Nina was right. He needn't worry. Still, getting back on plain ground, with both feet planted firmly at the same level would be welcome. And maybe Prisha and the daughter would love the park. He liked it when he was there with Ella and Nina. It was a nice park.

"There! Do you see it?" Nina exclaimed. "There's an opening there. It's small. See it?"

Niam saw it. There was a small break in the ether that was non-existence. The ether was dark, foreboding, still surrounding them, trying to get to them. The opening, Niam noticed for the first time, was lighter, slightly brighter, welcoming albeit with a good bit of caution. There was no other such opening around.

"No, there is no other such opening," Nina spoke out loud what Niam was thinking.

"What opening?" Prisha asked. She moved her head and squinted her eyes, trying to see what Nina saw differently than her. All she saw were shrubs and rocks on one side, and the stone path up ahead, meandering down in a somewhat sharp turn.

"There is an opening on the side of the hill. We can take it and be down sooner," Niam replied.

"I like the sound of that," Prisha said, and smiled.

"Good," Nina joined in. "Then let's walk down from here."

They broke from the main path and went almost straight down. A few steps later, they came back onto the stone path that had meandered down. Nina did not take it. She cut across it and continued downward. Her steps were now much firmer, her gait more certain. She looked like someone who had just determined her course of action after much deliberation, and wasn't going to waste time thinking much further about things.

It was, however, Ajani and the daughter who soon took the lead, and by many leaps. This caused no small amount of dread for Prisha.

"There, there!" The daughter pointed in the direction of a thick wooded area some distance down.

Everyone stopped to look in the direction she was pointing toward. They had missed it before because they were focused on the path and their immediate steps. When they had first looked down from the top of the high hill, everything below had looked very small. The vast land had also seemed to stretch out to the horizon, which is what most of them had concentrated on. It was easy to miss a wooded area at the base of the hill.

Ajani stopped too when the daughter shouted. He turned his head toward the forest. His eyes turned expressionless. His body tensed. The canopy of trees looked familiar. He tried hard to remember where he had seen it before. He raised his nose to smell. The smell emanating from there also appeared to be familiar. The air was slightly dense with the odor. There was danger there, for sure. But there was also something else. Something visceral, intimate. On the other side of the forest, he instinctively felt, would be something familiar. There was safety there. He realized it. It was safety. It was intimacy. It was his family. They were on the other side, he was sure of it. This was the canopy where he had first been trapped by Nina and Ella. This was where his journey had started, a journey he wouldn't have willingly wanted to take. It was a journey that did not change him in any positive way. It had only made him miserable. It made him dislike himself. But now he saw a chance to change things. All he had to do was rush toward and through the forest. On the other side, his clan would be waiting. That's where he belonged.

Ajani snorted softly. His body was still at attention, his attention was on the forest. He slowly raised his front paw, and put it back on the ground gently. He lifted the other front paw, and put that back on the ground too. Then he snorted loudly, and casting caution to the wind, he galloped down with the daughter still on his back. That's when Prisha let out a wail.

There was however little that Niam and Prisha could do to stop Ajani. Niam was the closest to him. He tried to reach out to the daughter instinctively when he saw Ajani move from the corner of his eyes. This was not because he had realized what Ajani was about to do, but simply because he did not want the daughter to fall off his back and hurt herself. But he was slow, and Ajani was a wild animal with determination and a clear way forward. In a few short seconds, by the time Prisha had stopped her loud howl, taken a short breath, and called out to Niam, Ajani and the daughter had already crossed the first line of trees in the forest. The next instant, they had disappeared behind them.

"Niam!" Prisha gathered all her strength. "Do something!"

The loud call by Prisha was the impetus Niam needed to come out of his paralysis. He looked at her, then turned to look at Nina, and then turned again to face the direction Ajani had run off to. He started running down the slope as fast as he could. It wasn't easy, though. A few steps later, he slipped and fell hard. He covered the rest of the way rolling and tumbling down. This was broken when he crashed into a tree, torso first. Fortunately for him, he did not break any bones. The bruising was also limited. He stood up slowly in a stupor, his brain struggling to get a semblance of balance. He saw Prisha and Nina staring at him, agape. He looked down at his clothes, and brushed some of the soil away from his pants. He stood straight back up and quickly realized why he was here in the first place. He turned and ran into the forest.

The forest was fairly thick with trees. Visibility was not more than a few meters in either direction. Niam stood in a small opening and looked around frantically. He wanted to call out to the daughter. But she had no name yet. He shouted "daughter" a couple of times. He shouted for Ajani a few times too. There was no response. He didn't know if his voice was even carrying far enough. The forest was very good at damping sounds. He was surrounded by complete silence.

In frustration, Niam decided to go back out to Prisha. He turned to determine the direction he had come from. He couldn't remember. He took a deep breath to overcome a sense of panic and to recollect his thoughts. He decided to walk in a direction he thought looked the most appropriate. Fortunately, he wasn't too far off. When he reemerged at the base of the hill outside the forest about half an hour after he had entered, he wasn't too far off from where he had gone in. Prisha and Nina had made their way to the edge of the forest by then. They were standing close together. Nina was holding Prisha's hand, gently patting it, trying to calm her. When she saw Niam, Prisha took her hand away, and ran toward him. She hugged him tightly. Niam looked over her shoulders to see Nina making her way toward them.

"We need to find her!" Niam shouted when Nina was close enough. "I couldn't see anything inside. We need to call out for help. I don't know if she's safe."

"I think she is safe," Nina replied in a reassuring voice. "The hyena has taken care of her so far. Let's try to remain calm. We'll find them eventually. Come, let's go into the forest. We can't stay out here for too long. It's gaining ground. Soon it'll take us too, just like it took the others."

Niam nodded his head. He pulled away from Prisha, and held her hands. He tried to comfort her with words. Prisha

195

eventually quietened down enough for Niam to be able to converse with her. Together they took a few steps, and were in the forest, covered by a verdant cloak.

Book III
Anomie

The three of them could not find Ajani and the daughter. Nina did not even try to look, though she did not impede their agitated search by Niam and Prisha. Niam and Prisha held their hands the whole time and went in whichever direction they could see beyond more than a few yards. They exhausted themselves eventually. Niam sat down crouched, with his back to a tree. He looked around helplessly. Prisha had still not given up. She was standing, distressed and agitated, turning around in circles, and occasionally shouting at Niam, asking him to do something. Nina stood some distance away, observing them.

Prisha's eyes caught a slight movement behind some trees. She stopped and looked hard in that direction. There it was again, a small shimmer in the air, easy to miss if one wasn't paying attention. The shimmer disappeared and came back. The trees around it appeared slightly distorted through a lensing effect. With a great deal of concentration, Prisha started moving toward it. She tried hard not to even blink, lest this thing disappear. Nina watched her with wary eyes. One instant, Prisha had been deeply perturbed and flummoxed. The next, she seemed very determined. Niam was still sitting under the tree and still looking down, not paying much attention to his surroundings. He had succumbed to physical exhaustion and anguish.

Nina did not try to stop Prisha until it was too late. She saw the shimmer only when Prisha was very close to it. She shouted at her, asking her to stop. Niam lifted his head to see Prisha walking slowly toward an opening between the trees.

Niam and Nina watched dumbfounded when in one quick motion, the shimmer opened up wide to engulf Prisha, and she disappeared.

"Yes, you're right. It wasn't non-existence that took her, and it wasn't non-existence that took the hyena and the daughter," Ella said to Niam when they met later at the park.

"So, what took them? Are they safe? Will I ever see them again?" Niam asked, her answer not making much of a headway in alleviating his agitation.

"They've gone back into the loops from where they came," Ella replied. "They're not too far from you. The hyena and the daughter came from one loop, and your wife came from another."

Niam stood still, trying to pay attention to her words. His thoughts were drifting in different directions.

"I didn't realize it then. But I do now. There are always loops. The hyena and the daughter are always together in a single loop. The two are intertwined. The loop itself is them. One cannot exist without the other. Never has, and never will be. They are forever together, or if not, then seeking each other."

"Prisha?" Niam uttered.

"Your wife? I don't know what kind of a loop she is in. You'll need to take the trouble to find out if you really care. You are in a loop too, by the way. It's much, much bigger than the other two loops. You're the one who sets up the loops. Forever."

"So, they're safe then?"

"I don't know what you mean by the word 'safe.' But you'll be seeing them again, if that's what you want to know. You can trust me and relax. Come, there's someone I want you to meet. He's been waiting for you for a while," Ella said, and reached out to touch Niam's shoulder.

After Prisha's disappearance, it had taken quite a bit of effort by Nina to calm Niam, and convince him to continue their onward journey. Niam had run around the spot where Prisha had disappeared. He had shouted her name as loud as he could. He had shouted at Nina, and even accused her of causing all this. When he had tired himself out and sat down again against a tree, Nina stepped in front of him, hunched down, and spoke to him in a kind and sensitive voice. She talked about Ajani and the daughter, and how they came to be in Paris. She talked about what had taken Prisha.

"I am sure she's fine, and I am sure the daughter is fine too," she told him. "I am certain Ella would help," she also said. "Let's go meet her."

It took a few different versions of those sentences, and a few more too, until Niam stood up, ready to walk.

He had tried to argue with Nina. "What if Prisha comes back here and doesn't find anyone?" he had asked. "What then? She would be scared and lost. Wouldn't waiting for her here be the right thing to do?"

But Nina had finally prevailed.

They walked for some distance, when Niam asked, "Do you even know where we're going? It looks all the same to me in all directions."

"This is true. But we still need to keep walking. We'll be out of this forest eventually. There has to be an ending." Nina smiled at him.

Soon enough they walked out of the forest and into the same park where Niam had met Ella earlier in the day. The sense of relief felt by both of them was almost tangible.

The park appeared exactly as Niam had last seen it. There were the ducks, the mother walking her baby, and the young couple in a tender embrace. Ella was standing with her walking stick in her hand, not more than a few yards from where Nina and Niam emerged.

"Good! Good!" Ella smiled and her face lit up. "You have no idea how long I've been waiting for you. What took you so long?"

Before Nina could say anything, Niam said out loud, "We need to find my wife and daughter. They've gone. I don't know where they are. We need to find them. Nina said you know how to help. Help me, please. We need to inform the police."

"I am sure they're okay," Ella responded. "I don't think the police can help you. Why don't you tell me everything? Let's take a walk. We'll do three rounds around the park once again. It's still a beautiful day. Let's make full use of it, while we help you get back to your wife."

They walked around the small pond. Nina told Ella the bulk of what had transpired, with Niam filling in some of the gaps and providing his perspective. Ella remained silent for most of the duration.

Ella asked Niam about Delphine, Nabil, and Hamoon, and she asked him about Prisha's disappearance. She told him her inference. She next informed him about someone waiting for him.

"I quite literally ran into him after we parted earlier. I think I may have even hurt him good with my stick. The poor guy. He was so nice about it, though. A perfect gentleman, I must say," Ella said. "While I was apologizing, I had this very strong feeling that he and you knew each other. He confirmed it when I asked him. I brought him here. He's been eager to meet you. I think he has something to say to you."

The three walked toward the bench where Niam had first found Ella earlier in the day. There was a man sitting there very still and very straight. He had his back toward them.

"Hello there! Here's your friend Niam you've been waiting for," Ella said when they were close.

The man stood up in one quick motion, again very straight, and turned around.

"Hello Niam! It has been a long time," Neel said, and smiled at Niam.

Niam stopped and stared at Neel in astonishment. Then a smile broke out on his face and he rushed to him. They gave each other a light hug.

Neel was just as immaculately dressed as Niam had remembered. Only now, the expensive designer casualwear was replaced by an expensive suit and shoes. Neel projected his professional accomplishments very well.

"Isn't it nice when two old friends meet again after a long gap?" Ella said. "Or I think it seems nice. I can't see very well, you know. Nina, are they glad to see each other?"

"As far as I can tell," Nina said.

"Yes, we are indeed very pleased," Niam responded. "You could have simply asked me instead of Nina."

"I know, I know," Ella grinned. "But I like it this way. How many years has it been since you two last met?"

"I don't know. It's been many years," Niam said and turned to Neel. "You completely disappeared. I tried to call you. I even tried to reach you through others, but no one seemed to know where you were. Last I knew, you went to Israel, right?"

"Yup, that's right. I was there, I am still there. I came to Paris for a business meeting. The meeting ended on Friday. I decided to stay for an extra day to go around the city and see a few people I know. That's when I ran into your friend, Ella."

"I think you two seem to have a lot of catching up to do," Ella said. "Why don't Nina and I take a walk? Nina? Are you up for some more walking? There's this new pizza place not too far from here. I didn't particularly like their pizza the last time. But it wasn't too bad. I have worked up an appetite waiting for you, and that not-so-great pizza looks like a good option. What do you say?"

"If it's pizza then I am all for it," Nina replied with an elated voice. "I love pizza!"

They left, walking side-by-side, with Ella tapping her guide cane on the paved path at regular intervals. Niam and Neel silently watched them take a turn around the pond and walk toward the park entrance. They sat down on the bench.

"What have you been up to all these years?" Neel asked. "You're still looking good. You haven't changed much."

"I've been okay," Niam replied. "Life's been okay. I got married. And now I have a daughter. I can't seem to find them both at the moment, though. But that's another story. I've been in Paris for a while now. I think about two years. It may be time to go back. What about you?"

"Wow! You're married. That's great. I still remember you talking to a girl on the phone. Are you still in touch?"

"I don't know, actually," Niam replied after some thought. "Maybe not."

"I don't get it! Either you're in touch or you're not in touch. You can't be doing both."

"I think it's complicated, and I am not very sure," Niam said. "But forget all that. What about you? You tell me about what all has happened in your life. You simply disappeared."

"I've been having the time of my life, I'll tell you that!" Neel beamed. "I'll be the last person to complain. The company I work for is great. They've made me a Director of Operations, and..."

"Director of Operations?" Niam interjected. "That sounds awesome. They must really like you."

"Apparently they do," Neel smiled. "Good title, good salary, a great benefits package, lots of vacation!"

"I guess the work must keep you very busy and with no time to party anymore?" Niam grinned.

"Come on, you know me!" Neel let out a small laugh. "I cannot stop partying. I have a big circle of friends there, too."

"And is there a woman in your life?"

"Woman? Nah. Women is more like it. I love Israeli women. And they love me."

"Somehow I had guessed it," Niam said. "I can't imagine you any other way."

They were silent for a few short moments trying to figure out the next question to ask the other.

"How's life in Israel? You're in Tel Aviv, right?" Niam broke the silence first.

"Yup. Tel Aviv. Great city, great people. The country is a nice place, I'll tell you that."

"Oh yes?" Niam said. "Tell me about it. Any fun things you've done? Maybe I'll visit you."

"Absolutely! Let's plan it out. You'll love it there. I'll show you around," Neel replied excitedly. "Maybe we'll even spend a few days at a Kibbutz! I've been to one. A friend of mine lives there. Some of us go over there during holidays, or when we get too burnt out at work. We crash at his place, enjoy the quiet days and nights drinking and smoking pot. There's a nice little stream near the Kibbutz. I always have a fun time swimming in it. And there's a good night life there, too. It's obviously not as great as at Tel Aviv. That city is one party place. But it's not bad. I am sure you'll like it, and I am sure my friend will be very happy to have you as a guest."

"Sounds like fun!" Niam Caught Neel's infectious smile.

"What have you been up to all this time?" Neel asked.

Niam told him about his life over the few years since they had last communicated. He left out all that had happened this present day.

"Any news about Arun? Are you still in touch with him? What's he been up to?" Neel asked, when Niam stopped.

"I don't know. I haven't been in contact with him for a while. He worked in London or somewhere for some time. Then his project ended, and he came back and worked in Delhi briefly. He left that job too, and then moved somewhere, maybe to Singapore or America. I don't exactly remember. Last I heard, he seemed to have been doing well."

"That's good," Neel said. "I liked that guy. I mean, he was difficult to handle with all his opinions and all. But he was good company if you were able to ignore that part of him. Do you think all this traveling has changed him? Do you think he'll approve of us two meeting up in Israel and partying and drinking and getting high?"

Niam let out a short laugh. "That would be something! But yes, I will search him up and find out what he's been up to. It would be nice to hear from him. We had a good time together at the apartment"

"Yes, we did. We had lots of fun. I had fun in college too, but I didn't have any money then," Neel said. "When we were staying at that apartment, we had the money to enjoy."

"Not too much!" Niam exclaimed. "But yes, we had some to spare!"

There was again a pause in the conversation.

"When is the last time you visited home?" Niam broke the silence again.

"Me? I don't know. It's been a few years," Neel said. He was not smiling.

"Oh really?" Niam said. "That long? I suppose life is indeed keeping you busy."

"I suppose so," Neel replied. He hunched slightly and looked down.

"Your family must have visited you during this time, I suppose," Niam continued.

"No, they haven't," Neel replied.

"Really?"

"Yeah. Listen, I don't talk about this much," Neel said with a grave tone.

"Sure. No problem. Sorry for asking," Niam responded.

"No, don't be," Neel said. "You're okay."

There was silence again. This time Neel broke it first. It was mostly small talk about life in Tel Aviv, and questions about

Niam's work and about his wife and his life in Paris. Niam repeated some of the things he'd mentioned previously.

Neel eventually let him in on his life and why he had broken contact.

"I was done with this fucking world and this fucking society. I was angry, very angry. Full of rage. I am still angry. But now I've learned to control it, and not let it control me," he told Niam. "I am not a bad person. Yes, I walked away when I saw someone dying from an accident on the road, or when someone was doing something bad. I understand that not doing anything to stop something bad is the same as doing something bad. I get it. I've done things that I am not proud of, and I will be the first to say I cringe now when I think about some of things I've done. But really, I am not a bad person. I really wish no one any harm, and I go out of my way to be good, to do good, too, or at least not cause any harm to the extent I can. After all this, why did bad things happen to me and my family? What had we done? What had I done to deserve this?"

Niam felt it best to remain quiet. Neel, he felt, would tell him, of his own volition, what he was comfortable with. He told him some more.

"My brothers were not some illegal or unlicensed traders. They were legitimate shop owners. They had done nothing wrong. They had a right to protest peacefully. They had a right to let their opinion be known. Tell me, did they deserve this?"

"Deserve what?" Niam asked.

"To die," Neel said, with a grave voice. He stared at Niam, as if Niam had the answer he was seeking.

"How did they pass away, if you don't mind me asking?"

"My brothers were tortured. They were brutally tortured for hours. They were beaten with sticks for hours. They were even penetrated with a big object. Maybe a big stick. Both of them in the same police station. When they died, their bodies were dumped in a ditch not far from our home. The police tried to pass it off as a simple case of robbery gone wrong. But we know what happened. We know they were both picked up by the police in the evening. It doesn't take a genius to figure this all out. My brothers had done nothing wrong. Maybe all they did was speak in a tone that the police or someone did not like. But is that so bad that they needed to be killed in such a brutal way? To teach them a lesson? What lesson? What lesson could be worth their lives?

"I was in Tel Aviv when this happened. I flew back on the next flight. I found my mother on her deathbed. The shock and grief were too much for her. When she saw me, she seemed to get better. Maybe there was that reassurance that at least one of her children was still alive. But she died. Within a day of my being there, she was dead. I cremated my entire family over two days."

Neel took a few deep breaths. Niam remained silent, his hands crossed on his legs. This was the only appropriate thing to do, he felt.

Neel continued, "My relatives tried to explain this to me. Some said this may have happened because of a recent falling out between my brothers and the son of our local politician. Some said this was perhaps a case of a psychotic officer going berserk. Whatever the reason may be, they were all clear on one thing. It was not safe for me anymore there. Killing me would mean wiping out an entire family, leaving no one to cause any problems, then or later. They asked me not to stay at my home for even a few hours more, and certainly not overnight; I should escape. I was in a daze, with no free will or free thoughts. I just followed instructions. After we came back from the cremation grounds, I packed my bags, picked up important documents I could quickly lay my hands on, and left my home through the back door in a relative's car. I took the first train out of there. I didn't much care where it was headed to. Fortunately, it was to the nearest big city. On the train, I bought the first available flight back to Tel Aviv. It all worked out very quickly. It was only after I had gone through the airport security check, and was firmly seated in the waiting area in front of the airplane departure gate, when the full reality of what had happened hit me. This was it, I realized. This was the end of my life in my own country. I was never coming back, and there was nothing I could do about it. I had become stateless."

Neel paused again and took some more deep breaths. He wiped an eye with his cuff.

"Once I was back in Tel Aviv, it took me a while to control my emotions. I had to do it alone. No one around me would understand. How could they? Fortunately, I had lots of work thrust on me from big projects. That and alcohol, and spending time at this Kibbutz I told you about with my friend, the only one I confided in at that time, helped me enormously to recover."

"I am so sorry to hear all this," Niam said after Neel took another pause.

"It's okay I guess. It's been a few years. I've moved on, the world's moved on. My relatives are mostly good people. They cleaned up my home and the shop, shipped important things to me, and helped find reliable renters for the properties. It's been a steady source of income for me. I get my taxes filed there, get the money transferred here. Maybe I am not so completely stateless. Maybe I might go back in a few years. Maybe never. I have an uncle in Johannesburg, in South Africa. I like him. He's been asking me to come to South Africa to help him in his business. I think if I don't get to stay permanently in Israel, I'll go to South Africa. When I was little, I always enjoyed time with him whenever he visited. He would bring all sorts of great gifts and tell us three brothers interesting stories from his travels and various safari trips. I remember once when I was a little grown up, maybe around thirteen or fourteen, he said something strange during one of his stories. He said that the world is controlled by Whites and Jews. I listened to him, and I didn't really understand what he meant. I had never personally met a white person at that time.

I had just seen them on television or in movies or read something in the newspaper or textbooks. As for Jews, I had no idea at all who they were. None. How comical is that? I am now living in Israel, surrounded by Jewish people.

"Now that I have seen and experienced this world, I think I know where he was coming from and just how poisonous such a thought is. Most people in this world are not Whites or Jews. For most, for the entirety of their lives, they only experience institutionalized discrimination by their own people. It's easy for the government to take attention away from this and claim it's someone else. Governments have a monopoly over violence, which is what I now believe governments fundamentally are, and they can exercise it. And a government is not some nebulous far away thing. The police who tortured and killed my brothers were representatives of the government. I ran away from my own government. I could not seek justice from my own government."

They sat silently for a while. Niam watched two ducks swimming in the pond. With one duck watching, another duck would dive into the water, and come out. The first one would follow. They repeated this for a while. To Niam this was somewhat redolent of human beings mimicking each other, doing something not because it needs to be done but because someone else is doing so.

He also thought of what to say to Neel. He could not find the right words. He simply put a hand on Neel's shoulder and patted him a couple of times. Neel did not look up.

The sun had begun to set. Shadows from plants and trees and nearby buildings were growing longer. Birds were chirping louder. The two young lovers had stood up and were now walking hand in hand. The mother with her baby was nowhere to be seen. She had probably left when Niam and Neel were talking.

As the sun was setting behind a row of buildings, it sent out long rays of light through the gaps to counter the shadows and let everyone know that it still existed. Soon those rays too disappeared, and evening firmly set in.

"That thing you talk about," Niam finally said, "that Kibbutz. It seems like a great place to hang out."

"Yes, it is. I love it whenever I am there," Neel said softly.

"Looks like I'll love it too. Maybe I'll be there the next long weekend. There should be one coming up soon, I think. We can talk about it and plan something out."

"I'll love that," Neel said as he turned his face up to look at Niam. He was still hunched over.

"Would it be okay if my wife also comes along? It'll be difficult to go to Israel without her, or anywhere for that matter. This is what marriage is all about," Niam said.

"I am sure it'll be fine. I'll get to meet her too," Neel replied. "Just let me know."

"Great! But what is a Kibbutz exactly? I've never heard of this word before."

Epilogue

"There you two are! I hope you won't consider us interlopers," Nina said. "You two seem so immersed in conversation."

"Yes Nina, that's what happens when long lost friends meet," Ella responded.

Niam and Neel turned around. Nina and Ella were standing behind them, each with an almost fully eaten ice cream cone in hand.

"We had a good time, if you must know," Nina said. "We had a slice of pizza each at that pizzeria. Mine wasn't bad, but it wasn't great either. The chicken topping on it was not the greatest. But it was okay."

"That's why I asked you to take the veggie one," Ella chimed in. "I like that one the best there. I love olives too."

"Maybe next time," Nina said. "Anyway, we were about to enter the park when we saw you two still immersed in conversation."

"You saw them, not me. I can't see that far, you know!" Ella smiled.

"Yes, I saw. Not her. I saw you both talking, and we decided to let you talk some more. We got ourselves ice cream from a nearby ice cream shop."

"Sounds like you two had fun," Niam said.

"We did," Ella replied. "How about you two? Did you two get a chance to catch up after all these years?"

"Yes, we did," Neel replied and stood up. Niam followed his action. "I think I should leave. It's getting late. I have a flight to catch tomorrow morning too. Listen," he turned to Niam, "I am very glad to have met you, thanks to your friends here. I wish I could stay longer and we could head for dinner or coffee or something. Hopefully next time."

"Hopefully," Niam spoke.

"Yes. And I'll message you as soon as I am back at Tel Aviv. We should absolutely meet there if you can. It's a wonderful place. I'll show you all the great places there. We'll have a great time!"

Neel shook hands with the three of them, said his goodbyes, and walked away toward the exit, and into the darkening skies and the bright city lights.

"Well, it was a great day today, I suppose!" Ella exclaimed when sufficient time had passed in silence. "I am exhausted. I think I'll have some wine tonight and a good long sleep. I deserve it. Nina do you want to join me for some wine? I'll need your help getting home too. Can't see well, you know."

"Absolutely! I'd love to have some wine. When did I last get drunk? Oh wait, it was just yesterday. Why not make it two days in a row! You know, this one time, I drank every night straight for thirty-three days. That was something. I'll never do it again. Do you want to join us for some drinks?" She turned to ask Niam.

"Maybe after Ella has helped me find my wife. I know you gave me your assurance," he said to Ella. "But I am getting very worried."

"Oh, your wife? How silly of me to forget to tell you." Ella let out a small laugh. "Your wife is back home."

Niam stared at her with suspicion. "How do you know? How did she get home?"

"That's where she went. Where else was she supposed to go? You don't believe me? Just call her up and ask," Ella said.

Niam pulled his phone from his pocket. He looked at Ella

and Nina. Nina was observing his phone. Ella was standing still, looking into the distance. He pushed Prisha's number. The phone rang a couple of times.

"Hello." He heard Prisha's voice.

"Hello, Prisha!" Niam exclaimed and broke out in a wide smile, almost from ear to ear.

"What happened?" Prisha asked.

"Nothing. What happened with you? Are you safe? Are you okay? You're not hurt, are you?" Niam blurted out his questions in quick succession.

"What are you talking about?" Prisha asked with a hint of suspicion. "Are you okay?"

"I am perfectly okay!" Niam replied, his voice still ecstatic. "I just…"

"Listen." Prisha cut him short. "When are you coming back? I need to ask you to do something on your way back."

"I'll be back home very soon. What do you need me to do?" Niam responded.

"Can you stop by a pharmacy and pick up something?" Prisha asked.

"What?" Niam became concerned.

"Nothing to be worried about," Prisha said when she sensed his concern. "I need you to pick up a pregnancy test kit. I think I am late by more than two weeks."

Nina and Ella said their goodbyes to Niam once they were out of the park. Nina watched Niam rush toward the bus stop. She held her arm in Ella's, and they both turned in the opposite direction.

"I know just the place nearby for the wine," Ella said. She gave her the name of the place and described the general direction it was located in.

"Do you think it's going to be a daughter?" Nina asked Ella.

"I am sure of it!" Ella said out loud with a small laugh. "And he'll get to name her this time. Something also tells me that he's going to be fortunate enough to be able to play with her and watch her grow up."

"And what about the hyena? I suppose he will come too?"

"Someone must always suffer. Always. Forever in the past, and forever in the future. He will come too, believe me. He is not done yet, or will ever be."

Acknowledgments

Once again, a huge thanks to the entire team at Madville Publishing for bringing this book to life. In particular, Kimberly Davis is a visionary leader who has selflessly dedicated herself to supporting authors. Mike Hilbig is not only an outstanding editor, but also a wonderful friend. Elizabeth Evans is an exceptional line editor. And of course, the marvelous layout of the book was made possible by Catherine Smith-Cox.

A special thanks to Natasha Murray for being the first to work with me on editing this book. A big thanks also to Vitiana Robert for helping with the French usage in the book. Their efforts have been instrumental.

About the Author

Amit Verma, 2022 International Book Awards New Age Finalist, is a resident of Houston, Texas, where he divides his time among things he is passionate about, including being a professor of engineering, a never perfect yard he often gives up on, and of course, being a writer. His opinion articles have appeared in print-media and other places. More information about his work and his media presence can be found on his website at amitvermaauthor.com.